"Why," Rose asked, "do you drink so much, Mister Thorpe?"

"The question is, Mademoiselle Gallant, why don't I drink more?"

"You should have faith," she told him.

"Faith that drink will not make my sorrows go away, or faith that things will get better?"

"Both," Rose said.

He stared into her brown eyes, only inches away, and whispered, "If only I had a semblance of hope."

Hearing him speak of hope as if she held the key made Rose gasp for air. She let herself look into his face . . . and fell hopelessly into a sea of vivid blue. "I really should go," she said. "You can walk me as far as the creek."

They walked without speaking through his fields, along the woods to the creek. When Rose reached the water's edge, she paused, wondering how to remove her shoes and stockings discreetly. Then, suddenly, two arms encircled her and lifted her up. Before she had time to object, Coleman had carried her across the stream to the opposite bank.

He did not put her down. He paused to gaze at her, still holding her tightly in his arms. She knew, somehow, that he was going to kiss her, and she wished with all her might he would.

You taste of heaven and earth, Coleman thought as he captured her lips with his, *like a cross between a cloud and a sweet apple pie.*

Rose leaned forward into the kiss, wanting it never to end. . . .

Dear Romance Reader,

In July, we launched the Ballad line with four new series, and each month now we offer you both new and continuing stories set everywhere from medieval England to the American West—the kind of passionate, romantic stories you love best, written by the most gifted authors. At the back of each book, we'll tell you when you can find subsequent books in the series that have captured your heart.

Rising star Joy Reed continues her charming Wishing Well trilogy with *Emily's Wish* as a spirited young woman fleeing her past stumbles into a celebrated author . . . and a chance at a love story of her own. Next Candice Kohl sweeps us back to the medieval splendor of The Kinsmen as *A Knight's Passion* becomes a breathtaking romance . . . with a Welsh heiress the king intends for his brother.

New this month is veteran author Linda Lea Castle's Bogus Brides series. The Green sisters must invent "husbands" to remain in the charter town of McTavish Plain, Nebraska—and love is an unexpected complication in *Addie and the Laird*. Finally, we return to the bayous of the Louisiana Territory as Cherie Claire offers the second book of the The Acadians. *Rose* dreams of romance . . . but loses her heart to the one man her family has forbidden. Enjoy!

Kate Duffy
Editorial Director

The Acadians

ROSE

Cherie Claire

ZEBRA BOOKS
KENSINGTON PUBLISHING CORP.
http://www.zebrabooks.com

To the "Ragin' Cajuns" in my family, my mother, LilyB Staehling Moskal, and my sister, Danon Dastugue. Thanks for always believing in me and for getting me west of the Atchafalaya.

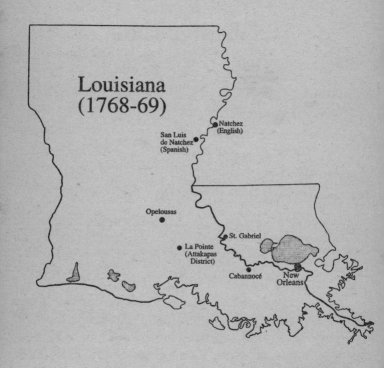

Louisiana
(1768-69)

Natchez
(English)

San Luis
de Natchez
(Spanish)

Opelousas

La Pointe
(Attakapas
District)

St. Gabriel

Cabannocé

New
Orleans

Chapter One

Opelousas Poste, Louisiana Territory
1768

Only hell could be hotter than Louisiana, Rose Gallant thought as the pirogue glided along the bayou, its smooth surface interrupted by an occasional burst of wind. The sky swarmed with dark clouds and rain was imminent, but still the heat continued.

Rose leaned out of the cypress pirogue, hoping the closer proximity to the water might provide relief. She dropped a hand into the tepid bayou water and relished its slight comfort.

"Better be careful, mademoiselle," said the hired

guide and owner of the pirogue. "There's gators in these parts. Not to mention poisonous snakes."

Rose quickly withdrew her hand, but not before an enormous insect popped her in the face.

"Best to sit still," her older sister Emilie offered.

Emilie detested the water. She sat as stiff as a tree trunk in the middle of the dugout, careful not to tip the pirogue in any direction, her head bowed to avoid flying insects.

"I wish something would dispel this unbearable heat," said Gabrielle, Rose's middle sister who was three years her senior.

Rose couldn't help but wish the same, even though she tried to enjoy the magnificent oaks draping Spanish moss over the tranquil bayou and the flocks of snowy egrets presenting a magnificent contrast against the blackened sky. Her neck ached from gripping the sides of the pirogue in an effort to balance herself, and every inch of her clothing was pasted to her flushed skin. The air hung so humid it might as well rain, Rose decided.

Within seconds she regretted her thoughts. The sky exploded, sending torrents of rain down upon them.

Rose shut her eyes to ward off the pellets of rain beating at her face. The droplets fell so large they stung her cheeks.

"How much longer?" Rose heard her mother shout to the guide, but the pirogue was already heading toward shore. Bayou Courtableau was a long narrow waterway, and it took only a few strokes to beach the pirogue on the left bank.

"There is a house over this ridge," the guide shouted to them over the thunder and rain. "We'll take cover there."

While flashes of lightning lit the dark sky, Lorenz Landry, Rose's brother-in-law, helped pull the pirogue to safety, then assisted Rose's mother, Marianne, out of the boat. Next came a cautious Emilie, Lorenz's wife, and Gabrielle.

Being the youngest and lightest of the group, Rose had been placed at the bow. And as she had done so many times before, she waited patiently for her family to lead the way.

They were traveling to the Opelousas Poste, a frontier stop in the southwestern prairies of Louisiana, in the hope of reuniting their family, separated during their exile from Nova Scotia thirteen years before. The English had occupied Nova Scotia since before Rose's father's birth, allowing the French inhabitants to remain on the Canadian peninsula as long as they supplied the English with food and vowed to remain neutral in wars between France and England.

But the Acadians were prosperous and multiplied, occupying the best lands. That they had steadfastly refused to renounce their Catholic faith and learn a new language remained a bone of contention with the English. Even though the Acadians complied with the English's wishes and faithfully followed orders, the English continued to regard them as enemies.

One afternoon, the English called all the men of Grand Pré to the village church to announce the "King's wishes" in the occupied lands of Nova Scotia. They trapped the men inside, while their wives and children were hauled to the shore, their houses burned and their livestock slaughtered. The men, women, and children were reunited on the beaches, only to be forced to board ships that would scatter them throughout the English colonies, the Caribbean, and Europe.

Rose was too young to remember that horrid fall of 1755. She barely remembered their father. Only that he was a kind man who smelled of apples and pipe tobacco.

But she had heard the stories.

Joseph had arrived at the embarkation area, waved from his place on the hill and headed toward them. Maman had even spoken to him, shouting above the masses waiting to be shipped from their beloved Acadian home. Then Gabrielle had wandered off and Maman, holding Rose in her arms and grasping Emilie with one hand, had left to search for her. Once they'd found Gabrielle and returned to their place on the beach, Papa had disappeared.

Despite her fervent pleas, the English forced Maman and her three daughters onto a boat, and rowed them out into Minas Basin, where they boarded a ship bound for Maryland. The soldiers assured her they would find Papa and bring him to the ship, but darkness came and he was nowhere to be found. The anchor rose and they sailed from their home, watching Nova Scotia disappear in the twilight and praying that Joseph Gallant would find them.

Rose remembered the huddled families crowded aboard the ship, the stench of dirty water and sickness, the cries of family members separated from their loved ones. Half of the ship's inhabitants died from smallpox and exposure. It was a wonder Rose survived, being so young. She remembered the fever as if it were yesterday.

The heat of a Louisiana August wasn't that different. The humid air choked her, made her head dizzy like the annoying mosquitoes that circled her head. The sweat that continually poured from her skin left Rose lethargic and constantly thirsty. It felt as if the Louisiana swamp had risen from the ground like a mist and plastered itself to her, turning her clothes into washrags.

It was nothing like the Maryland colony.

Thirteen years ago, they had been shipped to Port Tobacco, a small town lying inside a protected bay between the Chesapeake and the Potomac River. There were Catholics in Maryland, and Rose and her family were treated better than in other, less tolerant colonies of the Eastern Seaboard. Still, Maryland was hardly a garden of Eden. They lived in poverty, depending on others for help. Gabrielle and Marianne stitched clothes for extra money while Emilie and Lorenz farmed a meager plot of land. When word came last year that Joseph Gallant had been sighted in the Louisiana Territory, Rose was more than happy to be rid of Port Tobacco.

But they had arrived to find Joseph gone. And the Louisiana terrain was about to swallow her whole.

"Dépêche-toi, Rose," Emilie cried from the bank.

Rose slid over the side of the pirogue, finding herself up to her chin in the bayou. Despite its bathlike temperature, the water felt refreshing against her skin and she longed to remain. A long dark object floated past and Rose remembered the guide's warnings. Before she realized it was merely a twig, she had jumped toward shore, dragging her small bag of belongings.

As she slung the bag over her shoulder and attempted to climb the slight incline, the movement threw her off balance and her feet slid backward on the mud. Quick as the lightning piercing the sky, Lorenz grabbed her shoulder, effortlessly pulled her to his side, and helped her up the bank.

"Are you all right?" he shouted above the crash of thunder.

Rose could barely make out her tall brother-in-law through the sheets of rain, but she nodded and he caught her message. Lorenz was forever looking out for her, protective of the sister who could barely see past his shoulders. With one enormous arm draped about her, Lorenz could ward off all the evils of the world. She couldn't have asked for a better brother.

Lorenz had lost his parents during the exile, or *le grand dérangement* as the elder Acadians called it. Maman had insisted he live with them in Maryland, glad to have a man about. Only twelve at the time, Lorenz was grateful not to be alone. He and Emilie had been close friends since childhood and their relationship comforted them in exile. It was only a matter of time before Lorenz became an official member of the Gallant family, and it seemed appropriate that it happened in Louisiana, the land some were now calling the New Acadia.

As they trudged across the field toward a distant

house, Rose thought of Lorenz and Emilie's marriage in St. Gabriel, a town on the Mississippi River where her father was supposed to have been. It warmed her heart knowing that part of the family was finally finding happiness, but the memory of the wedding also reminded her of what she would never have.

"You're very quiet," Lorenz said.

"It's difficult to speak with all this noise," Rose answered, knowing that it was the pain searing at her heart that stilled her lips more than the thunder bellowing above them.

When they reached the house, Lorenz took Rose's bag and deposited it with the other belongings on the gallery.

"The commandant's home is up the road," the guide announced. "But the DeClouets will give us shelter."

"Do you think the owner's at home?" Marianne asked.

"No one would be going anywhere at a time like this," the guide said, gazing up at the clouds that had grown blacker, if that was possible. "Something's coming. Maybe a hurricane."

Before Rose could digest that thought, the gallery door swung open and a tall well-dressed man with rolled-up sleeves appeared before them. The troubled look in his eyes mirrored Rose's feelings.

"May I help you?" he asked impatiently.

"Monsieur DeClouet," the guide said, bowing, "I'm taking this family to the commandant, but the weather turned on us. May we rest at your house until this storm blows over?"

The man observed them quickly, glancing from their sparse belongings to their threadbare clothes. *We must look a sight,* Rose thought, *forever living on the brink of survival, forever traveling in search of Papa.*

"It doesn't look like it will blow over soon," the man replied with a frown.

"We can help you prepare for the storm," Lorenz suggested. Leave it to Lorenz to find a way around a situation, Rose thought with a smile.

The man brightened and held the door open wider. "My name is André DeClouet," he said as they filed past him into the foyer. "We will have to save pleasantries for later."

"What can we do?" Gabrielle asked.

André barked orders to a mulatto woman standing in the hallway, cowering every time a peal of thunder shook the house. "Go with Esther," he said, turning back toward the family. To Lorenz, he said, "Come with me."

Rose followed the other women toward the parlor, turning back to catch Lorenz's irritated expression before he headed out the door into the storm. Lorenz despised authority. It was a distrust he had learned in childhood.

"We need to bring the breakables away from the windows," Esther said, her head bowed so as not to meet their eyes.

Rose had heard that slaves were taught to speak and act as if they were inferior, and she felt a fire burn across her forehead. She didn't see herself as defiant of authority as Lorenz was, but slavery was an inhumane institution that she could not abide. She touched Esther's arm so the older woman would glance up. "Where should we start first?" she asked with a warm smile.

Esther responded with a smile of her own. "The crystal needs to be wrapped in cloth and placed in the hallways. No windows there."

"Then let's get started," Marianne announced. They began to remove the delicate bowls and vases, wrapping them in lengths of calico they would have been thrilled to use for clothing.

Rose heard Emilie sigh as she picked up a multifaceted crystal bowl that sent waves of rainbows about the room when it passed the candle's light. "I've never seen anything so magnificent," Emilie whispered to Rose.

Gabrielle cleared her throat and motioned with her eyes toward the floor. Covering almost the entire parlor was an exquisite Oriental rug. All four women paused when they realized the enormity of the value of the finely crafted rug and the wealth of its owner.

Slowly, their eyes moved about the room to see what other items appeared before them. Tapestries, mahogany furniture, family portraits, a crystal chandelier, and a marble mantel completed the parlor.

"Are they royalty?" Gabrielle asked no one in particular.

Esther laughed, then covered her mouth. "No ma'am. They be aristocrats though. Big family in France."

When the three sisters continued to stare, Marianne placed her hands on her hips and sent them a reprimanding look. "Monsieur DeClouet is offering his hospitality, allowing us a dry place to wait out the storm. Don't abuse it."

They all returned to their jobs wrapping breakables and filling the long foyer. Before Rose could send the ungrateful sentiment away, she wondered how a hospitable man could allow four women to remain soaking wet and dripping in his parlor.

By nightfall, the house had been stripped of its *objets d'art*, including the massive chandelier and enormous paintings. Furniture had been pulled away from the windows and crowded into the centers of the rooms. Curtains had been removed and stored on the second floor. Rose no longer shivered from the wet clothes wrapped around her like a mummy's shroud, but she continued to sweat from the heat of the boarded-up house. Her skin was clammy and uncomfortable. Lorenz and the guide returned, looking as if they had fought the hurricane single-handedly. André DeClouet followed, equally wet but not nearly so dirty.

When they entered the house the wind howled through the foyer, blowing papers around and knocking over chairs. They quickly shut the door, but not before Emilie rushed to Lorenz's side to make sure he was unharmed.

"I'm fine," he said, but he held her tight.

That simple gesture sent a wave of fear through Rose. The wind and rain had intensified since their arrival. Would it get worse? Did hurricanes blow houses—even fancy, expensive houses like the DeClouets'—off their foundations?

"Do not worry, mademoiselle," she heard a soft voice speak into her ear. When Rose looked up, she found André standing close. Very close. He seemed to examine her as if pondering some great question.

"Will it get worse than this?" she asked.

"Perhaps," he answered. "But I have seen worse. You will be safe in this house."

His eyes were blue, Rose noticed. Sky blue, just like Coleman's. She shook off the image as soon as it entered her head. She couldn't think of *him*. Not now.

"The worst part of a hurricane is sitting inside a hot, stuffy house," André continued, this time with a twinkle in his eye. "Too bad they don't come in the winter, when we wouldn't mind being stuck indoors."

Rose thought to mention that being as wet as she was in the middle of winter would not be more comfortable, but she held her tongue for fear of being rude. Somehow, her host read her thoughts.

"You are wet," he said. "We must rectify that."

André called Esther to fetch dry clothes. Although now that Rose thought about it, she doubted the man could accommodate four women of different shapes and sizes.

Emilie was by far the tallest, almost reaching Lorenz's height, and the one who always turned heads with her shapely figure and cascading brown curls.

Gabrielle resembled their father, Rose was told, with dark complexion, silky black hair, and deep-set sad eyes. Even though Marianne insisted the opposite, Gabrielle blamed herself for the family's separation on the beach that day.

Their mother stood somewhere in between. She was of medium height and had a lovely figure and chestnut hair. The stress of living thirteen years in exile had produced a number of gray hairs but failed to diminish her beauty.

Rose didn't favor anyone, except a great aunt who had moles and walked with a cane. She was tiny, for one thing, eye level with most people's chests. She lacked curves, and her brown hair fell straight about her shoulders when it wasn't wrapped in its obligatory braid. It was so fine that tiny wisps consistently poked free.

She was, in essence, an ordinary girl. Even though her mother insisted she owned a "delightful smile" and an easy-going, unpretentious nature, Rose labeled herself plain.

No man ever gave Rose a second glance. No man except one. And he might as well have been from the moon.

Esther returned from upstairs with blankets and an assortment of women's clothing, some finely tailored.

"We can't possibly wear these," Marianne said, gazing at the brocades and silks. "We will make-do."

André glanced at the clothes, unaware of her meaning. "They are my mother's and my sister's. They are in Pointe Coupée visiting relatives. They will not mind."

Marianne passed an appreciative hand across one dress. "I believe they will, monsieur. We have been traveling for days and are in no state to wear such fine clothes."

André shrugged. "Do as you please."

They stood in the stifling foyer wondering what to say next. They longed to change out of their clothes, take a bath perhaps, but didn't know how to approach the subject with such a wealthy host. None of them had enjoyed the company of an aristocrat before, let alone stand in one's foyer. Even Esther, her arms laden with clothes, was at a loss for words.

"Perhaps we can wait out the storm in a private room where we can remove our clothes and allow them to dry," Gabrielle offered.

André shrugged again. "Fine, but we will need something to eat."

Esther cringed at the sound of thunder exploding over the house. "How will we get to the kitchen?" she asked, clearly frightened at the prospect.

André appeared displeased. "Well, someone has to get the food. We can't starve while this storm bellows around us."

"Where is the kitchen?" Rose asked.

"Apart from the house," André answered. "There's a covered gallery between."

Esther whimpered and Rose took her hand and squeezed. "I'll go fetch us some food. I can assume it doesn't need to be cooked."

André frowned, clearly upset to have his routine disturbed, but he relented. "I suppose not."

"You can't possibly think to build a fire on a day like this," Lorenz said, the censure evident in his voice.

Again, André shrugged, then headed up the stairs. "I shall change. Do what you wish."

With their host gone and the wind roaring around the timbers, the Gallant family gazed at one another. Rose knew what they were all thinking: André De-

Clouet was a strange person and an equally strange host, and perhaps he was typical of his class.

Holding on to each other, Rose and Gabrielle braved the wind and rain that beat at them despite the covered gallery.

When they entered the kitchen, the storage bins were packed with many different types of foods, but mostly ones needing to be cooked. Gabrielle grabbed two baskets off the wall and began filling them with bread, peaches, figs, and two bottles of wine—foods they had not seen in a very long time.

"You've been thinking about him again, haven't you?" Gabrielle asked, breaking the silence.

"Thinking about whom?" Rose answered, even though she knew well her sister's meaning.

"You know."

Rose turned away to retrieve some pecans lying in a side bowl. Why did Gabrielle insist on speaking about Coleman Thorpe? He was a past acquaintance, one to be forgotten. Only Rose could not erase the man from her mind. And her sister could not stop bringing him up.

"Why must you worry about me?" she asked. "Coleman went west without so much as a good-bye, so I hardly think he cares for me. And we're here, looking for Papa's land grant where we will wait for his return." Rose turned and looked Gabrielle in the eye. "Besides, we both know he's an impossibility."

"I know," Gabrielle said with a sigh. "I just see the way you look sometimes and I know you're thinking of him."

Rose understood. She saw the same look in her

sister's eyes. "And you, Gabrielle, do you not think of Jean Bouclaire?"

A sadness overtook her sister's face, but she shook it off, then laughed. "We are a pair, are we not? Falling for an Englishman and a pirate. What on earth were we thinking?"

There was indeed something humorous in their choice of men, Rose thought. She turned and leaned against the sideboard, joining in the laughter.

"Do you think it might have been our circumstances?" Rose asked. "We were so desperate to find Papa. When Coleman and Jean came to our rescue, it was natural we would fall prey to their charms."

When word came that Joseph Gallant was in the Louisiana Territory, the family had chartered a ship from Maryland hoping to find their patriarch at a Louisiana Acadian settlement called St. Gabriel. But the Spanish government had other ideas. Longing to populate the frontier against English encroachment, the Spanish sent the Gallants upriver to a new settlement at Natchez.

While there, Coleman Thorpe, a neighboring English plantation owner, hired them to sew his shirts. It was clear he had feelings for Rose. He had even professed his love for her one day in their cabin. Rose hadn't been able to understand his words, since the man spoke only English, but his emotions that day crossed all language barriers.

Captain Jean Bouclaire was in Natchez on business when Gabrielle met him. The husky, mustached pirate—or smuggler as he would have it—assisted the family several times. Jean even became friends with Coleman before returning to New Orleans, where his ship and crew waited.

"Perhaps," Gabrielle replied. "But I have always been partial to ships, and you have always had a difficult time saying no."

Rose had heard this before, from every member of her family. She was too kind, too forgiving, too accepting of people. Rose never could understand how people could listen to one thing in church, then warn her against it the next day. How was it possible to be too nice, too accepting, too forgiving?

Gabrielle sighed and Rose hoped a lecture wasn't forthcoming. She had heard it all too many times. Her family was afraid Rose could be talked into anything.

"We were women alone in a new territory," Gabrielle said. "I was fearful that Englishman would convince you to run away with him."

Whenever they spoke of Coleman, Rose felt her cheeks flush. Whether from embarrassment or anger, she could not tell, but it was never an easy conversation.

"It wasn't like that at all," she said softly, trying to dispel the fire rising in her face. "He helped our family and he enjoyed my company. But he is English, so what does it matter?"

Gabrielle glanced down into her basket. "You're right," she said softly. "What does it matter? We're heading into Opelousas now, and leaving the memories of these two men behind."

If only it were that easy, Rose thought.

"Come on," Gabrielle said, with a renewed smile. "Our host awaits."

The two women giggled at the image of André DeClouet, a man so far apart from them in education, upbringing, and money. Rose wondered what he would think of the meager supper that looked like a feast to her.

As they expected, André was not pleased with dinner, but he ate quietly, dressed in a dry set of well-tailored clothes. Rose savored the bread and the tart sweetness of the pears, followed by sips of wine that warmed her all the way to her toes. By the end of the meal, she could barely keep her eyes open.

"It's time we retired," Marianne said.

André said nothing and continued eating. When all eyes fell on him, he wiped his mouth and leaned back in his chair. "Esther," he called, "show them to the guest room and to my sister's room."

The slave curtsied, then picked up a candle from the table. Marianne rose and the rest of the family followed, all except Lorenz and the guide. Emilie glanced back to the table in alarm.

"Don't worry about me," Lorenz said with one of his charming smiles. "We're going to wait out the storm in case anything happens."

Emilie hesitated, not wanting to let her impulsive husband out of her sight. Lorenz had a habit of placing himself in harm's way. But her mother snaked a hand through her arm and led her away.

Again, Rose followed at the rear, which gave her a chance to slip a pear into her pocket in case she got hungry in the night. As she passed André on the way to the stairs, he gave her another long look.

It didn't take long for the women to fall asleep,

despite the wind howling at the windows. Gabrielle and Rose took one bedroom, discarding their clothes across the chairs and slipping beneath the soft cotton sheets of a four-poster bed. High above their heads a canopy allowed the mosquito netting to drape around them. Beneath them was a moss-filled mattress. Gabrielle and Rose held their breath as they crawled into the bed, fearful that the experience might be only a dream. Before long, they were sound asleep.

The wind and rain didn't keep them awake, but the silence proved too much for Rose. She woke to find the wind and rain gone. There was not even a breeze. At first she thought she was dreaming until she heard familiar voices on the outside gallery.

She threw on her damp clothes and headed down to the first floor. When she left the back of the house, she saw Lorenz and their guide repairing the door to the barn. Surrounding the house and outbuildings was an endless sea of broken branches and roof tiles beneath a crescent moon.

"You shouldn't be out here," André said. Rose turned and found her host standing on the gallery.

"The hurricane's over?" Rose asked, ignoring his command.

"It's the center," André said, taking a long drink from a glass. "It won't last long."

Rose had heard about the eye of a storm, but she had never imagined it would be so peaceful. She leaned over the gallery railing and saw a sky full of stars.

André slid a hand about her waist and pulled her back toward him. He politely released her, but not before she felt the tight muscles of his large chest and the starched crispness of his shirt and inhaled the aroma of sweet tonic.

"You mustn't do that," he said softly. "When the winds pick up again, they will come around that side of the house with more force than before."

Rose nodded, uncomfortable with their sudden contact, and moved to return to her room.

"Mademoiselle," André called out.

Rose paused on the threshold. "Yes, monsieur."

"I wish to speak to you on a matter," he said.

Rose released her hold on the doorknob and returned to a spot on the gallery where she could make out André's face. He was probably hungry again, wanting more food from the kitchen. Then she thought of her pear and wondered if he had seen her put it in her pocket. Would he be angry over a pear, especially in the middle of a hurricane? she wondered.

"I have a proposition for you," he said. "I have inherited money from an uncle in France. But there is one stipulation: I must be married. It's a great deal of money and I would like to get my hands on it as soon as possible. This hurricane will only make it more necessary, if you understand my meaning."

Rose didn't understand his meaning at all. How many crystal vases did one man need? If he was short on cash, that Oriental rug alone would probably bring enough money to keep the family in pears for a year. Still, she nodded.

"You and your family appear to be in need of money," he continued. "Lorenz explained to me that while you were sailing for Louisiana to find your father, he sailed for Maryland when he heard of your whereabouts. Now you are here in Opelousas looking for his Louisiana land grant to await his return."

"Yes." Rose hated the irony of it all. Thirteen years without word of their father; and when it finally happened, they had practically crossed in the Gulf of Mexico. Praying he would make it back to them, the family set out for the land grant that Joseph had obtained in Louisiana the year before. They had two places to search—Opelousas and the Attakapas Poste to the south.

"His land grant's not in Opelousas," André said.

"I beg your pardon?" Rose's heart stopped beating; she was sure of it.

"I know every land grant in this district. Joseph Gallant is not one of them."

Rose felt the blood drain from her cheeks. She wished she had a chair to sit on. They had traveled so far, spent every last dollar. They knew there was a chance the land grant would be in Opelousas, but that most of the Acadian settlers had chosen the Attakapas Poste instead. The inclement weather had forced them north.

They would have to move on now. Head south. But their food supplies were gone and they had no money to hire a wagon. Walking to the Attakapas in August didn't seem to be a good option.

"As I said, mademoiselle, I have a proposition."

Rose looked up into the aristocrat's face and found kinder eyes than she had seen earlier. Perhaps she was wrong about André DeClouet. Perhaps he wanted to help after all.

"It would be a business arrangement," he said. "You and I would marry. I would receive the inheritance, and I would pay you handsomely for the transaction. You would have more than enough to travel to the Attakapas Poste. You would have enough to build a house and purchase cattle. And I would not require anything of you as my wife."

Rose felt her jaw drop. The man wanted to marry her! She had to be imagining things.

"You don't have to answer now," André said, before downing the contents of his glass. "But would you agree to consider my proposal?"

Rose heard Lorenz approach and prayed he hadn't heard the outrageous proposition. For some reason she was embarrassed that she was having this conversation. André leaned in close and she could smell the brandy on his breath.

"Think of your family," he whispered. "This would solve all your problems."

"And yours."

She couldn't believe she had uttered something so bold, but his question had shocked her.

"Yes, mademoiselle," André said soberly. "And mine."

Lorenz was saying something to their guide, but Rose couldn't make out the words. Oh God, what would Lorenz think? What did she think? The proposal seemed absurd, yet the prospect of money was tantalizing.

"Don't say anything now," André said. "Just promise me you will think about it."

Common sense left her at that moment, or perhaps it was the shock that numbed her ability to reason. Rose nodded her approval as the northwest winds of the hurricane returned full force.

Chapter Two

Coleman Thorpe gazed at the apocalyptic scene before him, wondering if God was having a good laugh at his expense. His first crops had been parched by a dry spring, and he had spent nearly all his money planting again in midsummer. Now his fields were ruined, drowned in the tail end of the hurricane and trampled by his cattle and pigs.

His barn, if one had the nerve to call it that, was leaning precariously to the left, waiting, it seemed, for a small breeze to finish the hurricane's work. Spying a rake head plunged into the ground, Coleman realized he should have brought the tools in from the shed—or better yet, built a tougher shed. The hastily constructed building was nowhere in sight.

If he had known anything about farming, he would have created stronger pens for the animals and a better drainage system for the fields. He should have done a lot of things differently, Coleman thought. But then he wasn't a farmer.

When Coleman emerged onto the back porch to assess the damage, the vibration of his steps caused part of the roof to collapse, sending a shower of water down on his head.

Yes, Coleman thought grimly, God was having a very good laugh.

He might be ignorant about farming, but Coleman knew one thing. He needed a drink. Now. And he knew where to find one.

Coleman entered his tiny cabin to change his clothes. He couldn't help thinking, as he did every time he crossed the threshold and saw his surroundings, that he was ignorant of too many things. Raised on a plantation, most of his concerns centered around Latin studies, music lessons, and riding. Farming and its weather-related problems were the concerns of the overseer. Cooking, cleaning, and mending were done by the house slaves. If he needed clothes, the tailor came from town. If he wanted lessons, a tutor was hired.

As Coleman removed his wet shirt, three buttons missing, he was reminded again of his many shortcomings. And of how much money could buy.

If he had stayed on the plantation when he came of age, he would have learned everything the overseer knew. He would have accompanied Ben, the eldest slave, on his daily duties and picked his brain about weather patterns and soil composition. He would have watched the planting, knowing how far apart to sow corn and indigo seeds. He would have paid more attention to the slave superstitions, the ones that dealt with full moons and planting on Good Friday—ideas his father called ludicrous that now made sense.

But he hadn't stayed. After his mother's death, he had fled to Williamsburg for schooling, traveling as far as possible from his father without going to England. If he hadn't hated his father's profession so much, England would have been the next stop.

University at Williamsburg had been a failure, the first in a long line; but it had given him distance from his father, something he desperately needed. Coleman returned to his Natchez plantation when his money ran out—and because his father had insisted on it—but there was too much anger between them for a reconciliation. It was only a matter of time before he left again. When Coleman turned twenty-one and inherited his mother's estate, he purchased a land grant in Opelousas and moved away.

Looking around the filthy cabin, its sink piled high with dirty dishes and scorched pots and pans, its chairs full of torn dirty clothing, Coleman wondered if this would be another one of his failures. Not to mention that money was running out.

Yes, he definitely needed a drink.

He threw on his shoes—expensive, fine-tailored ones bought in New Orleans, now caked with mud and splitting at the seams—and headed for the door. He grabbed his straw hat and left the dilapidated cabin. The sight from the front door rivaled the one from the back porch.

"A hurricane," he shouted toward the heavens. "Why don't you just send a tornado and finish me off?"

As always, there was no answer. God was too busy laughing.

No doubt everyone else in town was laughing too. They all took sport at Coleman's misfortunes. Being English, he was a good target. The outpost consisted primarily of Creoles from New Orleans looking for a chance at fortune or displaced French from Mobile evicted from their homes when the English took control of West Florida. A few Acadians had settled in the Louisiana prairies. Not as eager to become rich, these families were more interested in starting a new life on their own land.

Acadians.

The word reverberated inside his head. He caught his breath. Would there ever be a moment when he didn't think of her?

As he approached the outpost store, Henri La-Londe shouted, "Back so soon?"

Henri loved to taunt Coleman about his lack of farming knowledge, his lack of carpentry and cooking skills, and his recent passion for drink. Yet Coleman found it hard to dislike the chubby Frenchman. At least the man spoke English. That was more than the others were willing to do.

"My supplies were damaged in the storm," Coleman said.

Henri laughed, then spit on the ground. "Don't

think you learned how to cook during that storm, supplies or no.''

When Coleman reached Henri and the threshold of the store, he noticed Henri had been partaking of his alcoholic stock. "Of course I didn't," Coleman returned. "So why did you ask?"

Henri grunted and staggered back inside the meager cabin where half of the store's dry goods lay on the floor, ruined by a leaking roof. "What do you want this time, Englishman?" Henri asked. "Something to drink or something to eat?"

Now that Coleman thought about it, he hadn't eaten since the day before, when the weather turned. "Both if you got it."

"Marguerite?" Henri yelled out the back window toward the kitchen. A woman's voice yelled back, and the two began a long hurried conversation in French. Coleman understood little, but he caught his name, usually followed by laughter when it was mentioned.

"She's coming," Henri said, turning back to Coleman. "But you," he added, poking his finger at Coleman's chest, "you got to stop coming here every time you hungry."

Coleman removed his hat and shook the masses of blond curls that fell about his forehead. He loosened his tie and tried to harness the unruly hair that was in desperate need of a haircut.

"Why must I stop coming?" he asked Henri, who watched his movements intensely. Most of the people in Opelousas seemed fascinated by his blond hair and blue eyes, features not usually found on the French. "You don't seem to mind taking my money."

Henri straightened, as if reminded of some important fact. "You're right. I don't." He then produced a bottle from underneath the counter and poured them each a drink.

This is strange, Coleman thought. Henri drank with many of his patrons, but never with him. Although they both had a common reason to drink this afternoon. They saluted with their glasses, then downed the contents. The rum left a welcome burning down Coleman's throat and he anticipated the numbness that would soon follow.

"You need a wife," Henri said, leaning on the counter. "You need someone to help you clean that filthy cabin of yours and cook you dinner."

Coleman couldn't help but smile. "Why, Henri, you're concerned about my welfare."

Henri straightened and snorted. "What do I care what the hell you do? I'm sick of seeing your ugly English face in here, that's all."

Coleman took the bottle and poured them both another drink. "Then I'll come to the back window where you can take my money without looking at my ugly English face."

"It's not funny," Henry said soberly. "You look like, what's the English word for *merde*?"

Merde was the one French word Coleman understood. "Shit," he answered.

"Sheet," Henry replied, pointing again. "That's what you look like, *L'Anglais*. Horse sheet."

Marguerite appeared through the back door with a bowl of stew in her hands. She placed it before Coleman but held the spoon and napkin until he gave her two silver coins. *"Merci,"* he said before devouring his meal.

Marguerite and Henri began another heated conversation that Coleman couldn't follow; he was too busy concentrating on the delicious stew to care. In between bites of bread he heard his name mentioned, but he ignored it. The French always spoke about him in his presence. They knew he couldn't understood them. When Henri and Marguerite finished talking and silence fell, Coleman looked up to find the couple staring at him.

"My wife agrees," Henri stated. "You need a wife."

Coleman stared back aghast. The last thing he expected was Henri and Marguerite LaLonde playing matchmaker. He hardly expected them to speak to him.

"I'm capable of taking care of myself," Coleman said.

Henri released a rush of breath through his lips that resembled blowing out a candle. It was a gesture the French were fond of using to express disapproval. "A wife would get you settled, help with the chores and the cooking. Maybe keep those pigs where they belong."

Dear God, Coleman thought, the man was serious. The last thing he needed right now was a woman in his life.

"I appreciate the thought," Coleman began, "but . . ."

"But nothing. Are the women in Opelousas not good enough for the likes of an Englishman? You don't like French women, is that it?"

Now Coleman really had to smile. The only women he had ever loved was French, Acadian to be exact, and that was one reason he had come to Opelousas. To try to force her out of his mind.

He would move mountains if it meant marrying Rose, but the prospect was unthinkable. What Acadian woman, expelled from her home in Nova Scotia by the English, would wish to marry an Englishman? Even if Rose felt the same way, her mother would never approve. Nor would anyone else in her family.

Coleman's smile disappeared as the familiar pain seized his heart. A cloud descended upon him as it did every time he pictured Rose's small oval face sprinkled with freckles and graced with an adorable upturned nose. She was hardly a beauty, yet she shone with an inner radiance that had captivated him, had literally taken his breath away. Those brown eyes, perfectly round and full of wonder and light. How they sparkled when she spoke. And a voice like an angel.

But it didn't matter. Rose Gallant was as far removed from him as heaven from earth.

"There are nice women in Opelousas," he heard Henri say through the fog. "You might like them if you give them a chance."

Coleman stared down at the bottom of his glass, wishing it wasn't empty. He needed more rum to deaden the pain.

"I have met the finest of women, sir, and I am not able to have her," he answered softly. "I mean no disrespect to the women of Opelousas, but I doubt anyone will ever capture my heart again."

Henri stared at him hard, then refilled his glass.

"I only paid for two drinks," Coleman stated.

Henri said nothing, then mumbled, "It's on the house."

Stingy Henri LaLonde offering a free drink to an Englishman? The day was full of surprises. What would happen next? Coleman wondered.

"Don't give up," Henri said. "You never know. Your wife may be the next woman who walks through that door."

Coleman forced a smile, knowing how far-fetched that idea was. Rose Gallant was safe with her family in St. Gabriel, reunited with her father at last. But he saluted his host. "Good health to you and your wife," he said before drinking his fill.

"And to you and yours," Henri said as he downed his, a smile breaking at the corners of his lips.

The door opened and a patron entered, so Henri ushered over to help the man with his supply list. The two men left the building, chattering in French as they headed for Henri's stables. Coleman turned and leaned against the counter, tilting his head back to enjoy the effects of the rum, glad for the solitude. He closed his eyes, wondering, as he did every night at Henri's counter, why the rum refused to ease the pain tearing at his soul.

When he heard footsteps at the back door of the store, Coleman realized he wasn't alone. He pulled his head forward and opened his eyes. Standing before him was the woman he had been dreaming of for months, the angel who had stolen his heart.

* * *

Rose glanced down at her supply list and tried to focus on the elegant handwriting. After a restless night, she was too exhausted to care about eating. But André had insisted.

Only hours after the hurricane's fury had abated, André DeClouet had put everyone to work. The main house had been spared, but the barn and chicken coop had significant damage and the fields were ruined. While the others helped restore the household and the slaves worked in the fields, Rose and Lorenz had been sent to the outpost store for lumber and tools. And food to make a "proper dinner."

Rose couldn't help thinking that what they all needed after their long journey from St. Gabriel and the sleepless night from the hurricane was rest. Especially Lorenz. He hadn't slept in two days, working nonstop for André through the storm. He barely stayed awake on the wagon trip to the store.

But Rose didn't wish to be ungrateful. André had insisted they live in his guest cabin until they raised enough money to travel on to the Attakapas Poste. In return for helping with the plantation's chores and farming, they would receive two meals a day along with the board. In addition, André promised a small salary that would be enough to hire a wagon in about six weeks' time.

Gazing around the small store, Rose stared at the meager supplies and the ruined dry goods on the floor. She stepped over a puddle and a spilled barrel of flour. So this was the frontier. The few items lining the shelves, the chickens visible through the holes in the floorboards, and the squalor didn't bother her. She was used to it. But André had given her a long list of items, some quite rare in rural areas, and there were few to be had in the store this day.

Rose loosened her bonnet's tie at her neck, feeling perspiration roll down the front of her shirt. The store was stifling, but she dreaded facing her host without the requested supplies. She turned down another aisle and found a barrel of sugar, giving thanks for one item to cross off the list. Now if she could only find some salt and flour.

When she checked the bottom shelf, she noticed a pair of shoes in front of her at the counter and realized she wasn't alone. She knew the polite thing to do was make slight eye contact with the man and introduce herself, but the shoes caught her attention and she couldn't tear her gaze away. Although they were well worn, the shoes sported brass buckles, large ones with an elaborate design. They were so familiar, like the kind Coleman used to wear.

Rose shut her eyes, trying to will the memory away. She had to stop thinking of him. She was going to marry André DeClouet and help her family settle in a new frontier, in a safe place where Papa could find them. They would start over with cattle, seeds to plant, and a new home. She would help her sisters with their children, care for her parents in their old age, and be satisfied, knowing her marriage of convenience had brought her family happiness in their time of need. And she would stop thinking of the man who had passionately declared his love for her before leaving for the West. The man who had claimed her heart.

"Rose?"

Dear God, Rose thought, shutting her eyes tighter, she could even hear his voice.

"Rose?"

Suddenly there were hands gripping her arms, forcing her eyes open. Standing before her was Coleman Thorpe, his cerulean eyes examining her from head to foot as if he, too, doubted they stood in the same room.

"What are you doing in Opelousas?" he asked.

The realization hit Rose full force. It *was* Coleman. She might have brushed off the first sight of him as a product of her imagination, a specter conjured up from her desires, but his fingers on her arms were real. *He* was real. His clothes were torn and dirty, his hair too long with blond curls falling about his forehead, but it was Coleman. Her Coleman.

"I, ah . . ."

Rose didn't know what to say, and the few English words she knew seemed trapped inside her brain. Coleman Thorpe was the last person she expected to find in Opelousas. She had been told he had moved west, but she imagined it was one of those distant places in the interior with bison, prairies, and wild Indians. Opelousas offered prairies and natives, but it was only a few days' journey from New Orleans and Natchez, hardly Rose's picture of the American West. Perhaps Coleman was merely stopping at the outpost to pick up supplies on his trek to somewhere else.

"You were supposed to be in St. Gabriel," he

insisted, concern evident in his voice. "Why are you here?"

Rose's mind began to clear. She forced herself to concentrate. "Papa wasn't at St. Gabriel. He left for Maryland when he heard we were there. We crossed paths on our way to Louisiana."

Coleman dropped his hands and Rose instantly missed the warmth they had provided. He shook his head in disbelief. "Oh Rose, I am so sorry," he said.

The pain returned, landing like a lead weight upon Rose's heart. Finding Joseph Gallant gone had devastated Marianne when they had finally reached St. Gabriel. Emilie had taken to her bed for days. If only they had stayed in Maryland a few months longer, they would have been reunited. But they couldn't think of what could have been. They had to move on, to travel to his land grant and wait. They had waited in exile for thirteen years. They would wait again.

"We came to Opelousas to find his land grant and wait for his return," Rose continued, finding comfort in Coleman's eyes. Regardless of what Lorenz and Marianne said about the English, Coleman Thorpe was a fine and caring man. She was certain of it.

"His land grant is here?"

Did she detect the sound of hope in his voice? Was it possible he lived in Opelousas and wished the same for her? Would he show her the same attention he showed her in Natchez? Rose felt her heart jump. She dared not hope for such things.

"No," she answered. "We think it may be in the Attakapas Poste, so we will be traveling there next."

"When?"

"In several weeks' time, I believe."

He stared at her so intently, Rose had trouble breathing. "Where are you staying?" he asked.

For a moment, Rose's mind went blank. She forgot everything—her family, her host, her reason for being at the store that day. As she gazed into his eyes, the whole world floated on an ocean of blue.

"Rose?" he repeated.

"André DeClouet," she blurted out, waking her from her thoughts. "We are staying with André DeClouet."

Coleman's countenance darkened, or perhaps she was imagining things. As she recalled her agreement to consider André's marriage proposal, Rose felt her spirits drop as well. What would Coleman think of her marrying another?

What difference did it matter what he thought? she chided herself. He had left without so much as a good-bye. Obviously, he wasn't in love with her, no matter what proclamations he had made to her that day in Natchez. And his words had been English so he could have been declaring his love for her seamstress abilities, for all she knew. And then there was her family. They would never allow an Englishman to court her. Never.

No, she would marry André DeClouet, regardless of the fact that Coleman Thorpe and his entrancing blue eyes now stood before her.

But the thought of it was breaking her heart in two.

"Why are you here?" she asked him.

Coleman's eyes brightened. "I live here," he said.

She couldn't help herself. Joy claimed her soul and rose to her face. Rose was powerless to stop it. A smile began at the corners of her lips and broke free.

Coleman reacted with a smile of his own, hesitant at first, then spreading across his face like wildfire.

When Lorenz reentered the store, he found Rose and Coleman staring silently at each other, grinning like lovestruck fools.

Chapter Three

She must have been quite a site, Rose thought, when Lorenz found her smiling adoringly at a strange man in a rugged outpost store in the middle of the Louisiana frontier. The look on his face changed from shock to outrage and back again.

"Lorenz," she said, praying that the heat pouring across her cheeks wasn't a visible blush. "Lorenz, this is . . ."

"Coleman Thorpe," Coleman announced enthusiastically, offering a smile and an outstretched hand. "I have heard so much about you."

If her actions in the store weren't shocking enough to Lorenz, realizing that the man of her attentions was English surely was. His eyes grew enormous with alarm and he refused to accept Coleman's hand.

"Lorenz," Rose admonished him.

Coleman instantly realized his boundaries and returned his hand to his side.

"Then Lorenz and Emilie returned safely?" he asked Rose.

"Yes," Rose answered softly. "They were . . . What is the English word?"

"Married?" Coleman suggested.

Such a simple word, yet it sent a shiver through Rose, especially coming from his lips. "Yes, married. At St. Gabriel."

Coleman turned toward Lorenz, raised his hand again, thought better of it, and crossed his arms. "My congratulations, sir."

Lorenz frowned and started to answer, but Rose intervened. "They are newly married, only a few weeks."

Coleman glanced back toward Rose. "And your mother, Gabrielle—are they in good health?"

Rose smiled, comforted somehow that he remembered her family. "They are well, thank you."

Coleman leaned toward her, too close for polite company. Rose wondered if the flames streaking her cheeks were a result of her blushing or of the scalding look Lorenz was sending. "And you, Rose, are you well?" he asked so sweetly, she nearly melted.

I am now, she thought, but instead she turned her eyes toward the floor to escape the spell his eyes were casting on her. *"Oui, merci,"* she said wondering too how his fancy shoes had deteriorated so much in so short a time.

"Rose," Lorenz barked. "We must go."

Rose wasn't ready to leave yet. She wasn't ready to say good-bye. "We have supplies to purchase," she answered him in French.

"We have to leave *now,*" Lorenz said.

"I have to find flour and salt, and there is an item here I have never seen before . . ."

Lorenz grabbed her elbow. "We have everything we need. *Allons!*"

Rose pulled away from his grip, which shocked her as much as it did Lorenz. She had never objected to his instructions. She had never objected to anyone. "Why are you being so rude?" she demanded.

Lorenz leaned in close, his face red with anger. "I have to talk to you now."

"But the list?"

Coleman moved between them and lifted the paper from her fingers. "I'll see that it's taken care of. Henri can bring the supplies by later."

"That's not necessary," Lorenz said to him in English, grabbing the list from his hand.

Coleman looked at Lorenz hard, but not in anger. They seemed close in age and stature, although Lorenz was a good two inches taller. Would they be friends if their nationalities didn't stand between them like a gaping chasm? Rose wondered. If Coleman hadn't spoken English, he and Lorenz would probably be talking about shooting rabbits and the price of corn.

"If I know André DeClouet, it's very necessary," Coleman retorted and held out his hand.

"Oui, Monsieur Landry," Henri agreed from the back of the store. "We will take care of it."

Lorenz glanced at Henri, then at Coleman. Still sporting a disapproving look, he shoved the list into Coleman's hands, grabbed Rose's elbow, and headed for the door.

Rose looked over her shoulder and uttered *"Merci,"* before Lorenz pulled her across the threshold.

Coleman watched the heavenly image disappear and wondered if the rum was playing tricks with his mind. When he heard Lorenz calling the horses outside and wagon wheels creaking into action, he knew she had been real. Rose Gallant, looking every bit as charming as the day they met, had stood before him. He had even held her in his arms.

The familiar cloud descended again. Only this time, its darkness was ten times more acute.

He felt Henri's hand on his shoulder and a bottle of rum being slipped into the crook of his elbow.

"Go home, *mon ami,*" Henri said. "It will all look better tomorrow."

Coleman nodded, but he knew things were never going to get better. God was having too much fun.

Lorenz whipped the horses again, urging them on. He was hell-bent on getting away from the store, which only fueled Rose's anger.

"Why are you doing this?" she demanded. "How can you be so rude?"

"How can *I* be so rude?" he barked back. "How can you be so blind? That man is English, in case you haven't noticed."

"You refuse to shake his hand because he's English?"

Lorenz stared down at her so hard the hairs on the back of her neck prickled. He gritted his teeth in frustration, then reined in the horses. When the wagon came to a stop, he placed an elbow on his knee to make his eyes as level with hers as possible.

"That's him, isn't it?" Lorenz asked. "That's the man."

Rose had an idea what Lorenz was talking about. He had caught her crying one day in St. Gabriel, and she had hinted of meeting a man in Natchez, but she had refused to give him details. She never expected to meet Coleman again. Why give Lorenz and her family something else to worry about?

"What man?" she said, hoping he would drop the subject.

"The man who broke your heart, the one you wouldn't talk to me about, remember?"

Rose stared down at her lap and ran her finger along the stripes in her skirt. "He didn't break my heart."

"Stole your heart, then."

Rose looked up and squared her shoulders. "He's my friend. He hired me to mend his shirts in Natchez, that's all. We talked some. We went for a walk. He came to the village one night and played music for us all. What's the harm in that?"

Lorenz looked heavenward as if asking God for support. "He's English!" he yelled when he looked back.

"He calls himself an American," she insisted.

The veins in Lorenz's neck were about to burst. Rose couldn't remember when she had seen him this angry. "I don't care if he calls himself the Pope, you are to stay away from him."

This was it. This was the moment she was waiting for. The point when everyone knew what was best for her, when they instructed her how to act, what to do. Only this time, she wasn't listening.

Rose hopped down from the wagon, grabbed her basket, and began to walk toward the DeClouet plantation.

"Where are you going?" Lorenz called after her, but she refused to turn around. Her skin tingled from the anger of the injustice, and her eyes burned from the tears she fought to control.

"Rose," Lorenz called out again, this time pleadingly.

Rose refused to turn. Marching ahead, she heard Lorenz utter a few choice words and descend from the wagon. Within seconds his hands were on her shoulders, stopping her and turning her around.

"Rose, talk to me." His voice was softer, but the anger still simmered in his eyes. "Pumpkin, how do you expect me to react? I walked in the store and found you two gazing at each other like lovers."

"He's my friend," she insisted.

"You were crying over this man."

Rose looked away and wiped her eyes with her sleeve. "I suppose I am now too," she said with a grim smile.

"Why? What could you possibly see in this man?"

Rose knew why Lorenz detested the English. His

mother, in fragile health, had died in his arms after the English soldiers evicted her from her home in Grand Pré, then burned it. His father died onboard ship en route to Maryland and was buried at sea. Even if they could return to Canada one day, there were no graves to visit, no village left standing to show the Acadians had once lived there. All because of the English.

But Coleman Thorpe wasn't responsible simply because he was born English. Why couldn't Lorenz understand that?

"I don't judge people because they were born one way or another, Lorenz," she said. "I know you think that's naive, but I judge people by their hearts instead."

Lorenz captured a loose hair and tucked it behind her ear. "I know you do, Pumpkin. That's what we all love about you."

"But it's also what you don't love about me." Rose walked over to a nearby log and sat down. "You appreciate my accepting nature except when it interferes with your wishes."

Taking a place next to her on the log, Lorenz took her hand. "That's not true, *mon amour*. We worry someone will take advantage of you."

"Is that what you're worried about now? I assure you, he's my friend."

Lorenz ran his hands through his hair. "I don't trust the English. I never will." Gazing over at her, he added, "And neither will your maman."

Rose shook her head. "Coleman Thorpe is not

responsible for our exile, Lorenz. Why would you distrust him so when you don't even know him?''

"Because I'm afraid one day I'll turn my back and he will convince you to marry him.''

Rose laughed thinking of the irony. "No, that's what the Creole French do.''

Lorenz moved his body so he was almost facing her. "What do you mean?''

She took a deep breath, then let it out slowly. "André DeClouet has asked me to marry him.''

Rose didn't think it was possible for Lorenz's eyes to stretch any farther than they had in the store, but he stood and stared down at her with eyes the size of walnuts. He blinked, looked away briefly as if suspecting he'd heard wrong, then turned back to her, his mouth wide open.

"It's not what you think," she offered.

Lorenz smirked, then shook his head. "What else does asking you to marry him mean?''

Rose shut her eyes briefly, weary of the confrontation. But sooner or later they had to discuss this.

"He's inherited some money from an uncle in Europe. Only he has to be married to receive it. He asked for my hand as a business proposition. In return, our family will be given enough money to travel to the Attakapas Poste and start a new life. He said he would give us enough to purchase cattle and seeds and build a new home. I haven't agreed yet. I just promised to think about it.''

Lorenz placed his hands on his hips and his face grew stern. "Over my dead body," he said so gravely that Rose shivered.

"It's the answer to our prayers," she argued.

"It's the answer to that pompous aristocrat's prayers," Lorenz shouted. "The rich bastard will be able to spend his life fornicating with any woman he sees and you will die an old maid. I will see you married to that damned Englishman before André DeClouet marches you down the aisle. Do you understand me?"

Rose had to admit that the idea of being married to self-centered André DeClouet, despite the fact that it would enable the family to start anew, both scared and repelled her. Regardless of what he promised or how generous he had been to the family, she would be his wife. And his property.

"Do you understand me?" Lorenz repeated.

Rose nodded, realizing that having a brother looking out for her welfare was a good thing, after all. Maybe she was a stupid naive girl who was incapable of making decisions. Maybe she was too trusting of people. Maybe she had no sense at all.

A lone tear trickled down her cheek. Lorenz sat down and brushed the tear away with the back of his hand. "Why would you give up your chance at happiness?" he said softly. "I appreciate your thinking of the family, but it would have meant your never having a family of your own."

A sob made its way up her chest, threatening to choke her. But Rose wasn't going to be defeated today. She breathed deeply and exhaled the emotion. "My chance of happiness has already come," she whispered. "And you refused to shake his hand."

Lorenz dropped his hand from her face and turned

forward again. He leaned his elbows on his knees and placed his fingers at his lips like a steeple.

Dear, dear, Lorenz, Rose thought, knowing he agonized over their conversation. He was her champion, and she had given him the toughest of conflicts.

"I'll make a deal with you," he finally said. "You say nothing to André, agree to nothing. If he insists on an answer, you tell him he must talk to me. I'm the patriarch of this family right now, and I have to approve whom you will marry."

"And Maman," Rose inserted.

"Yes, of course, your mother too." Lorenz was silent for a moment, then gazed into her eyes. "You mustn't tell your mother about this."

"About DeClouet or Coleman?"

"Either one. She has enough to worry about these days. Let's keep this between us."

"And what is the rest of the deal?" Rose asked.

Lorenz frowned. He was probably hoping she wouldn't have remembered. "I'll go talk to this 'American' of yours."

Sunlight poured in on Rose's heart and she couldn't stop the smile erupting on her face. "Oh, Lorenz, you promise?"

"Talk," he insisted, his voice stern. "I'm not promising anything else."

It was a small gesture, but a start. Rose nodded, then slid an arm through his and placed her cheek against his shoulder. "Thank you," she whispered.

Lorenz grunted, clearly unhappy at the idea of meeting Coleman. But he was relenting, Rose thought. What was the saying? Rome wasn't built in a day. They had several weeks. Could a bridge between two nationalities be built in that short amount of time?

The afternoon dragged on. The women fought off fatigue with coffee while they returned the house's furniture and fixtures to their rightful places. Water had leaked in through the hallway, so Gabrielle and Emilie spent hours scrubbing the floors. Marianne was sent to the kitchen where supplies were thrown everywhere while Rose worked the back gallery, covered with branches and debris. Upon their return from the store, Lorenz began repairing the barn and was not seen again that afternoon.

"I don't want to sound ungrateful," Rose heard Emilie say, "but Lorenz desperately needs sleep. He's been working constantly since we arrived. I can't help thinking we're all being taken advantage of here."

"I want to see this guest house Monsieur DeClouet has for us," Gabrielle said. "Every hour and every new job he finds for us, my hopes diminish. I'm beginning to wonder if we'll be sleeping in the barn."

"And poor Maman," Emilie added. "If only Papa's land grant had been here. She is so tired of being dependent on other people's generosity, having to deal with their every whim, every request."

"As am I."

Rose paused at her sweeping and leaned against the side of the house. Lorenz was right about one thing. She didn't think things through. She was capable of letting people talk her into the most ridiculous situations. She had considered André's proposal in order to allow her family freedom, but accepting his money would have been another form of charity, another person to be indebted to. And what of her freedom? André would be able to live a normal life, even produce legal heirs outside the marriage bed, but she would be forced to remain single for the rest of her life.

"A penny for your thoughts." André's voice startled her and she jumped.

"You surprised me," she said, trying to dispel the anxiety churning in her stomach. She glanced around the yard hoping Lorenz was nearby, but they were alone.

"You were deep in thought. I hope it had to do with our conversation early this morning." André approached her and took the broom from her hands. He stood close. Too close.

"No," Rose said, backing up a step. "I was simply taking a break. We are all very tired from the journey and the storm."

André mumbled, then stared out over the fields. "Perhaps we should break for supper." He turned back and stared at her hard. "Did you have time to consider my proposal?"

Rose's throat constricted. She hated telling people no; she never knew where to start. She was always cornered into buying items she didn't need because she couldn't turn down the seller's entreaty. André was a grown man, capable of accepting rejection, especially since there was no love between them, but Rose hadn't the heart to tell him no.

Then a thought came to her.

"We can't start supper yet," she said. "Henri LaLonde is bringing the supplies from the store. I won't be able to help with dinner until he arrives."

André's eyes bored into her. He was about to ask again, Rose knew it, but a couple of men on horseback approached.

"André," the tall muscular one shouted. "I have some interesting news for you."

The smaller one, sporting a beard and clothes as fine as André's, dismounted. "You won't believe what has happened to our Englishman now."

Rose's heart stopped, imagining they spoke of Coleman, while André broke into laughter. "What has the poor excuse of a farmer done now?"

The tall one dismounted as well, and they met André at the bottom of the gallery's stairs. "It's not what he's done," the tall one said. "It's what the hurricane did to him. He's ruined."

André tilted his head back and laughed again, then slapped the man on the back. "Well, that's about the best news I've heard today."

With a side glance, André caught Rose's eye and sent her a stern look. For a moment, she sensed it was a warning. But that was impossible. André DeClouet couldn't possibly be depending on her to retrieve his inheritance. There must be dozens of women throughout the region itching to be his wife. Now that she thought of it, why on earth had André asked *her*?

"This is Rose Gallant," André introduced her to the two men, who immediately bowed. "She and her family are helping out on the plantation for the next month or so." To Rose, he said, "Monsieur Delahoussaye, Monsieur Latiolais."

Then he dismissed her and turned toward the men to continue the conversation. "So what happened?"

"His fields are a mess," Latiolais said with a grin. "And this is the second crop he's planted this year."

"And the animals?" André asked.

The two men laughed. "Everywhere," Delahoussaye answered, "And if a pig leans against that shack he calls a barn, it will come crashing down. In fact, a good breeze has probably destroyed it today."

The men laughed again and Rose's heart dropped. Could they be speaking of Coleman?

"Is there more than one Englishman in this district," she asked them.

The men stopped laughing and Rose wished she could retract her question. It was one thing to be introduced to a man, but another for a woman to speak when not addressed.

"There is only one, mademoiselle," Latiolais said curtly. "One is enough."

"Not for long though," André said, eliciting a smile among the threesome. "Not if I have anything to do with it."

Chapter Four

Rose agonized during dinner, waiting for a moment to catch Lorenz alone to tell him what she had heard. As soon as they finished eating, André ordered several slaves to take them to their sleeping quarters. The house had once belonged to a former overseer. Then the new overseer's house was built.

"So we get the old house that's not good enough for the current overseer, a single man," Emilie said as they followed the slaves' lanterns through the fields.

"What's your point, Emilie?" Marianne asked.

"A house that's not good enough for one man doesn't sound too appealing for a family of five, particularly four grown women and a man."

"Don't be ungrateful," Marianne said. "I'm sure Monsieur DeClouet is offering the best he has."

Gabrielle sent Emilie and Rose a look that said, "Doubtful," but they all remained silent. Truth be told, with the way they were feeling, a pig sty would have been a welcomed site.

When the house came into view, Rose wondered if they weren't that far off.

"This is it?" Lorenz asked, gazing at the dilapidated building.

"Yes, sir," said the slave holding the lantern. "Monsieur André had us clean it up this morning."

"You mean it looked worse?" Emilie asked.

"I'm sure the inside looks better than the outside," Marianne said, taking the lantern from the man's hands and sending everyone a reprimanding look.

To the slave she said, "Thank you," and then led her family down the path.

They filed into the tiny house, treading gently on the weathered floorboards. The inside was in better shape than the outside. André had sent over several piles of linens, which were stacked on the bed.

"The house is in good shape," Emilie said, "but there is only one bed."

Marianne peered through the back window. "There's a large gallery off the back leading toward what looks like a kitchen."

"Why must all the kitchens be in some other building?" Gabrielle asked. "We're always having to go outside to get something to eat."

"To keep the house cooler," Lorenz answered, "and also to protect the house, if there's a fire."

"Well, I'm for anything that keeps a house cooler,"

Emilie stated, fanning herself with her hat. "I'd sleep outside if I could in this insufferable heat."

Marianne set the lantern down on the house's lone table. "I'm glad you said that, Emilie, because that is where you will be sleeping."

"What?" Emilie asked.

Marianne didn't have to explain. Lorenz caught her meaning instantly. "It means, my dear, that we are to sleep on the gallery and your mother and sisters get the bed."

"I'll sleep on the gallery if you wish," Rose offered.

Gabrielle pinched her arm. "Don't be silly. This way they have some privacy," she whispered.

Rose glanced at the newlyweds, who were grinning at the idea of being alone. They had lived together for so long, with Lorenz practically a member of the family, Rose sometimes forgot he had married Emilie. Lorenz grabbed an armload of linens, and the couple quickly disappeared out the back door.

"You didn't have to tell them twice," Gabrielle said, and she and Rose began to giggle.

"Your day will come," Marianne said, handing them the rest of the linens.

Gabrielle's eyes clouded over and she sighed. Rose knew exactly what she was thinking. They threw the sheets across the bed, tucking them in at the corners while Marianne took the pillows outside to beat out the dust.

"Do you think Maman will make us count the bed's joists again?" Gabrielle whispered to Rose as they worked.

When the cabin had been built for them in Natchez,

Marianne had insisted they count the joists, so they would dream of their intended grooms the first night in their new house. It was a silly superstition, one of the many Acadian tales passed down through the ages. But it had brightened Marianne's spirits that night, giving her hope that her daughters might find happiness.

But their dreams had been disturbing.

"Do you remember my dream?" Rose asked softly. "The blond man working in the fields and singing?"

Rose looked up at Gabrielle who was bent over her work. Either her sister was being polite or she had forgotten one essential detail. "It was Coleman Thorpe," Rose said.

"You don't know that. You said you didn't see his face."

"I didn't have to see his face, Gabrielle. The man spoke English."

Gabrielle threw the blanket over the bed, then grasped Rose's hand in hers. "You must forget about him, *chère*. The man went west and we're on our way to the Attakapas Poste. You must stop thinking about him."

Rose longed to confide in her sister, the one person who understood what it was like to care for the wrong type of man. But Marianne entered the room and began getting ready for bed.

The three women undressed down to their chemises and slid into bed. Although it was a snug fit, they quickly fell asleep.

Except for Rose, who stared off into the darkness,

reminded of a warm smile and the enchanting color of blue.

Rose woke to the sound of singing, a song she had not heard her mother sing in years. From the angle of sunlight shining on the bed, the day had advanced. It was more likely close to noon.

"Wake up, sleepyhead," Gabrielle said, throwing a pillow at her.

"I can't believe I've slept so long," Rose said, wiping her eyes. She still felt groggy, despite the many hours of sleep.

Gabrielle was fully dressed, her sleeves rolled up from cleaning. She sat at the edge of the bed and offered Rose a cup of coffee.

"You are the dearest sister," Rose said, taking the steaming cup.

"I know," Gabrielle said. "I'm your favorite middle sister."

"Where is everyone?" Rose asked. "I hear Maman."

"Maman is busy washing clothes after a delicious breakfast that André brought over. The man paid us for our work yesterday, so Lorenz and Emilie have gone to the store to purchase supplies."

Rose sat up in bed, suddenly wide-awake. "André was so kind?"

"Amazing, isn't it?" Gabrielle leaned back on an elbow. "Yesterday he seemed so demanding, I was beginning to wonder if he didn't imagine us his slaves. But I suppose he had his plantation to consider and wanted to get it functioning as soon as possible. He's not such a bad man after all."

Unlikely, Rose thought. Ever since she had witnessed André laughing with the other men at Coleman's expense, Rose's opinion of him had deteriorated.

Rose rubbed her forehead in frustration. What was she doing siding with an Englishman against a man who had taken them in, given them a place to rest and food to eat?

"Are you well, Rose?" Gabrielle asked.

Wanting so badly to confide in her sister, Rose looked up and grasped her sister's hand. "I have to tell you something."

The door opened and Marianne appeared, followed by Esther and a plate of food. "Good morning, sweetheart," Marianne said smiling. "Monsieur DeClouet brought over some food." She placed the tray on the bed. "Some beautiful fruit, bread, even butter."

Rose looked down at the platter filled with treats and her stomach growled. "How wonderful!" she said. "How long has it been since we've eaten this well?"

"A very long time," Marianne agreed. "And when you're finished, Monsieur DeClouet has asked to see you. Esther said she will go up to the main house with you."

A sense of dread fell on Rose. Lorenz was at the store so she would be alone with André.

"Can't it wait?" she asked her mother. "I need to help with the washing."

"Gabrielle and I can finish the washing."

"But I've just risen."

Marianne studied her. Rose knew what she was thinking. Her youngest daughter was never one to shun responsibility. "He's been generous to us, Rose," she said sternly. "It's the least you can do."

Rose stared down at the plate of fruit before her. She was so hungry. "What could he possibly want of me?"

"I told him what a great seamstress you are," Marianne said. "Perhaps he needs someone to mend his clothes."

Rose would have gladly offered her services, but she dreaded being alone with André, alone with his questions. If only Lorenz hadn't gone to the store. "Yes, Maman," she said softly.

"This isn't like you," Marianne said, pushing a wild strand of hair behind her ear. "Are you not well?"

Rose ached to say yes, but she could never lie to her mother. "I will go as soon as I finish my breakfast."

"More like lunch," Gabrielle added.

Marianne studied her harder, then placed a hand on Rose's forehead. Convinced her youngest didn't have a fever, she turned to Gabrielle. "Let's let your sister eat. We'll finish the washing."

The two women left the house while Esther stood uncomfortably in the doorway. "Esther," Rose said, making room on the bed. "Come join me."

Esther's eyes widened in shock. "Oh no, Mademoiselle Rose, I could never do that."

She might be André's slave, but as far as Rose was concerned, master and slave didn't exist in the Gallant household. "Of course, you can. Please. You are my elder and I would never sit while you stand."

Esther cautiously sat down on the edge of the bed.

"Would you like something to eat?" Rose asked. "I can't possibly eat all this food."

Esther's countenance began to relax with the casual conversation. "You are so petite, mademoiselle," the plump woman said. "Don't you eat enough?"

Rose broke off a piece of bread and handed it to Esther. "I eat plenty. I'm afraid I will never be larger than this."

"Someday you will be big with child," Esther offered. "Someday soon, perhaps."

Children. Would she ever experience the joy of her own children? Not if André DeClouet had his way.

"Esther," Rose asked, "do you know where the Englishman lives?"

Esther swallowed and nodded. "He's your neighbor."

Rose felt a lump in her chest and wondered if a piece of food had lodged there. "My neighbor?"

Esther nodded. "He lives on the other side of the woods. There's a stream back there," she said, pointing toward the west wall. "That's the boundary of his property. Just over the creek and up the embankment is his house."

So close, Rose thought. Coleman lived and slept within a short walk from the house. "Have you seen him?"

Esther wiped her face. *"Oui*, mademoiselle. Monsieur André pens his animals for him."

That seemed strange. Why would Coleman pay

someone else to keep his animals? "Why doesn't he pen them himself?"

Esther shrugged. "They keep getting loose and Monsieur André captures them and puts them in a pen. I've heard him brag that he makes a lot of money selling those animals back to the Englishman."

That sounds more like it, Rose thought. Suddenly, her doubts about choosing Coleman's side disappeared. She bolted from the bed and retrieved her clothes.

"Esther, I have a small chore to do," Rose said, as she hurriedly pulled her vest over her chemise and laced the ties. "It will only take a minute. You go on to the main house and I'll be up shortly."

Esther stood and took the empty platter with her. *"Oui,* mademoiselle," she said.

"Esther, please call me Rose."

Esther sent her a wide grin. "Rose," she answered.

Rose hastily buttoned her petticoat and stepped into her skirt, then tied her hair behind her head. She had no time for braids. She had to see him, warn him somehow. She placed her bonnet on top of her head and tied it underneath her chin. Grabbing the two remaining apples and stuffing them into her skirt pocket, Rose headed for the door. "Please tell Monsieur I am on my way."

"Oui, Mademoiselle Rose."

Rose wanted to correct Esther again, to assure her she didn't have to be subservient with the family, but she didn't have time. With her sister and mother occupied with the wash, Rose left the house and headed for the woods.

The path was easy to follow. The hard rains of

the hurricane had washed away much of the ground foliage. It wasn't long before Rose found the stream, its waters high from the recent weather.

She removed her shoes and stockings and waded across. The cool water felt good against her shins, as welcome as the slight breeze blowing up the stream that teased the perspiration lingering at her collar and breastbone. Not for the first time that summer, Rose wondered if Louisiana would ever cool off.

On the opposite bank, Rose slid on her stockings and shoes and made her way up the slight incline. When she left the cover of the woods, a wide prairie stretched before her. At its far end were cultivated fields next to a house that was in worse shape than the overseer's house. Part of the roof was missing over the back gallery. Two pigs roamed free through the rows of corn, enjoying the ears scattered on the ground. Arpents of land were filled with every imaginable debris, from branches to farm tools.

Where was Coleman? She expected him to be busy repairing the hurricane's damage, as André had done the day before. The scene was eerily quiet, the only noise the grunting of pigs gorging on corn and the sound of thunder brewing in the west.

As she got closer to the house, Rose recognized Coleman sitting on the gallery, leaning against the side of the house, his eyes closed and his hands outstretched as if in prayer. When she stood before him, she realized he was asleep.

"Monsieur Thorpe," Rose whispered, trying not to startle him. "Mister Thorpe," she said louder in English when he didn't stir.

When she received no answer, Rose leaned down and studied him closer. She tilted his hat back with the tip of her finger and his eyes opened slightly.

"Mister Thorpe, are you not well?" she asked him.

Coleman said nothing, offered a lazy smile, then closed his eyes again. His head fell forward on his chest and he began to snore.

It was then Rose noticed the bottle and the laceration on his arm. She pulled the empty rum bottle from the cradle of his elbow, taking care not to aggravate the wound. Then she gazed around the back gallery littered with tools and a makeshift ladder. It appeared as if Coleman had tried to repair the roof only to injure himself, give up, and start drinking.

"Oh, Coleman," Rose whispered to him in French. "How do you expect to live out here by yourself with no one to help you?"

He said nothing, and Rose wondered if she should leave him there. The roar of thunder behind her made her think otherwise.

"Mister Thorpe," she said, raising her voice. "Mister Thorpe, you have to get inside."

He didn't move.

"Mister Thorpe," Rose said, shaking him. "You have to wake up."

His eyes blinked, and then looked hard at her. He smiled lazily again, and closed his eyes.

"Mister Thorpe," Rose said, grabbing the front of his leather vest and shaking him harder. "You must get up."

Coleman finally woke up, staring at her as if dreaming. "Rose?" he muttered.

"Yes, it's Rose." She stood and grabbed his vest again, pulling him forward to get him on his feet. Coleman tried to lift himself up. But when he stood, he staggered and fell backward. Rose quickly grabbed his vest again and righted him. Then she slid beneath his arm so he was leaning against her.

They made their way slowly into the cabin, Coleman's arm draped about her shoulders and Rose struggling to keep them both from falling down. As they approached the bed, Coleman turned and gazed down at Rose, his brow creased in thought.

How odd this must seem to him, Rose thought. Yet it felt as natural to her as the rain beating against the roof. Why was that? Why did she feel comfortable around a man whose nationality was so far different from hers?

"A few more steps and we're there," Rose said.

Coleman smiled again, his blue eyes hazy with the effects of the rum but twinkling as they did every time he looked at her. Then suddenly, his eyes rolled back, as did his head, and his legs began to buckle.

Rose had to think fast. Coleman was a few inches taller than she; if he fell to the floor, she would not be able to stop him. In all likelihood, she would fall with him.

Before Coleman slipped from her grasp, Rose grabbed his vest once more with both hands. As he lost consciousness and began to drop, she swung him around letting him fall backward onto the bed. Falling onto the mattress, he grabbed her and pulled her down on top of him.

Suddenly, Rose found her chin resting on top of

his broad muscular chest. Her hands on either side of her face still clung to the front of his vest. Coleman sighed, his eyes shut in slumber, but his hands caressing her back, bringing her even more firmly against him.

Dear God, Rose thought, feeling every solid inch of him, including the rock-hard thighs pressed against her hips. He needed a bath, but something about the manly scent of hard work intoxicated her. His large hands roaming her back felt possessive and loving, and it thrilled her to think he might feel this way sober.

Rose had to remove herself, but for a moment she tilted her face and let her cheek rest against the soft cotton of his shirt. She closed her eyes and listened to the beating of his heart while one of his hands swept the hair from her face in a soft gentle circle.

When both hands fell against his sides and he started to snore again, Rose gingerly lifted herself and left the bed and the comfort of his embrace. Taking a deep breath, she pulled his long legs onto the bed and righted him, then removed his shoes and stockings. She ripped a piece off her petticoat and bandaged the cut on his arm.

Gazing down on the sleeping Englishman, his blond curls falling about his face in a mass of yellow, Rose studied the shape of his nose and the honey glow the sun had created on his cheeks. Feeling brave, she slid her fingers through his hair and pushed the intruding locks away from his eyes. She swore that if they met again, she would insist on giving him a haircut.

But she had come to deliver a message. Now what would she do? Perhaps she would leave a note.

Rose glanced around the cabin for pen and parchment. What she found instead made her mouth drop in astonishment. Coleman's clothes were scattered everywhere. Most were filthy and lying in piles. Dishes caked with food were piled on the kitchen table. The floor was covered in mud, no doubt from the hurricane, and two chickens perched in a rafter on the opposite side of the chimney. She was thankful they were not above Coleman and his bed, but their droppings were quickly discoloring the floor beneath them.

Rose turned toward the sleeping man as if to reprimand him for the squalid condition of his cabin, but he was fast asleep. That didn't stop her from sending him a disapproving look.

"Well, I'm not going to stand for this," she said, picking up a broom. "And the first thing to go are those chickens."

Rose shooed the hens outside, then began to sweep the floor, picking up clothes and tools in the process. She built a fire, put a pot of water on, and filled a tub for cleaning first the clothes and then the dishes. When she knelt down against the tub to give his shirts a good scrub, the apples inside her skirt pocket interrupted her actions.

A wonderful idea came to Rose. There was hardly any food about the place, just some sugar, flour, and dried beef. How the man survived on his own, she couldn't fathom. She could do wonders with two apples and his meager supplies.

Rose stoked the fire to get it at the right temperature, then set about making a pie. When she had filled the pastry shell with a mixture of tart apples and sugar, she placed it inside the fireplace, grinning at the prospect of surprising Coleman with a hot apple pie.

By the time she had finished her creation, the rain had stopped. Rose returned to her cleaning, hanging the clothes outside on a rope she found on the gallery.

After several hours, Rose stood back and admired her handiwork. The rugged cabin had a long way to go before it was livable by her standards, but at least it was clean. Coleman now had clean clothes, clean dishes, and a warm meal.

Rose pulled a sheet over Coleman's sleeping form and left the cabin. Dusk was beginning to settle on the prairie, casting a warm orange glow about the live oak trees and waving prairie grass. Rose removed her shoes and stockings to cross the creek, then hurried home before darkness fell.

When she emerged from the woods, she nearly collided with Marianne. Her mother stood on the front gallery, her arms crossed in front of her.

For the first time since Rose had awakened, she remembered that André had called for her. She gasped, thinking that her host might have waited all afternoon.

"I can explain," she said to Marianne, but she doubted she could.

"Where have you been?" her mother asked.

Thoughts flew through her head like the flocks of

white egrets that passed their way every afternoon. *Choose one,* her mind demanded. *But which one?*

"I found a stream," Rose began. "There's a lovely creek through these woods."

Marianne frowned. "You've been at the stream for hours?"

"No, Maman," Rose said. "I have been exploring all over."

Marianne looked puzzled. It wasn't like Rose to ignore her responsibilities. It certainly wasn't like her to hide her actions either. What would she not admit if Marianne probed deeper? "Have you forgotten about Monsieur DeClouet?"

Rose looked shocked, which wasn't far from the truth. She *had* forgotten. "Oh, Maman, I am so sorry," she exclaimed. "I completely forgot. I shall go up to the main house immediately and offer my apologies. Is Lorenz at home?"

Marianne appeared as if she would continue her questioning and Rose cringed, waiting for the worst.

"She doesn't need to go to the main house," Lorenz said as he walked on to the gallery. Winking at Rose from behind Marianne, he added, "I have taken care of everything."

Rose should have been relieved that André De-Clouet would now leave her alone, but all she could think of was Coleman, drunk and alone, lying against the side of his crumbling house with his fields ruined.

"Well, I suppose so," Marianne said. "But next time you go wandering off, tell someone. I don't like you exploring these woods. We don't know what's out there."

"Yes, Maman."

Marianne frowned again, hesitating at the threshold as if not sure she had said enough. Then she opened the door and strode inside.

"Merci," Rose said to Lorenz.

Lorenz smiled broadly and bowed. "That's what big brothers are for."

"But there is the other part of the promise," Rose suggested.

"What other part?"

Rose sighed. She knew Lorenz would not visit Coleman without a shove. "You promised me you would visit the other person in question."

Lorenz winced. "I will."

"When?"

"Soon."

"When?"

Lorenz removed his hat and beat it against his leg. "Lord, Rose, I said I will and I will."

He turned to leave, and for a moment Rose saw again the state of Coleman's cabin and the horrible shape of his fields. "He needs us, Lorenz," she said.

At first Lorenz said nothing. He just stared at her the way her mother had when she emerged from the woods. Then his brow furrowed, as if he contemplated his own set of questions.

"I must run," Rose said, hoping to avoid more interrogation.

Before Lorenz could utter a word, she was safely inside the house.

Chapter Five

Coleman knew dawn was approaching when Pierre Blanchard's rooster crowed in the neighboring yard, although the heat in the cabin belied the fact that it was only six o'clock. Or something close to it.

A watch, Coleman thought. When was the last time he had worn his watch, the one his father had given him when he turned sixteen and made his way to the College of William and Mary?

Sitting up in bed and anticipating the pounding it was sure to cause, Coleman placed his head in both hands and sent the thought away. He wasn't going to think of his father now. He was not going to be reminded what a failure he had become. His father had warned him he would amount to nothing if he left for the Opelousas Poste. How proud Richard Thorpe would be now.

Coleman threw his legs over the side of the bed and felt a pendulum of rock swing inside his head from one ear to the other. Rum produced such a quick intoxication, but it delivered the worst hangover. Definitely not worth the brief hour of pleasure. Only Coleman always figured this out the morning after, and refused to learn from it.

"I'm such a fool," he muttered, placing a hand on his forehead as if to keep it from shattering.

Feeling nature's call, he made his way to the porch, relieving himself over the edge. He leaned against the side of the house, keeping his eyes focused on the ground. He was weary of looking at the devastation before him and the broken-down excuse for a house. He was tired of the hours of work spent producing nothing. He was tired of being cheated by André and ignored by the rest of his neighbors.

He was tired of thinking of her.

Funny, Coleman thought, he could have sworn Rose had stood on that very porch the day before. He could see her face now, beaming up at him from his embrace.

Coleman buttoned his breeches and rested against the wall. Was the rum still burning through his veins? Now he was delusional.

Suddenly something caught his eye and he turned toward his fields. Several of his shirts and a pair of breeches were tied on a rope between two trees, swinging in the breeze like ghosts. Coleman stared at them for several moments, trying to make sense of the scene. Had he washed his clothes the day before? Doubtful. He had spent a good part of the morning chasing animals and penning them in a makeshift corral, only to have them escape once again—including the two blasted chickens that fled into his house. Then he tried rescuing his crops, but the fields were waterlogged. Close to noon, he had attempted to repair the roof, only the wooden pegs in the last two rungs on his bloody ladder had loosened and he had crashed onto the porch.

That was when he took Henri's bottle, gulping the rum down as fast as he could swallow. He didn't remember much beyond that.

So when did he wash his clothes?

"I'm losing my mind," Coleman said and entered the cabin. The scene before him was even more disconcerting.

The floor was neatly swept, the chickens no longer roosted in the corner, and all of his dirtied pots and dishes had been removed from the table and placed upside down on the sideboard to dry. In the dishes' place was a round pan covered with a cloth, next to a piece of parchment.

Coleman swallowed to relieve the cottonlike coating filling his throat. Was he dreaming? If his head didn't hurt so much, he would have sworn he was sleepwalking.

Then he noticed the material on his arm. That was a memory he could latch on to. He had injured his arm falling off the ladder. Yet, he didn't remember bandaging the wound.

Coleman lifted the cloth from his arm and stretched

it out. Damned if it wasn't the bottom of a lady's petticoat. Now he knew he was dreaming.

Still clutching the delicate cotton, Coleman sat down at the table and cautiously removed the cloth from the pan. Whoever was having sport at his expense was doing a grand job. An apple pie? Who would think enough of him to clean his cabin, bandage his arm, and bake him something?

Fear gripped Coleman's heart thinking of the possibility. No, she couldn't have come here last night, he thought madly. She couldn't have seen him this way.

Coleman stretched out the fabric once again. Holding the two ends together, he could tell it was the petticoat of a petite woman, a woman the size of Rose Gallant.

"Dear God, no," he muttered, placing his head in his hands.

Staring up at him was the note, with crude handwriting on the front reading: "Mister Thorpe."

Coleman picked up the note and unfolded it. Inside were the words of his angel, yet it pained him to read it.

> *André De Clooé not a fren. He means harm you. Do no trust him.*
>
> *—Yor fren, Rose.*

Coleman raised the note to his lips and inhaled, hoping the scent of her fingers still lingered there. "What must she think of me now?" he said, remembering the state he had been in the evening before.

Glancing around the cabin that still repulsed him,

yet now showed a semblance of hope, Coleman vowed he would be a success. Vowed he would make his land profitable, his home a place to welcome company. He would make Rose proud of him, no matter that she could never be his.

He would stop feeling sorry for himself and make something of his life.

He would never let her see him that way again.

Marianne lugged two pails down the path toward the stream Rose had described. It wasn't long before the creek came into view, justifying Marianne's fears.

Where had Rose gone the day before with the stream so close to the house? She had spent hours away from the family and Marianne didn't believe she had been "investigating" the woods.

A pain gripped Marianne's heart. Rose had never lied to her before; she was the one person who could be trusted unconditionally. Not that Emilie or Gabrielle gave her reasons to worry, but there were always times when each daughter retreated into her own world, confiding less and less in her mother as she grew older, perhaps more confident to settle her own problems. But never Rose.

Rose was her baby. She told Marianne everything.

That made it doubly hard to imagine she might be hiding something, at a time when they were all experiencing another disappointment and planning on traveling to yet another frontier.

Maybe she was worrying needlessly, Marianne thought as she filled the buckets. The stress of the past thirteen years, and especially the past few months, had been hard on everyone. Perhaps Rose had taken the afternoon to revitalize her spirits after their brutal trip to Opelousas and the tiring day of rebuilding after the hurricane. She had always loved the outdoors.

Yes, that was it, Marianne concluded. There was nothing to fear. Rose was such a gentle soul. It would be reasonable to assume she was intimidated by André DeClouet, escaping to the woods for peace from the overbearing man.

Rose would never lie to her. It wasn't possible.

Suddenly, footsteps sounded on the opposite bank. A stranger approached carrying his own set of pails. Marianne straightened, waiting to make introductions with her neighbor. When the man face's hit the patch of sunlight shining through the trees, Marianne's fears grew tenfold.

Coleman Thorpe looked up at the same time Marianne recognized him. At first he almost smiled in greeting, until he read the shock on her face.

"Madame Gallant," he said, removing his hat and bowing politely.

It took great care to keep her mouth from falling open, but Marianne swallowed hard and tried to concentrate. Coleman Thorpe? The Englishman who had hired Rose and Marianne to mend his shirts, then appeared one day lovesick and rambling on about his affections for Rose? Marianne suspected Rose cared for him as well. She saw the way she had looked at him the night he brought his fiddle to the dance and gave the village music.

But he was English! Not someone she would consider allowing Rose to marry. He was supposed to have gone west!

"Monsieur Thorpe," Marianne answered, trying to keep the anxiety from her voice.

Coleman paused at the stream, unsure of what to do next. He filled his buckets and placed them on the shore.

"Do you live here?" Marianne asked. She knew he spoke no French, but perhaps he understood a little.

Coleman caught her meaning. *"Oui,"* he answered, pointing up the embankment toward the east.

A lump lodged in Marianne's throat. Not only did a man she hoped to be far removed from her daughter live only an arpent away, but Rose had lied about meeting him the day before. This was bad news. Very bad news.

Feeling a rush of anger rise to her face, Marianne grabbed her buckets and hastily left the stream. She spilled much of the water on the way to the house, but she didn't care. Her daughter, her baby Rose, was being courted by an Englishman. And Rose had fallen for the man's charms.

Most of the washing had been finished the day before, but so much of it needed mending. Rose collected the clothes in a pile and began to sew them in order of importance, enjoying the slight breeze that cooled the back gallery.

She was working on Lorenz's workshirt, the one torn while he repaired André's barn, when Marianne rounded the corner of the house. With one look, Rose knew something was wrong.

"Maman," Rose said, rising. "What has happened?"

Marianne soberly placed the buckets at the bottom of the porch steps and crossed her arms. "Perhaps you tell me," she said.

The anxiety in her mother's voice caused Gabrielle to stop cleaning dishes and emerge out on the gallery. Something was wrong, and Rose had a feeling it had to do with her.

"Were you going to tell me about him?" Marianne asked. "Were you going to tell me that you two have been meeting secretly?"

How could she have known? Rose thought madly. Did André, in his anger over Lorenz's refusal to allow them to marry, talk to her mother about the marriage?

"I was going to tell you, but we thought it best not to worry you about it right now," Rose said.

"We?" Marianne shouted. "What has that man been telling you?"

"It's not what you think, Maman. He wants to marry me, but it's an honest proposal. At least I believe it is."

Marianne turned pale and reached for a step. Gabrielle took her mother's elbow and helped her sit down. Looking up at Rose, Gabrielle asked, "Someone asked you to marry him?"

"It was more like a business proposal," Rose said.

Marianne swallowed and looked at Rose with pain in her eyes. "And you never thought to tell me? This man lives next door and you never thought to tell me about this?"

Rose felt remorse for keeping quiet and wished Lorenz was there to support her. "Lorenz and I thought it best not to tell you. Lorenz said he would speak with him."

At this, Marianne rose and towered over her. "Lorenz knew?" she shouted.

"I'm not going to marry him, Maman," Rose assured her. "Not unless you think I should."

Marianne blinked as if she was confused. "As if I would ever suggest such a thing!" she said menacingly.

"Who is this man?" Gabrielle asked.

Marianne took a deep breath and exhaled. "That damned Englishman from Natchez."

Now it was Rose's turn to sit down. She felt the blood rush from her face. "Coleman?" she whispered. "You're speaking of Coleman?"

Marianne turned away, gazing out over the yard, her arms still firmly crossed against her chest. "Who else would I be referring to?"

A guilt so intense filled her that Rose had trouble breathing. "I thought you meant André DeClouet."

Both Marianne and Gabrielle turned and stared. "André DeClouet asked you to marry him?" Gabrielle asked.

Rose nodded.

"When?" her mother asked incredulously.

"The night of the hurricane," Rose said.

Just then, Lorenz and Emilie appeared, their laughter a stark contrast to the grave conversation at hand.

When they glanced at the threesome on the gallery steps, their smiles quickly faded.

"What's the matter?" Emilie asked.

But Marianne's focus was on Lorenz. "Did you know André DeClouet proposed marriage to Rose?" she asked him.

Lorenz stood before them like a deer caught in a hunter's path, not knowing which way to run. "I did. But it's not what you think."

"He will be able to collect an inheritance if he is married," Rose offered and everyone rested their astonished gazes on her. "He said he would share the money with us if I helped him."

"By marrying the man?" Emilie demanded. "Rose, are you out of your mind?"

"I thought it would help," Rose argued. "Give us some money to get to the Attakapas Poste."

"But you would have to marry the man," Gabrielle said.

"I know, but consider this," Rose countered. "It will be fall when we arrive there, we will need money to make it through the winter."

Marianne stared at Rose while a cacophony of exclamations rose from the others. A pounding began inside Rose's head, and she felt as she always did when her family discussed her future—like a helpless fool who couldn't decide her fate for herself.

"And yesterday," her mother said softly, causing everyone to stop talking. "Yesterday, you were not talking to André all those hours in the woods."

Suddenly, Rose didn't feel helpless. She thought

of Coleman and somehow it gave her strength. "No, Maman, I was at Coleman Thorpe's cabin."

"What?" Lorenz shouted.

"I heard he was our neighbor, so I went to look. I found him ill and his cabin in shambles. I helped him, that's all."

"I saw him at the stream minutes ago," Marianne said. "He didn't appear ill to me."

Rose looked down at her feet. "He was drunk yesterday, Maman."

"Drunk?" she asked. "You were helping a drunkard?"

Rose knew what they were all thinking, that not only was the man English but a disgrace as well, but she didn't think less of him because of it. "He had reason," Rose argued. "He lost his crops, and André and his neighbors are trying to cheat him out of his stock." Softly, she added, "Then to top off all his misfortunes, I came to town."

"Who is Coleman Thorpe?" Emilie asked.

"A man who showed affection toward Rose in Natchez," Gabrielle said quietly.

Emilie stepped closer, almost eye to eye with Rose on the gallery. "Why, Rose, that's sweet."

Rose wanted so much to smile, to rejoice with her sisters that a man loved her, a man she believed she loved in return. But it wasn't meant to be.

"He's English," Rose heard Lorenz say behind Emilie and Emilie's smile disappeared.

"English?" Emilie said, her shock evident. "You can't be serious."

"Rose never led him to believe she cared for him,

Emilie," Gabrielle said in her defense. But when Gabrielle turned toward Rose, she was just as shocked that Coleman lived so close, that Rose hadn't told her.

Marianne climbed to the gallery's top step and stood at Rose's side. "You are never to see him again. Do you understand me?"

Rose's head began to throb. "Which one?" she asked, crossing her arms. She hadn't meant to sound sarcastic, but she was tired of being the center of attention, the center of everyone's consternation.

"Thorpe," her mother said, clearly upset that she should ask. "I'd rather you not see DeClouet either."

"I've spoken to André," Lorenz said. "I've taken care of everything."

"Good," Marianne said. "I'm glad you're here, Lorenz."

"And don't worry about Coleman," Gabrielle offered. "We'll be moving out in a few weeks' time."

There it was again. Her family was discussing her life as if she were invisible. As if she were incapable of making one rational decision. Didn't her opinion matter in anything?

"I won't do it," Rose said, before her mind had time to censor her words.

"What did you say?" Marianne asked.

Rose stood and faced her mother, her heart pounding in her chest. "I know marrying Coleman is an impossibility. I am not naive enough to think otherwise, as you all assume. In case you have forgotten, Coleman is a gentleman, someone who would never think of marrying *me*. But he is my friend, and there is no reason I should not see him, help him, or speak to him while I live in this poste.''

Rose didn't wait for her family to retort. She took advantage of their shock, grabbed her bonnet, and fled through the house and out the front door.

It was halfway to noon, while Coleman finished the repairs on the animal pen, that a jolt of hunger overtook him. Food was just what he needed, now that the morning headache and thirst of his hangover were dissipating. He thought of visiting Henri, but remembered his vow. The way Marianne Gallant had stared at him at the stream renewed his determination to make a success of his farm. Or maybe it was the delectable apple pie he had consumed that morning that made him yearn for finer foods.

Besides, hunting would do him good, clear his mind. He had seen some wild turkeys in the backwoods of his property. Roasted turkey would make a nice supper. This time, he would watch the fire more carefully, try to have more patience with the spit. Trouble was, Coleman hated cooking. He couldn't stand spending the time necessary for a good meal. But if he wanted to survive in the wilderness, it was time to learn. Money was quickly running out. He needed seeds to plant a spring crop—and spring was several months away.

Coleman trod lightly through the fields, spotting the turkeys instantly. With exquisite aim, he landed a fat bird before the flock disappeared onto André's property.

Coleman picked up the bird and headed home, thinking of ways to improve his homestead. If he could build a larger henhouse, perhaps he could purchase more chickens and sell eggs to Henri during the winter. He needed a rooster too. His last one had mysteriously disappeared and one just like it had popped up in André's yard.

André DeClouet. Rose had come by his house to warn him of his conniving neighbor. Even though she had seen him in such a drunken condition, it warmed his heart to think she cared enough to cross the invisible boundary between nationalities to keep him from harm. Coleman slid his hand to his bandaged arm and touched the soft piece of cotton tied there. If only he could see her again, talk to her.

As he crossed the road heading back toward his cabin, he spotted a figure marching down the road, her bonnet bent toward the ground and her hands clenched into fists. The woman was almost upon him when he realized it was Rose, but then she quickly turned and walked in the other direction.

Had she seen him? Most likely, her mother had warned her never to talk to him again. He shouldn't be surprised. But Coleman felt his heart break as he watched her trek back toward her house.

He threw his gun over his shoulder and crossed the road, still determined to make a difference with his life. Even if Rose never spoke to him again, he would be satisfied knowing he was worthy of her approval.

At that moment, Rose turned again and headed back in his direction, her eyes still focused on the ground before her. She nearly collided with him before Coleman cleared his throat. Rose jerked her head up just in time to stop in front of him.

"Are you lost?" he asked her.

Rose's round chestnut eyes grew enormous, then she looked down at her feet and frowned. "I am angry," she said softly. "I'm never angry. I don't know what to do."

Guilt pressed on Coleman's heart. No doubt he was the cause of her problems. "Your mother?" he asked.

Rose nodded.

"I am so sorry," Coleman said, lightly touching her arm.

Rose shook her head. "No," she said with a force he had not witnessed before. "You are not the reason for our exile. She has no right to dislike you because you are English."

Coleman slipped the gun from his shoulder and leaned against its barrel. "But I am to blame," he insisted, "in their eyes. You are too young to remember, but it's still vivid in their minds."

Rose folded her arms across her chest. "That's not fair."

Coleman tilted her chin up so that their eyes met. "Life's not fair, *chèrie.*"

Rose stared at him for several seconds, her anger still brewing. Then she exhaled and offered a slight smile. "Why don't you speak French?" she asked, breaking the awkward silence that had developed.

"My father spoke French," Coleman said. When Rose looked up, confused, he knew an explanation was necessary. He hated speaking of his father. He hated speaking of himself. But somehow, being next to her, his angel, the woman of his nightly dreams, he longed to speak of his past.

"My father is a spy for the English," Coleman explained. "He came to the Louisiana Territory hoping to take control of the Mississippi for the Crown, to divide the continent, keep the French from expanding west. Now that the Spanish own Louisiana, he hopes to gain control of the river from the Spanish."

Rose said nothing, staring at him with wide eyes while her fingers twisted a button round and round on her vest.

"I refused to learn French because I didn't want to give my father and members of my family ammunition to persuade me to join the army. Basically, I never wanted to be like my father."

Coleman studied Rose for a reaction, but none came.

"I don't understand your English," she finally said. "You talk too hard."

Coleman couldn't help himself. He laughed. It was the first time he had spoken his feelings aloud regarding his father and Rose couldn't comprehend his words. When a pained expression crossed her face, he regretted his outburst.

"I don't speak French," he said, grinning, "because I'm a stupid Englishman. Ask anyone."

Still, Rose refused to smile. "You're not stupid," she insisted.

Where had God created this one? Coleman thought.

Was she an angel someone had dropped to Earth? He didn't care. She was here, standing in front of him, believing in him when no one else would.

"Oh, Rose," he said softly. "I know I am ruining your life, but you are the best thing to happen to me."

He knew she didn't understand him and he was thankful for that. The sun disappeared and thunder cracked above them, making them both jump.

"It every day rains," Rose said incredulously.

Coleman smiled, thinking how weird that had seemed to him when he had first moved to semitropical Louisiana. "It won't rain long."

When she stared off into the dark clouds hanging low on the horizon, Coleman knew her anger and hurt still lingered.

"Don't be mad at the weather, too, *chèrie,*" he said. "It won't do you any good. Trust me."

She raised her perfectly round eyes to his and nodded. She did trust him. Completely. Why was that? Why did Rose Gallant trust him while his neighbors, who had known him longer, did not? Equally puzzling were his feelings toward her. They hadn't known each other long in Natchez before he knew he wanted to spend the rest of his life with her. It was a feeling of comfort, a sense of ease. As if his twin had been wandering the world and he had finally found her.

The thunder crashed again. He should walk her home. See her safely down the road. But he couldn't find the strength to say good-bye.

"My cabin is close," he said. "Would you like some tea, wait out the rain?"

Rose bit her lower lip in contemplation. He shouldn't have asked, put her in such an awkward position. If she followed him, it would cause more problems with her family.

Coleman started to rescind his offer, to remind her of their differences and her family's objections, but Rose thrust her chin forward. *"Oui,* Mister Thorpe," she said confidently. "I would love some tea."

Chapter Six

Rose removed her bonnet and placed it on the table while Coleman started a fire. From the corner of his eye, he noticed her surveying the cabin, no doubt searching for the remnants of her handiwork. He wanted to tell her the pie had been the finest dish to pass his lips in months, but he dreaded reminding her of his drunken state.

Coleman filled the teapot and placed it on its hook inside the hearth. Standing, he found Rose examining his secretary, the lopsided desk he used for studying and writing. What was she looking for?

When Rose turned, she realized Coleman was staring and blushed. "I was wondering . . ." she began.

Coleman moved to the cupboard and removed two

pewter mugs, trying to act nonchalant to put her at ease. "Yes?" he said with his back to her.

"Where is your violin?"

A warmth spread through Coleman, remembering how she had asked about it in Natchez and how he had visited her village that night, playing music for hours. Music was one thing Coleman excelled in—his only talent.

"It's in the chest," Coleman explained, pointing to the trunk that contained everything dear to him. "I put it away when the hurricane hit. It was my father's. It's my most precious possession."

Besides you, he thought. When he glanced at her again, he could swear she had read his thoughts. Rose's cheeks blossomed with a fiery blush, and she turned and stared at the floor.

"Why didn't you say good-bye?" she asked softly.

A hope Coleman dared not imagine filled his heart. He had left Natchez to avoid being reminded daily that as an Englishman he had no right to court his angel. He left because he couldn't bear watching another man marry her, which was sure to happen in time. "I thought it best that way," he said.

Rose looked up, her mahogany eyes reflecting a sadness Coleman knew only too well. "Best for whom?" she countered.

Coleman wanted to explain, but how? Discussing such intimacies would be treading on dangerous territory. "Would you like some tea?" he asked instead.

Rose nodded, then approached the table while Coleman found a tin of tea. "Why does André DeClouet dislike you?" she asked.

Coleman placed the tin on the table, then pulled a chair out for her. "I'm his neighbor," Coleman said as Rose sat down. "He covets."

When he placed a strainer over her cup and filled it with tea, Coleman caught the puzzled look on her face. "He wants my land," Coleman explained in easier English. "He's hoping I will be a failure so he can seize it. Of course, he may try to take it before that day."

"What do you mean?" Rose asked.

Coleman walked to the hearth and removed the teapot, then sat down by swinging a leg over the wobbly chair. "He takes a little land here, a little land there, moves a fence, claims a boundary is farther than it really is. Before we know it, André's land is a little bit bigger and the rest of us have land that's a little bit smaller. Do you understand?"

Rose nodded. "Have you told the commandant?"

Coleman poured the steaming water into her cup. "The others are scared of him. They won't prosecute. And he hasn't harmed me yet."

"He takes your pigs."

Coleman laughed. "That's because I am a stupid Englishman." Rose began to object, but Coleman placed his hand on hers. "Anyone who fails to keep his pigs penned deserves to be cheated."

Rose glanced down at his callused hand over hers. Coleman picked up the tea strainer from her cup and placed it over his. He had to be careful. Ever since he first saw her in Henri's store, Coleman burned with a desire to caress her golden skin, kiss those adorable freckles gracing her cheeks, hold her petite body close to his. At that moment he wanted nothing more than to meet those tempting lips with a kiss.

"What if he does take your land?" Rose asked.

Clearing his throat in an effort to clear his thoughts, Coleman focused on the conversation. "I'm not scared of André DeClouet."

"But what if he steals your land?"

"He won't."

"How can you be so sure?" Rose insisted.

Now that he thought about it, there were *two* things Coleman excelled at, even if he never finished law school. "I may not be a farmer, but I studied law at William and Mary, a college back East. I know the law. And I have friends of influence in New Orleans."

Rose raised the cup to her lips and sipped gently. Then she sucked in her lower lip to capture the drops lingering there. The simple gesture nearly undid him.

"André wants my land because of my spring," Coleman continued, hoping to get his mind off the tension in his breeches. "I have a spring and a well. André has had trouble with his water supply. Sugar?"

"Yes, please."

Coleman pulled his leg over the small chair and walked the two steps to his cupboard to retrieve the sugar bowl. "Plus my land is magical," he added.

As he placed the sugar in front of Rose and she filled her cup, her brow deepened. *"Pardon?"*

Sitting down, he offered a sheepish grin. "I go to sleep at night and fairies clean my house."

Her cup was poised at her lips so he couldn't see her smile. But her eyes glistened with merriment.

"Maybe you had too much to drink and you're imagining things."

Whatever joy he had in teasing her disappeared when he remembered on his actions the night before. "Perhaps," he said soberly.

Rose placed her cup before her, then balanced her elbows on the table and leaned her cheek on one hand. "Why do you drink so much, Mister Thorpe?"

Her sweet face exhibited neither censure nor disapproval, yet Coleman was filled with shame. He wanted so badly for her to understand. "The question is, Mademoiselle Gallant, why don't I drink more?"

"You should have faith."

Coleman smiled grimly. "Faith that drink will not make my sorrows go away or faith that things will get better?"

Finally, a smile played on her lips, one that spoke of understanding and acceptance. "Both," Rose said.

"I wish I could," Coleman replied, thinking she would never be his. He stared into her brown eyes only inches away and whispered, "If only I had a semblance of hope."

Rose felt the hairs on her arms rise. She was having a devil of a time keeping her breathing normal when his blue eyes gazed into hers. Hearing him speak of hope as if she held the key made her gasp for air.

Ever since she had walked back into that cabin, Rose worried about her self-control. She convinced herself she wasn't in love, that she longed for Coleman's company because he was the first man to show her attention, that they were friends with a few common interests. But then she would look into his face. Fall hopelessly into a sea of vivid blue.

Gazing into those azure eyes now, Rose wondered how his callused hands would feel cupping her face, how those sun-bleached lips would feel exploring her body. If only he would touch her again.

"I really should go," Rose said, nearly knocking over her tea when she bumped the table. "It's getting dark and my family will worry."

Coleman rose as well. "I'll walk you home."

She hated leaving him, dreaded saying good-bye when she knew they would likely not meet again. Her thoughts were diving into dangerous waters.

"No, it's not necessary," Rose told him, although she couldn't help hoping he would insist.

Coleman didn't disappoint. "I insist," he said.

Rose picked up her bonnet and twisted its ribbon between her fingers. "You can walk me as far as the creek."

Grabbing his own hat, Coleman opened the door, waiting for Rose to walk through. "Agreed."

They walked without speaking through his devastated fields, then along the woods to the creek. When Rose reached the water's edge, she paused, wondering how to remove her shoes and stockings discreetly. She would wait for him to leave, she decided, and turned to tell him so when two arms encircled her and lifted her up to his chest. Before Rose could object, Coleman carried her across the stream to the opposite bank.

For the brief moments Coleman's arms were around her, and her hands were wrapped around his neck,

Rose studied his profile peeking out from beneath his planter's hat. He had a regal nose surrounded by a strong, yet kindly face now tanned from the sun. His hair, tapered into a tie at the nape, hung down his back. Blond curls fell about his forehead, almost hiding those cerulean eyes.

When they reached the far bank, Coleman paused to gaze at her, still holding her tightly in his arms. For a moment, Rose thought he might kiss her. And she wished with all her might he would.

But they were only minutes from her house.

Rose reached up and tugged at his hair. "You need a haircut, Mister Thorpe."

Coleman released her, gently placing her on the ground but capturing one hand. "Please call me Coleman," he said as his thumb slid across her fingers, "when we're alone."

A bead of perspiration slid down her bodice and Rose swore she could hear her heart beating.

"Good day, Coleman," she whispered, then hurried down the path toward the house without looking back.

Marianne waited for her on the front porch, sitting on the top step attempting to snap the ends off beans. When Rose came closer, she saw that her mother was nervously snapping the beans in half rather than ridding them of their stalks. Guilt raked her.

"I'm sorry, Maman," Rose said when she stood before her. "I should never have spoken to you that way and I beg your forgiveness."

Marianne raised her eyes and Rose felt doubly guilty

when she saw the worry and pain reflected there. "We have been worried sick," her mother said.

Lorenz came out on the porch after hearing Rose's voice. He, too, appeared distressed and sighed heavily when he saw her.

"I'm sorry," Rose said again.

Marianne and Lorenz exchanged looks. "Well, it's water under the bridge now," Marianne said. "We won't speak of it again."

Rose felt the blood rise to her face when she realized her opinions were going to be ignored one more time. "We must speak of it," she insisted. "I cannot agree with either of you. Coleman Thorpe needs us. His fields are in ruins; his barn was destroyed in the storm. He has no one to help him."

Marianne frowned and roughly set the bowl of beans on the floorboards. "That Englishman's perfectly capable of taking care of himself, Rose."

"He's all alone, Maman," Rose argued. "No one will help him *because* he's English."

"Then maybe he should stop spending his time drinking and start making friends with his neighbors."

Rose closed her eyes, hoping to find a way to convince them that Coleman Thorpe wasn't the enemy. When she opened her eyes, she turned them to Lorenz pleadingly. *"We* are his neighbors," she said softly.

Lorenz expelled a breath of air and frowned. "I'll go visit this Englishman," Lorenz said. "I'll offer my help and see what kind of man he is."

Rose's spirits lifted, but she dared not smile until

her mother gave her blessing. Marianne stood and folded her arms defiantly. "I don't want you near him," she said to Rose.

Folding her own arms, Rose straightened her back, bit her lower lip and met her mother head-on. For the first time in her life, she felt like an adult.

"I'm not going to run away with him, Maman. I only want to be his friend. He helped us in Natchez. Why shouldn't I return the favor? Besides, it's better than spending my days around André DeClouet."

Marianne unlocked her arms and placed one hand at her hip and the other over her chin. She was relenting. "I don't know," she said.

"He brought his fiddle," Rose offered.

This tidbit caught Lorenz's attention. "He has a violin?" he asked.

Rose nodded with a grin. Fiddles were hard to come by for people who had been exiled with only the clothes on their backs. And Acadians so loved their music.

When Rose's eyes met Lorenz's, she found him staring at her with an admiring smile. She was growing up and Lorenz was finally acknowledging it. "She can come with me," he said. "I doubt he will seduce her in my presence."

Marianne looked at Lorenz, and threw up her hands. "If you say so, Lorenz, then I'll agree for the time being." Turning back to Rose, she added, "But don't ask anything else of me with this man. I have my limits."

"Yes, Maman," Rose answered.

Marianne picked up her beans and entered the

house, her skirts rustling. Lorenz sent Rose a wink and followed.

Things were improving. The wall was falling, if only by a brick.

Lorenz stood at the edge of the woods, gazing out on the Englishman's fields. He promised Rose he would talk to the man, but leaning against the trunk of an oak tree, he wondered where to begin.

Rose had been right. The man needed help. Most men needed help in establishing a new farm, building barns and harvesting crops. That's where neighbors came in handy. Only this man was English, hardly a person Lorenz would rush to assist.

Examining the Englishman's land, Lorenz might have felt sorry for the man. The hurricane had ripped apart his crops and flooded the fields as far up as the pitiful excuse for a house. Or maybe the land refused to lose its water because of the poor drainage of the rows. In fact, there was no drainage system in place. What had been rows of corn, indigo, and cotton were poorly planted. They were half the height they might have been at this time of year if tended properly.

The man was an idiot, a *couyon*. But then again, he was English.

"Looking for someone?"

Startled by the voice, Lorenz turned and found Coleman approaching with two empty pails. His filthy clothes were torn from hard work. His hair was overgrown and wild about his face. If he hadn't spoken English, Lorenz might have been sympathetic.

When the blue-eyed man came closer, he could tell Lorenz wasn't offering a friendly visit. He sighed and his eyes turned cold. "She isn't here," he said.

Lorenz narrowed his eyes. "I know. Do you think I would let her come here alone?"

The Englishman studied him, but there was no malice in his gaze. "No, I suspect you wouldn't."

The men said nothing. They simply stared at each other until Coleman passed Lorenz and continued down to the stream. Lorenz knew he needed to talk to the Englishman, but what would he say? He had never spoken to a possible suitor before; he had no idea how to broach such a topic. Besides, they were moving in a few weeks' time, there was nothing to consider. Still, when Coleman returned up the path toward the fields, Lorenz knew he had to break the ice between them. He blurted out the one thing he felt comfortable discussing.

"You're a lousy farmer," Lorenz said, stopping Coleman dead in his tracks. "You're doing it wrong."

Surprisingly, Coleman didn't appear offended. "Which part?" he asked sincerely.

Lorenz smirked. "All of it."

The Englishman deposited the pails at his feet and placed his hands on his hips. "Can you be more specific?"

Lorenz had to admit that the man took criticism well. Probably because he faced starvation. Another crop like this one and the Englishman was doomed.

"First, you have to pen your pigs or they will make it worse," Lorenz explained, pointing to the sows rummaging through the damaged crops.

Coleman turned his blue eyes toward Lorenz, a smile lurking at the corner of his lips. "How can it be worse?"

Lorenz wanted to laugh. How indeed? And for a moment, Lorenz imagined the Englishman wanted nothing more than to have someone to laugh with.

Shaking off the congenial feeling, Lorenz pointed to the barn leaning precariously to the south. "You need to replace that as soon as possible."

Coleman followed his gaze to the ruined barn and nodded.

"I take it that small hill is manure," Lorenz asked, pointing to the mound lying exposed on the far edge of the fields.

"Yes," Coleman answered.

Lorenz shook his head at the man's stupidity. "You're wasting it. You might as well throw it away."

At this, the Englishman crossed his arms over his chest. "I use it to fertilize the fields."

"Oui," Lorenz answered, "but sitting out in the sun will only diminish it, and the rain will wash it into the creek where you get water."

"I have a cistern," the Englishman offered.

"So you let your horse drink such water?"

Coleman ran a lazy hand over his cheek. "So what do I do?"

A rush of excitement overwhelmed Lorenz. He couldn't explain it, but having the opportunity to teach this Englishman farming filled him with a sense of purpose. He was a good farmer and proud of it, but André preferred setting him to menial tasks like hauling hay and repairing roof shingles, constantly barking at Lorenz as if he were a servant. The Englishman may be a *couyon*, but André could go to hell.

"You build a shed for it," Lorenz explained. "A small one, with a roof. Four poles, space to throw in the manure, a gate on one end. Maybe a door."

Coleman nodded as Lorenz talked, then smiled gravely as the explanation continued. "I'll do that," Coleman said. "Right after I finish draining the fields, replanting my crops, and building a new barn, chicken coop, and hog pen. Of course, I have nothing to eat tonight, so I have to find time to hunt and shoot a turkey, but that shouldn't take long." Gazing down at his clothes, he added sarcastically, "And then there's the cleaning and mending to consider."

"Do you want my help or no?" Lorenz asked.

The Englishman didn't hesitate. "Yes," he said.

"Then shut up and come on."

Lorenz grabbed a pail and headed toward the house. Coleman picked up his own and was at Lorenz's side in two strides. "I can pay you," he said. "I don't have much left considering the seed I have to purchase, but I can pay you . . . "

"I don't want your money." Lorenz hadn't meant to sound so biting, but the idea was insulting.

"Then why?" Coleman asked.

Because I promised Rose, Lorenz thought, *and the chance to get my hands into that fertile earth you're destroying*. To Coleman, he lied, "Because we're neighbors."

At this, Coleman did laugh. "Since when did being a neighbor mean teaching an Englishman how to farm?"

When they reached the remnants of the barn, Lorenz placed the bucket down and stared at the mess. He suddenly understood Coleman's pessimism. But with two people working, they could reconstruct a solid barn in a day or two, or at least erect a frame to give the horse shelter.

"She put you up to this, didn't she?" Coleman asked.

Lorenz wanted to answer that wild horses couldn't have dragged him here today, but Rose Gallant's chestnut eyes could. He lied again, "I'm here to help."

"Why?"

"Because you're going to starve without it."

Coleman threw his bucket on the ground, spilling some of its contents. "So let me starve. That will solve all your problems."

Lorenz felt the hairs on the back of his neck straighten. They would finally exchange words and he was glad for it. "I'd love nothing better," Lorenz said.

"Then why are you here?"

Lorenz wanted to punch the Englishman, surround those blue eyes with a shiner, break a few bones, preferably the one in his aristocratic nose. But he thought of Emilie, who detested his impulsive violent nature. He thought of sweet Rose and the promise he had made.

And for some insane reason, he found it difficult to hate the Englishman as much as he would like.

"How can you speak of death so nonchalantly?" Lorenz asked, trying to change the subject. "Who are you to be so flippant toward what God has granted you?"

Coleman's blue eyes grew dark. "Look around you," Coleman said soberly.

Now, Lorenz really wanted to plant a fist in his face. "You whimpering idiot," he said. "Everyone in Opelousas has lost their crops, and their homes. You can replant. You can rebuild. But you sit here feeling sorry for yourself."

Coleman started to retort, but Lorenz's veins were boiling. "If this is the most of your worries, you're a piss-poor excuse for a man. Talk to me when someone robs you of everything you own. When they steal your homeland and scatter your family around the world, where half of them starve to death or die of pox. Talk to me when you watch your own mother die in your arms."

He knew the Englishman would not stand to be insulted, would move to action soon enough, but Coleman took the punishment Lorenz unleashed on him. Until Lorenz mentioned his mother. Coleman's eyes flew open and he grabbed the front of Lorenz's shirt, pushing him hard against the side of his house.

"How dare you mention that to me," Coleman shouted between his teeth. "Who told you of my mother?"

This was the moment Lorenz had waited for, the point when fighting would have been justified in Emilie's and Rose's eyes. If the Englishman wanted a fight, he would gladly accommodate him. But Coleman's comment unnerved him.

"Who told you?" Coleman shouted again, his blue eyes blazing with fury.

"No one," Lorenz shouted back. "I know nothing of you, Englishman."

Coleman jerked his shirt harder. "Then how did you know of my mother?"

Lorenz had had enough of this manhandling. He pushed Coleman backward and straightened, even though they remained inches apart. "My mother died on the beach at Grand Pré," he said. "Thanks to the likes of you."

Coleman stepped back, the blood draining from his face. He hadn't meant to react so strongly, hadn't dreamed of raising his hand against Lorenz. But the mention of his mother had lit a fire inside him, one that had burst into flame.

"I'm sorry," Coleman whispered. He walked to the porch and sat down, rubbing his forehead with one hand, trying to regain his composure. "Forgive me, I haven't spoken of her in years."

As if the hurricane's forces had not destroyed him enough—or the prospect of Rose being so close and yet forbidden—the image of his mother and infant brother dying in his arms renewed his belief that he was a defeated man.

Lorenz picked up his hat that had fallen during their confrontation and sat down next to him on the porch. "What happened?"

Was Coleman hearing things or was Rose's brother-in-law being kind? Lorenz Landry had to be a fine man; Coleman couldn't image anything less in the Gallant household. But he knew Lorenz's limits. And he didn't blame the man for being angry with the English.

"My mother died giving birth," Coleman said softly, shocked that he was actually speaking the words. He had not mentioned his mother's name since the day he had accused his father of murder and left home. "I was there when it happened."

Lorenz cleared his throat, uncomfortable with the conversation. Coleman decided to change the subject and save them both embarrassment.

"I'm your worst nightmare, aren't I?" he asked.

At this, Lorenz looked up unemotionally. "You're not exactly what I had in mind for Rose, no." He turned his hat round and round in his fingers. "But you're not my worst nightmare."

Coleman smirked, wondering who could be a poorer candidate for husband.

"André DeClouet," Lorenz said, reading his mind.

The fire returned, burning up Coleman's neck. "What would André have to do with Rose?"

Lorenz must have heard the fury in his voice, for he stared hard at Coleman. "He wants to marry her," he said finally.

The world stopped spinning, the sun disappeared, and the hurricane returned inside Coleman's head. As his heart sank into his chest, he heard the walls of the barn snap and the building come crashing to the ground.

This time, Coleman ignored God's laughter. He

refused to feel sorry for himself, to care about anything but his beloved Rose.

"Over my dead body," he said to Lorenz between gritted teeth.

For the first time since they had met, Lorenz smiled.

Chapter Seven

"You don't appear glad to see me and I nearly lost my life in that hurricane."

André sighed and planted a kiss on his mother's cheek. "I would be happier to see you if you weren't loaded down with every trinket and dress this side of the Mississippi."

Marguerite DeClouet extended her fan and cooled her face. "That was the point in our going to Pointe Coupée, was it not? Winter will be here before we know it and we must have material for new clothes."

A throbbing began in André's temple, a dull pain that emerged every time he tried to reason with his family and their relentless desire to spend beyond their means. "Mother, we have had this conversation too many times."

"So we don't need to have it again." Marguerite grabbed her daughter's elbow and headed toward the house. As the two passed André, Marguerite lightly touched his arm. "You'll take care of it."

André shut his eyes in an effort to keep his anger at bay, but the attempt was fruitless as he watched his slaves empty the wagon of three more chests. Winter clothes? Endless beads of perspiration soaked the back of his cotton shirt, reminding him all too well that winter was a long way away. What would they live on until then?

Thank God for the Gallants, André thought, still amazed at how they had appeared when he needed them most. The hard-working family proved an asset during these days of restoring the plantation, but then they were Acadian, farmers accustomed to living off the land and making the most of meager resources. André's Creole neighbors were not as practical. Like his mother and sister, they were used to having work performed for them and became irritated at interruptions in their routine.

Not that André was any different. He enjoyed luxury as much as they did. But after his father passed away, he was shocked to learn the family had been spiraling into debt for years. When they were forced to leave Mobile after the English took over the territory, his family expected to continue their high standard of living at Opelousas. The house, the fixtures, the furniture—everything was to be reproduced in this godforsaken frontier, even though they had sold half their slaves to finance the journey and spent most of their money starting new crops. Crops that were now destroyed.

At least they would starve through autumn in the latest fashion.

Remembering Rose, he trotted toward the kitchen. He had to talk to her again, force some sense into her. After all, the arrangement would benefit them both.

When André entered the stifling kitchen, Rose stood alone at the massive stove. One hand captured her hair from behind and stretched the auburn mass up over her head while the other hand wiped the sweat glistening on her neck. It was such a simple gesture, one everyone was doomed to repeat several times a day. Yet Rose's graceful movement at her neck made her appear like a goddess caught in a quiet passionate pose.

What was she thinking? She appeared in a trance, removing the perspiration as if imagining someone else's fingers touching her there.

André watched the small woman lost in thought. Hardly a beauty, which was why he had asked her to marry him in the first place, Rose exhibited a passion he had not seen before. For an instant, before he dismissed the idea as absurd, he wanted to kiss the moist skin at her nape.

Rose sensed his presence and turned, dropping her hair in the process. André expected his fervent image to disappear when her plain face came into view. Instead, he found her eyes sparkling, her cheeks burning red, and he reacted again at the sight of her.

"Monsieur DeClouet," she said, thrusting her chin forward slightly.

She seemed more confident than that first night in his house, which excited him further. Why hadn't he seen this side of her before? "I wish to talk to you if you don't mind." He had to calm his senses and relieve the tightness in his trousers.

"My brother has insisted you speak with *him.*"

My, she had grown *very* confident since that night when she stood shaking on his gallery. "I appreciate his concern for your well-being, mademoiselle, but I thought this was an agreement between you and me."

"We agreed that I would consider it. Nothing more."

André walked closer, amazed at the intensity of the heat within the small kitchen. Beads of perspiration broke out on his forehead as he gazed down into Rose's face. Without thinking, he placed a hand on her burning cheek. "Think about it," he whispered heatedly.

Rose gasped and stepped back, surprised as much as he was at the seductive note in his voice. André cleared his throat, turned, and began to handle a plate on the sideboard. His reaction to this homely girl was outrageous.

"As I said before," he continued in his usual authoritative tone, "I will be generous. Your family will want for nothing. It will solve all your problems."

"And as I said before, it will solve all of yours."

André turned and stared. Rose had become quite feisty. "It will help us both."

Rose removed the pot that was now boiling from the stove. "You, monsieur, will return to a normal life, but I will have given up my chance at happiness, my chance for a family."

Now that they were arguing, André felt his old self returning. He understood command; he always got his way. "Look at yourself, mademoiselle," he said. "You are small, plain, and poor. What are your chances at happiness?"

Rose's eyes widened at his honesty, and André almost regretted the hurt he had inflicted. Almost. The girl might have elicited lust from him for one small instant, but money was money.

"Why do you think I offered marriage in the first place?" he continued. "Do you think a pretty, sophisticated woman would agree to such an arrangement?"

Rose's face paled, despite the temperature of the room. Silently, she removed her apron.

"Think about it," André insisted. "You will have enough money to get to Attakapas and start your own farm. How are you going to do this otherwise? Even if your father returns, who will have the funds to buy seeds, to buy tools, to feed you through the winter?"

Rose placed the apron on the sideboard and moved to leave. André caught her arm and stood so close he could smell the herbal scent about her. "I'm your best offer," he said sternly.

The confident stance now gone, Rose gazed up at him timidly, then pulled her arm free and left the building.

*   *   *

The sun began its daily descent past the lime green cypresses in Coleman's woods, but the heat continued. A short afternoon shower had provided some respite, but now its moisture lifted from the ground like steam.

"It's like rain in reverse," Lorenz said, as they lifted a board into place to finish the last side of the pigpen.

"You get used to it," Coleman said, handing him a wooden peg. "After a few summers, you hardly notice it."

Lorenz laughed, gazing at Coleman's drenched shirt and red face. Who was he kidding?

"You're right," Coleman said with a grin. "I lied. You never get used to it."

"Well," Lorenz said as he beat the peg into the wood to hold the board in place. "At least we won't freeze in the winter."

Now that the pen was constructed, all they needed was rope to tie the gate closed. For the life of him, Coleman couldn't find the coil he had purchased from Henri three weeks before.

"I'm going to check the cabin one more time," Coleman said. Lorenz nodded and Coleman wondered if the Frenchman had understood. Surprisingly, Lorenz understood quite a bit of English, although there were times when Coleman rattled on too fast and a glazed look passed over his neighbor's face. "Rope," he added. This time, Lorenz's nod appeared sincere.

"Bring water," Lorenz said, then reminding Coleman of his need to learn French added, *"L'eau."*

Coleman repeated the French word for water and entered his house. Somewhere in all his belongings sat a large coil of rope.

Approaching Coleman's property, Rose heard the door to the house creak open. But she stopped at the newly constructed pigpen when she heard a hammer beating there. As she walked closer, Lorenz pushed up his head and smiled proudly. "What do you think?" he asked.

If Rose's heart hadn't been sitting at the bottom of her chest, she would have been proud of his accomplishment. It was a fine pen, one that would keep Coleman's animals well contained. Rose summoned her best smile to let Lorenz know how proud she was, even if she didn't feel like smiling. "It's lovely," she said.

Lorenz might have noticed her sadness had he not been enthralled at his handiwork. He stood there gazing at the pen, his hands planted on his hips and a wide grin playing about his lips. "Didn't take us more than an afternoon," he said.

Again, Rose smiled, offering him encouragement even though her heart was breaking. "Where is Coleman?" she asked.

At first, Lorenz didn't answer and Rose wondered if he had heard her. "He's in the house," he finally said, checking the sturdiness of a post. "He's looking for some rope."

Rope. The image fired her into action. Had he forgotten she had used his rope as a clothesline? She raced into the house and found Coleman rummaging through his trunk.

"It's outside," Rose said. "I used it for washing."

When Coleman looked up and their eyes met, his gaze bore into her. He quickly crossed the room and studied her closely. "What's wrong?" he finally asked.

Lorenz had not noticed her discomfort, yet Coleman sensed it immediately. Not for the first time, Rose wondered if an invisible string stretched between them, a connection that transcended nationality. Maman had visions, images that spoke of the future. Perhaps Rose had inherited this second sight, only she shared it with Coleman.

"What's wrong?" Coleman asked again.

Rose examined the floorboards at her feet. "Nothing."

A gentle finger touched her chin and lifted her eyes skyward. "What did that bastard say to you?"

Rose felt the tears lingering at the back of her eyes, but she dreaded setting free the emotions raging inside her. Instead, she leaned forward, tilting her head slightly so her cheek rested gently on his chest. Instantly, Coleman slid an arm about her waist and pulled her close.

She thought to consider Lorenz, to worry that he might catch them in such an intimate embrace. Yet standing there in Coleman's arms felt as natural as rain. Rose closed her eyes and enjoyed the warmth Coleman's arms offered her. He smelled of freshly cut wood and hard work. His strong arms felt like pillars of stone surrounding her, keeping her safe from the harsh words of André DeClouet. With his free hand, he caressed her hair while leaning a cheek against the top of her head.

"What has happened, my dear?" he asked her.

The question, along with the sudden beat of Lorenz's hammer, jolted Rose, and she pulled away. Even though Coleman's affection had eased the sting of André's insults, the fact remained that the arrogant Creole was right. "It doesn't matter," she said.

Coleman attempted to catch her arm, to draw her back, but Rose moved to the other side of the table. *Best to keep some distance between us,* she thought, *especially in my current state.*

Coleman planted his hands on top of a chair and leaned forward across the table. The passion in his eyes caused Rose's breathing to quicken.

"Rose, I have always known you would marry someday; it was something I had always expected. But you cannot marry André DeClouet."

She agreed with him. But for some reason, she felt a need to explain. "He's offered to help my family. It's a business arrangement."

Coleman gripped the top of the chair. "How can you say that when you sat at this table and said André was not to be trusted?"

"That was different."

"How?" Coleman asked heatedly.

She wanted to say because Coleman was English, but Rose wasn't sure of anything anymore. André's proposal seemed sincere. How could it not be? They would both gain from the agreement, even if Rose would spend the rest of her life an old maid.

Coleman moved around the table and grabbed her arms. "Don't do this," he said.

"It's only for money," she whispered, her heart beating madly at his body so close to hers.

"You'll be his property," Coleman said, pain reflecting in his eyes. "André likes people bowing down to him. He'll use you any way he can."

Rose had thought of that before, but she didn't think André would ask to bed her. She imagined them marrying, then her leaving for the Attakapas Poste and never seeing André again. But he had a right to ask anything of her, including sharing a bed anytime he desired it. And today in the kitchen, there was a moment when . . .

"Suppose you get rich on your father's homestead," Coleman continued. "He has the right as a husband to everything you own." Coleman reached up and pushed a loose strand of hair off her forehead. "Don't you want a family of your own?"

Rose could imagine children all right, children with curly blond hair and azure eyes. But that was the problem. She couldn't have what she wanted, if indeed Coleman desired her more than as a friend, which he more than likely did not. It wasn't just nationality that separated them. There was education and economics as well. André had made that point clear. And there would not be anyone else asking for her hand.

"I'll never be married," she whispered.

Coleman stared hard at her. "Why would you say that?"

Rose stepped back far enough to free herself from

his grip, then she crossed her arms in front of her chest in an effort to hold the heavy emotions inside. "Because I'm small, plain, and poor. Who would want to marry me?"

The shock that crossed Coleman's features was immediate. He looked as if he had been slapped. Then a sadness took over, one so intense Rose could almost feel the pain inside him. For that brief moment before Lorenz crossed the threshold, Rose swore Coleman was in love with her.

And a hope filled her like no other.

"What's going on here?"

The accusing tone in Lorenz's voice made Rose wonder if he would challenge Coleman to a fight. Surprisingly, Coleman showed more anger.

"You said André would not bother her again," he shouted at Lorenz.

Lorenz's eyes narrowed as he turned toward Rose. "Did he talk to you?" he asked her.

Rose thought to nod in agreement, but she feared Lorenz might challenge André instead. "It isn't what you think. He only wanted to ask me if I made up my mind."

"The answer is no," Lorenz shouted. "I made that clear to him."

Rose almost argued the same points she had offered to Coleman; that his proposal solved their financial problems and that she was not likely to be asked into marriage again. When she gazed up at Coleman and found affection swimming in those sea blue eyes, the idea of marrying André seemed ludicrous. She wanted nothing more than to return to the safety of his arms.

A slight smile began at the corners of her lips when she thought of how he had embraced her as she lay on top of his drunken form. A shiver of desire ran up her spine.

Coleman must have understood, for she could have sworn his eyes smiled in return.

"Don't worry," Coleman said. "André won't be bothering you anymore. Lorenz and I will see to it."

Lorenz and I? Could it be possible these two were friends? Rose glanced toward Lorenz, but he immediately began a long stream of brotherly instruction in French. While Lorenz lectured her about never being alone on the DeClouet property, Coleman placed three cups on the table and filled them with water. Lorenz gulped his water down without interrupting his speech, and Coleman refilled it three times. Finally, Rose had heard enough.

"*Merci*, Lorenz," she said, touching his arm. "I understand."

"Do you?" Lorenz asked with a touch of sorrow.

Suddenly, Rose knew Lorenz shouldered the blame for what had happened that afternoon. As patriarch of the family, he bore the responsibilities for them all, including patching up pigpens for English neighbors. After all the horrors the English had inflicted on Lorenz and his family, the last thing he wanted to do was assist Coleman in establishing his farm. Yet here he was.

Rose slid her arms about her tall brother-in-law's

waist and hugged him. "There is nothing to worry about," she whispered.

When Rose peeked over Lorenz's arm and caught the passion still lurking in Coleman's eyes, she instantly doubted her words.

"I'll fix the gate," Coleman said, heading out the door.

Lorenz pulled away and tilted her face to his. "What did that bastard say to you?"

She heard what Lorenz said, but her attention followed Coleman as he made his way toward the pen, one hand pulling the blond curls from his forehead. "He needs a haircut," Rose answered.

"What?"

Rose looked at Lorenz, still bristling from their conversation. "It's not important, Lorenz," she said. "What he said is not important."

"I thought I told you not to be alone with him."

Now that she thought about it, where had Lorenz been all day? He usually was within earshot whenever she worked at the DeClouet house. "I was waiting for you to walk me home."

A guilty look crossed his face. "Guess I got involved in the pen. You know me and projects, I can't seem to quit once I get started."

Rose felt a warm glow begin at her center. "You like him, don't you?"

Lorenz shrugged. If he did, he would be the last one to admit it. Rose raised herself on her toes and kissed him on the cheek. "I love you, Lorenz."

Lorenz threw his arms around her and hugged her

again. "I love you, too, Pumpkin. But now that I satisfied my promise, may I go home?"

Rose felt her hope slipping, but she refused to relinquish her grip. "What about those fields? Who will help him with those fields?"

Placing his chin on the top of her head, Lorenz stared out the window toward Coleman's waterlogged crops. "He's absolutely the worst farmer I have ever seen," he said. "Who in his right mind would plant corn so far apart?"

"So that means you will help him?" Rose asked.

A silence ensued, one that lasted several moments. "I have to work with André in the mornings," Lorenz said bitterly. "I suppose I could help out here in the afternoons."

Rose slipped from his embrace, picking the cups off the table and placing them in a pail for washing. "I can come straight after my work at the house and help out." Lorenz started to protest, until Rose added, "That way I could fix you both something to eat."

A flicker of interest appeared in Lorenz's eyes and Rose couldn't help but smile. Lorenz loved her cooking as much as he loved farming. How could he resist such a combination?

"We'll see," he said, leaving the cabin, but Rose knew victory was close at hand.

As the sun dipped below the horizon and mosquito hawks darted through the sky announcing twilight, Rose, Coleman, and Lorenz rounded up the pigs and secured them in the new pen. Lorenz beamed at his new creation and Coleman stood gazing at his corralled animals in disbelief.

"Amazing how easy it is when you know what to do," Lorenz told him.

Coleman extended his hand. "I owe it all to you."

Lorenz stared at the outstretched arm as if it were laced with pox. Then he accepted the Englishman's hand and shook it. As she watched her two favorite men exchange civilities, Rose's hope, so long buried inside her, began to blossom.

"It's time to go," Lorenz said.

"Just one minute," Coleman said and rushed into the house. When he emerged, he carried a long rifle and a handful of bullets. "There are turkeys in my woods," he said, handing Lorenz the rifle. "They come out this time of day. Perhaps you'd like a shot at them."

Never since the day Lorenz married Emilie had Rose seen his face light up so brightly. Years. It must have been years since he last used a gun, perhaps as long ago as Canada when he and his father hunted the woods around Minas Basin for deer. Lorenz took the rifle, running an appreciative hand up and down the barrel.

Lorenz wanted to accept—Rose could see the desire in his eyes—but he must have felt uncomfortable taking such a gift from an Englishman.

"If you hurry, they should be right over the ridge by the bayou," Coleman added.

Suddenly, Rose realized they would be alone, if only for the short time it took Lorenz to shoot a turkey. "Roasted turkey," Rose heard herself say, although she doubted she was speaking such bold words. "You go shoot a turkey, Lorenz, and I'll give this Englishman a haircut."

Lorenz stared hard at Coleman, probably assessing whether the man could be trusted to be alone with his ward. His hardened stare made Rose doubt he would relent. Then his eyes turned to hers and he seemed to melt.

"I'll be right back," he said as a warning.

"She'll be fine," Coleman said with a grin. "I have my other rifle handy and will shoot any man who comes near her."

Lorenz acted as if he didn't understand the humor in Coleman's statement, but Rose saw the edges of his lips curling in a smile.

"So now I have two big brothers to contend with," Rose said, folding her arms in mock defiance.

Coleman didn't waste time replying. "Yes, you do," he said, taking Rose's arm and leading her toward the house.

"I won't be long," she heard Lorenz shout at them. But when Rose turned, Lorenz had disappeared into the woods.

"That was very kind of you," she said to Coleman.

Coleman wanted to laugh. It wasn't kind at all. He knew Lorenz would jump at the chance of shooting a turkey and that allowed him time alone with Rose. "It wasn't altogether altruistic," Coleman said.

"Pardon?" Rose asked.

When they reached the light of the cabin's lantern, Coleman stared down into her angelic face, always astonished at the sweetness there. If only he could kiss those freckles, breathe in the scent that had conquered his senses that afternoon when he had been able to hold her. How would he ever sleep again? For so many nights her image had filled his mind, keeping him awake with a relentless desire. Now the memory of her scent and embrace would make sleep impossible.

"Wash," she said, taking him in from head to toe. Then blushing, she added, "And put on a clean shirt."

"Yes, ma'am," Coleman said, bowing.

Rose blushed a deeper red and smiled innocently. Coleman fought an intense longing to lean forward and taste the honey of those delectable lips.

"I'll get the scissors," Rose said, then entered the cabin. "Call me when you're ready."

Coleman's smile broadened thinking of those petite hands cutting his hair. He went to the cistern and drew water, then removed his soiled shirt and plunged his head into the pail. The chilled water refreshed him, making him forget his aching muscles. Rose's smile made him feel as if he could conquer the world.

After scrubbing himself with the soap Henri's wife had given him, Coleman realized he had neither a clean shirt nor a towel. He heard a throat clearing and turned to find Rose holding both in her hands while she discreetly looked away, a blush and smile still gracing her cheeks.

"*Merci*, mademoiselle," Coleman said, accepting the outstretched garments.

Rose stared toward the opposite horizon. "You must learn French, Coleman," she said.

The sound of his name spoken with her soft accent made his heart constrict. If he wasn't the worst likely candidate for a husband, Coleman might have imagined Rose a witch, casting a spell on him and capturing his heart. For indeed his heart was lost.

"Will you teach me?" he asked, throwing the shirt over his head.

Rose finally looked his way. "I've been thinking," she said.

"Yes."

Rose walked to his side and motioned for him to sit down on the porch. They were now eye to eye, although Coleman had to stretch his legs around her so she would be able to reach his hair.

"People like it when those who are different have misfortunes," Rose said, combing his hair. "They take pleasure in it, although I don't know why."

"Because it makes them feel less unfortunate," Coleman added.

Rose nodded, sliding her comb through the curls Coleman had spent a lifetime trying to tame. "If you were more like them, they would treat you better."

"So if I speak French, my neighbors would be friendlier."

Rose stopped to make eye contact. "Not just speak French, be French."

Coleman had to laugh. As a native-born American, he might not consider himself English, but he was a far cry from being French.

"I'm serious," Rose insisted. "You must eat like us, act like us."

"You mean use a lot of facial expressions," Coleman said with a grin.

"What facial expressions?" Rose insisted with a pout, and Coleman fought a desire to laugh again. The French could speak volumes without opening their mouths.

"Will you teach me?" he asked her again.

Rose began cutting. "If Lorenz will allow it," she said softly.

While the scissors snapped about his head and wisps of blond hair floated to the ground, Coleman tried to focus his eyes away from Rose. But she stood so close, her face only inches from his. He could smell the peppers she had cooked for lunch, the hint of lemon on her fingertips. He could see the soft line that lifted her cheekbones high on her face. The graceful lift of her nose. The cinnamon eyes so perfectly round, infused with light.

"Rose Gallant," Coleman whispered. "You are adorable. And any man who thinks otherwise is a fool."

Rose hesitated at his forehead, refusing to meet his eyes. She swallowed, then continued cutting.

"Your violin," she said with a catch in her throat. "Don't forget your violin. Acadians love music. I can teach you some of our songs."

Remembering Natchez, when he brought his violin to the Acadian village and played long into the night, Coleman knew Rose was right. Even Marianne had reacted to the music, laughing and dancing with the others who thrilled at the sounds coming from his violin.

But more important, Coleman realized, Rose was giving him information that would help break down the wall between them. For the first time in years, Coleman's faith returned.

Rose stepped back to gaze at her handiwork, then ran two fingers through the hair at his forehead to judge its length. Before Coleman's logic could intercede, he captured her hand and pressed his lips against the inside of her palm. Once there, he couldn't help himself. He planted kiss after kiss along her lifeline, her fingers, the delicate skin at her wrist.

Rose gasped, then leaned forward so her forehead touched his. She placed her free hand, still holding the scissors, on his shoulder. Coleman knew he was treading on dangerous ground, but he had to feel her. He pressed his thighs against her body, then slid his face into the curve of her neck and inhaled deeply.

As he pressed his lips against the soft skin below her ear, a shot rang out in the distance. Rose pulled away at the sound, refusing to meet his eyes.

Coleman thought to apologize; his actions were reprehensible. But he wasn't sorry. He would only regret his kisses if they had insulted his angel. When Rose's eyes finally turned his way, glazed with a mix of excitement and guilt, he knew the same conflict of emotions raged inside her.

"I got the fattest turkey this side of the Mississippi," Lorenz shouted from the darkness.

They had only seconds before Lorenz came into the light. Before he gave himself time to think, time to chase off the desire eating at his heart, Coleman took Rose's face between his hands and kissed her.

She tasted of heaven and earth, a cross between a cloud and a sweet apple pie. Her warm lips trembled against his, but she didn't refuse him. Rose leaned forward into the kiss, appearing to savor the taste of him as well.

Way too soon Coleman pulled back and exhaled, feeling like a man thrown to the cold outdoors after a night by a warm hearth. His large hands still held her delicate face, and he slid a lazy thumb over her moist bottom lip.

They both heard Lorenz approach at the same time. Rose grabbed her basket and moved aside and Coleman stood, exhaling heavily in an effort to ease his pronounced heartbeat. When Lorenz arrived, he was too preoccupied with his catch to notice any discomfort between them. "Nice, eh?" Lorenz asked proudly, holding up a fat turkey.

To her credit, Rose responded naturally. "You've had quite a successful day."

Lorenz beamed at the compliment. Then he offered Coleman the rifle. "Thanks. I haven't had the pleasure in a very long time."

"Keep it," Coleman answered. What was he thinking, giving away his rifle? A strange sensation overtook him. He wanted Lorenz to have his prized firearm, as if they were brothers, or something close to it.

"I can't do that," Lorenz argued.

Coleman slid a hand along his neck, amazed at how good a haircut could feel. He glanced at Rose whose eyes still glowed with that constant wonder, whose smile told him he had a chance—even a slight one—at making her his.

But first he had to become French.

"I want you to have it," he said to Lorenz. "I have another. Maybe we could go hunting together sometime."

Lorenz stared longingly at the rifle in his hands, and Coleman realized there were some things that transcended political boundaries. Simple things like waking up before sunrise and shooting a deer while enjoying the good company of a friend. Bringing home supper after a day in the fresh air.

Or the smell of lemon and a woman's gentle fingers at your forehead and the taste of her lips.

"You will come back?" Coleman asked Lorenz, sneaking a peek at Rose whose pert little face caused his breath to quicken.

This time Lorenz didn't hesitate. "We'll be back tomorrow afternoon."

Chapter Eight

"So, what's he like?" Gabrielle's breath felt warm at Rose's ear, but Rose refused to turn over.

"What's who like?" Rose answered.

Gabrielle wasted no time in leaping out of bed, crossing the room, and squatting before Rose's face. "How many times do we have to play this game?"

Rose sighed and lifted herself up on one elbow. "He's the same man we knew in Natchez, only poorer."

Gabrielle folded her legs, making herself comfortable on the floor. "Just like your dream. Remember, you said the man in your dream wore clothes that were worn; he was working a field and singing happily."

Rose laughed. "I can't image he's happy with his fields right now."

Silence lingered between them, a hush of unspoken questions. Finally, Gabrielle spoke the words Rose had been dreading to hear. "Are you in love with him?"

Rose sat up in bed and leaned back against her pillows. Loving Coleman was not something she wanted to think about, let alone speak of, but confiding in Gabrielle seemed to remove the heaviness from her heart.

"I don't know," she whispered. Then turning to Gabrielle and finding comfort in her sister's sympathetic face, Rose added, "Yes, I think I am."

Gabrielle's reaction ranged from alarm to understanding. She leaned forward and grasped Rose's hands. "What are you to do?"

Staring down at their intertwined fingers, Rose was glad for the lifeline, for her ship was surely sinking. Coleman's kiss the night before had made her forget all her troubles, but in the light of day, the old conflicts reared their ugly heads. "I don't know," she said.

"What can I do?"

"You can talk to Maman," Rose suggested. "Make her realize Coleman isn't the one responsible for all our troubles."

Gabrielle frowned, uttering the next words as if they burned her tongue. "He's English."

Rose removed her fingers and crossed her arms. She shut her eyes praying those two words would disappear forever. "I know what he is, Gabrielle. His father is an English soldier, too. Did you know that?

For all I know he could be related to the governor of Nova Scotia. That doesn't change my mind."

Now it was Gabrielle's turn to cross her arms across her chest. "That's because you don't remember the exile."

Rose threw back the covers and jumped out of bed. "Yes, I know," she said bitingly.

"Why are you mad at me?" Gabrielle asked, rising and standing beside her.

Taking a deep breath to relieve the anger, Rose tried to clear her thoughts. She couldn't remember the last time something had angered her before coming to Opelousas. Yet in one week she had spoken harshly to practically everyone in her family. Still, the anger failed to dissipate.

"Because I'm always told I don't remember the exile," Rose said. "I'm too nice. I don't know how to judge people. I'm too accepting. I can't make rational decisions because I may be taken advantage of. I can't be trusted to go into town because I might pay too much for food. Even though the one time I did that, the storekeeper's son had been jailed and he needed the money for bail. But I wasn't allowed to make that decision. I was too naive."

"Rose . . . "

"Now I love a man who's the wrong nationality. I'm mistaken for feeling this way about him because I don't remember the exile."

Gabrielle stepped back as if slapped. "That's not fair."

"Nothing's fair," Rose said, remembering Coleman's words on the road that night. "It wasn't fair what happened to us, what happened to Papa. It's not fair that you love a man you may never see again." Gabrielle's eyes widened at the mention of Jean Bouclaire, and Rose reached out and took her hands. "But I love him, Gabrielle. Don't I deserve a chance at happiness? Don't you?"

Gabrielle reached out and hugged Rose tightly. "Oh, Rose," she whispered. "If only he were French."

The two sisters held each other, rocking gently. "With my help, he soon will be," Rose whispered back.

Rose stared at the kitchen window that opened on to André's barnyard and fields. Lunch had been served to the DeClouet women and preparations finished for supper. Where was Lorenz?

For weeks they had worked at Coleman's fields, building a drainage ditch that emptied into the stream and, on the far side of his property, into the wider Bayou Courtableau. The barn had been reconstructed in record time and a shed over the manure pile finished in an afternoon. Rose still wondered how Coleman and Lorenz did it. They barely spoke a word, yet they seemed to understand each other and what was needed to complete each project. Every once in a while, they would fail to lift a board, find themselves up to their knees in mud, and share a laugh. It was at those moments Rose believed the two men liked each other, despite their differences.

Yesterday afternoon, when a pig escaped its pen during feeding and it took over an hour to catch the animal, all three found themselves laughing hysterically. Everytime they cornered the pig and one of them lunged, it somehow managed to evade them and race through their legs. It didn't take long before they were all caked in mud. At one point, they gave up, lying defeated in the dirt, laughing at the sight of one another.

Afternoons at Coleman's were the highlight of Rose's days. She and Lorenz endured the commands of the arrogant DeClouet women, who outdid André in their patronizing tones, then escaped through the woods with leftovers from the table. While Lorenz instructed Coleman about farming, Rose cooked a late lunch. Then she taught Coleman French as the three enjoyed their makeshift meal.

Today, Rose was particularly eager to leave the house. One of the slave boys had brought in a bucket of crawfish, which Madame DeClouet immediately dismissed. Always at home in a kitchen, Rose was eager to experiment with the tiny crustaceans so she hid them under the cupboard along with some discarded onions. Rose still had the hot peppers her Spanish friend had given her in Natchez. The combination of ingredients might prove a tasty meal.

If only Lorenz would come.

"Pumpkin?" Lorenz's voice registered just before Rose caught his face at the window.

"Lorenz, you won't believe what I have for lunch."

"I'm afraid I can't make it today," Lorenz said, squinting in the sun. "André needs some help with his fences."

Rose pushed a wooden crate under the window

and stepped onto it to meet Lorenz's eyes. "He works you too much."

Lorenz frowned again and nodded, but they both knew they were fortunate to have the work and the chance to get to Attakapas. "Tell *L'Anglais* I'll see him tomorrow."

A chill ran through Rose even though the temperature was scalding. Being alone with Coleman, possibly having his lips on hers again, took her breath away. The thought both scared and excited her. "Alone?" she whispered.

Lorenz studied her hard. "Is there a reason I shouldn't let you go?"

There were dozens, one being that the man held her heart in his hands and, the way she reacted to his touch, was liable to hold other parts of her body as well. Two weeks had passed and she never stopped dreaming of his kiss that night. In fact, the more time passed, the stronger the desire for more.

"No," she answered, trying to sound confident. "I will bring him lunch and return home."

Lorenz hesitated, sliding a hand across his chin.

"What could happen?" Rose asked, offering an innocent smile. "He's busy with the fields. Besides, he's out of food. We used almost all of his money for seed last week and I cooked all the vegetables for that soup two days ago. He's bound to have eaten it by now."

Finally, Lorenz nodded. Rose knew he approved of Coleman and wanted what was best for his neighbor, but he would never admit it.

"Well, don't stay too long," he said. "Maman will have my hide if she finds out."

Rose leaned out the window and planted a kiss on her brother-in-law's rough face. "You need a shave," she said. "And thank you for trusting me."

There was a rule Coleman and the Gallants kept: if they weren't at his cabin by two o'clock, they weren't coming. It was close to three, so Coleman finished his work in the fields, then went inside to wash and enjoy the last of Rose's vegetable soup.

He had spent so much time during the past two weeks replanting and rebuilding, he had neglected his violin. Now, with the skies turning gray and a long rain imminent, Coleman took his instrument from the chest and began a ballad he had penned since first meeting Rose. By the time he placed the violin onto his shoulder and raised the bow, he and the instrument had become one. He pulled the bow across the strings and music spilled forth, as if it took life straight from his heart.

It had always been that way, a natural talent since the day his father had passed on the legacy. His father had taught him old English songs, showed him the positions on the strings and how to hold the bow. Watching his mother's eyes brighten as his father played her favorite songs by the fireside was the highlight of his childhood. Now that he considered it, those were the only happy times he had witnessed between his parents.

When did the light leave his mother's eyes? Coleman wondered. Had it been before his father turned to the army for satisfaction, spending his every waking moment away from the family? Most definitely, she had changed when they left family and friends in Georgia and moved to godforsaken Natchez. His mother had been with child then, alone and miserable at their isolated plantation, while his father, the bastard, took every opportunity to visit neighboring towns, particularly New Orleans.

Coleman stopped playing and stared down at the violin in his hands. Though he detested his father and would probably never speak to him again, he treasured this instrument as much as his memories.

"Please don't stop," Rose said from the doorway.

Coleman looked at his beloved's face, glad for the company and the interruption of such painful thoughts.

"You have brought me something," he said, smiling at the basket of food in her arms. "I'm afraid I have eaten already."

"En Français," Rose said, reminding him to speak French.

"Où est Lorenz?" Coleman asked, wondering why Lorenz hadn't bounded through the door parlaying instructions for the day.

Rose placed her basket on the table and bit her lower lip nervously. "He has to fix some of André's fences. He won't be coming."

Coleman must have misunderstood her. His French had improved significantly over the past few weeks, perhaps he had heard wrong. "Lorenz isn't coming?" he asked.

To his surprise, Rose lifted her head and met his eyes confidently. "No," she said simply, and began pulling items from her basket.

"Is he coming later?" Coleman asked, hope pouring through him. He would give an eternity for an afternoon alone with her.

"No," Rose repeated. "Do you like crawfish?"

Coleman's mind was so busy racing through the possibilities, he wasn't sure what he agreed to, but he nodded.

"Bon," Rose said, and began assembling an assortment of pots and pans on the cupboard. "Would you mind starting a fire?"

No need, Coleman thought. A fire burned so intensely inside him, she could cook a dozen meals. *"Oui,* my love," he said with a sly grin. "For you, anything."

Rose lifted her eyes slightly, offering her own flirtatious smile, a gesture so sensual it was everything Coleman could do not to bolt out of his chair and lead her straight to his bed. Instead, he cleared his throat and headed toward the fireplace.

"I'm surprised Lorenz let you come here alone," Coleman said as he placed kindling onto coals still hot from breakfast. Thinking back on his behavior the night she cut his hair, guilt consumed him. "I'm surprised you came."

"Why wouldn't I?" Rose said as she chopped an onion.

Coleman stood and watched the wood burst into flames. He leaned an arm on the mantel and stared at the exploding log, wondering if his self-control was that flammable. "As much as I like to think I am a trustworthy man, I'm afraid I cannot be trusted. My actions the first night you were here proved that point."

Rose stopped cutting, sighed, and looked up. "You're speaking English again and I don't understand."

Perhaps it was the twinkle in her eye or the coquettish way she rested her hand on her hip, but Coleman doubted she misunderstood. He started to repeat the explanation in French, but instead began to think of ways to eliminate the space between them and capture those lips again. "You're not safe with me," he said softly in French.

The twinkle disappeared. A look of apprehension crossed her face, and Coleman wished he could retract his words. He hated thinking she might fear him. "Why do you say that?" she asked.

Coleman decided to be honest. What else could he be with Rose? "You know how badly I behaved when you cut my hair. If I ever hurt you, I'd never forgive myself."

"You didn't hurt me," she answered.

A silence developed between them, but neither looked away. "Rose," Coleman finally said. "You must know by now how I feel about you."

Rose blushed and smiled tentatively, then looked down at her hands. "You made it clear that day in my house in Natchez."

A knife in his chest might have hurt him less. Coleman winced, thinking back on that afternoon when a passion so powerful overtook him that he spewed forth his feelings in front of Rose, Gabrielle, and

Marianne. At the time he prayed the Earth would open up and swallow him whole. "I was hoping you hadn't understood my English," he said.

Rose's hesitant grin spread into a broader, yet still shy, smile. "Some things don't need translating," she said quietly while her cheeks burned crimson.

Coleman inched forward, placing his hands on the back of the chair opposite her. He would always remember them standing that way, no matter what their future held, as if the table represented the many differences that separated them.

"I couldn't help myself," he said, finding the confession comforting. "That day I met you at the fort, when your beautiful eyes looked at me with alarm yet you accepted my hand in greeting, I knew my heart would never be the same. Something happened to me, Rose. I can't explain it."

Rose placed her fingers on the table, rubbing the tips of them back and forth inside the wood's grooves while her eyes followed her actions. "I felt the same way when you played the violin that night," she said softly.

A hope so intense filled Coleman that he imagined he stopped breathing. "May I conclude, Mademoiselle Gallant, that you might care for me?"

Rose looked up, her chestnut eyes glowing with warmth and affection. "Of course I do," she whispered. "Isn't it obvious?"

Coleman reached out his hand and Rose slipped her fingers into his palm. He stared down at their hands, wondering if he would awaken from this fantastic dream and Rose would be gone. Or maybe it was

God who was sleeping, allowing Coleman a chance at happiness at last.

"Are you going to stand there," Rose asked softly, breaking Coleman from his thoughts, "or are you going to kiss me again?"

Coleman smiled so broadly his cheek muscles ached. "Perhaps I'm not safe with *you*, mademoiselle," he joked.

Rose tilted her chin skyward in mock defiance, shaking her head. "No, you're not."

Pulling her hand forward, Coleman led Rose toward him while he moved around the table and met her halfway. As soon as their bodies were within reach, Coleman's hand was on her cheek and his lips were tightly pressed to hers.

Whatever hesitation Rose felt about being alone with Coleman disappeared when his hand touched hers. She couldn't wait another moment, snaking an arm about his neck as soon as he drew near.

Coleman was equally eager, pulling her close with a hand at her waist while his other hand roamed the length of her back and his lips devoured hers. At first he playfully nipped at her lower lip, then consumed them with a heated passion. After what seemed an eternity, Coleman pulled away, planting kisses across her cheeks and down her jawbone to the soft skin at her neck and up beneath her earlobe.

While Rose gave his searing lips room to work, she stretched her arms about his neck and savored the scent of his hair, still wet from his bath. She pulled his tie loose and set his blond curls free, her fingers threading the silken mane. As his teeth bit and sucked at the soft skin beneath her chin, Rose raised herself on her toes to pull herself firmly against his chest.

Coleman moaned and immediately sought solace at her lips. This time his tongue urged her lips apart and danced its way inside, savoring the inside of her mouth and gently meeting her own.

The thrill of their bodies pressed together and their mouths in unison made Rose's knees weak. She rolled her head to the side in an effort to catch her breath while still moving her hands across his rock-hard chest. He felt so good, so incredibly good. Feminine places deep inside her began to throb, happy for the sensations but unsatisfied and demanding more.

Rose considered surrendering when Coleman lifted her and carried her to the bed. As he placed her gently on the mattress, she saw the conflict in his eyes.

"No, my love," she said, running her fingers across his lips. "I want this."

Coleman grasped her hand and kissed each finger, as if for the last time. "And I want this more than you know," he said with such passion Rose shivered. "But we must take care."

Now that space had come between them and Rose was able to take a steady breath, she began to think more clearly. Wild, foreign sensations roared through her veins, but her mind was able to decipher them for what they were. She nodded and leaned her head against his chest, listening to the pounding heartbeat through his cotton shirt.

Coleman lay back against his pillow, sighing heavily

as he wrapped an arm around her and began caressing her hair. "I love you, Rose," he whispered.

Rose slid an appreciative hand up the front of his shirt, admiring the strength and safety of his embrace. "I love you, too, Coleman," she whispered back.

His fingers traced circles around her face, smoothing the hair from her forehead and tracing the lines around her eyes and cheeks. Every so often Rose leaned back and stared into the warmth of his eyes while Coleman cupped her chin and brought their lips together once more.

They spent the afternoon touching each other, sharing casual kisses until they erupted into passion. Then they would lie in each other's arms, enjoying the comfort of their embrace, the sound of each other's heartbeat.

By the time the fire burned into embers, the afternoon sun approached the horizon and it was time for Rose to return home. Time for dinner. Time for her nightly chores.

But as daylight began to wane, Rose slipped into a dreamy slumber.

And that was how Emilie found her.

Chapter Nine

Life was so peaceful in the world where Rose dwelled. A gentle ocean breeze stirred the willow trees around her and she pulled a shawl about her shoulders to ward off a chill. The marshland grasses waved in the afternoon sun as the men moved through them on their way home from the fields while chimney swifts darted among their heads on the journey back to their nests.

All was good in the world, including the blond head resting in her lap.

He was teasing her, calling her pet names in French. Laughing, savoring their happiness.

Suddenly, Coleman became serious, the light fading from his eyes. "Rose?" he asked.

"Rose?" the voice demanded louder.

Rose bolted upright in bed when she realized the voice's owner.

"Emilie," she said, quickly glancing around the cabin.

"Looking for someone?" Emilie asked soberly.

Where is he? Rose thought. The cabin was deserted. Only her sister stood in the middle of the floor, hands folded dramatically across her chest.

"What are you doing here?" Rose asked Emilie, surprised to find herself irritated at being interrupted. Rose knew she had crossed the threshold of appropriate behavior that afternoon, but she felt neither guilt nor remorse.

Emilie responded by sending her a scathing look. "I was looking for Lorenz. He hasn't returned home yet."

"He's helping André with his fences," Rose answered, trying to rub the sleep from her eyes. "I must have fallen asleep."

"You're here alone?" Emilie sighed, fury beating beneath her calm exterior. Rose knew it would be a long walk home. "Get your things, Rose. We're leaving."

Rose wanted to touch her sister's hand, to relieve her anxiety and convince her she had done nothing wrong. But she *had* kissed Coleman, lain in his bed, enjoyed his embrace.

"It's not what you think," Rose began, even though she knew it was fruitless.

"Get your things," Emilie stated firmly, then left the cabin.

Grabbing her basket, Rose followed Emilie out the

door. As they reached the edge of the porch, Coleman rounded the corner of the house with a pail of water. He saw Emilie first, surprised at the sight of another woman on his property, then glad to make her acquaintance when he realized who she was. Rose winced, anticipating their conversation.

"You must be Emilie," Coleman said in French, extending his hand. "I have heard so many things about you."

Like Lorenz in the store that day, Emilie's eyes grew wide with shock. Not only did she not accept his hand, she stepped back in horror. Coleman instantly realized his mistake and glanced to Rose for support.

"I'm sorry," Rose told him in English. "She's not ready."

Emilie turned at the sound of English being spoken and branded Rose with a look so scorching the August heat was cool in comparison. Rose could almost feel her skin bake.

"Allons à la maison," Emilie uttered between gritted teeth.

Emilie passed Coleman without looking at him, but Rose paused on the bottom step.

"I have caused problems between you and your family," he whispered. "I should never have let you come here today."

Rose shook her head. "It doesn't matter. She is angry at the English, not at you."

Coleman raised his hand to touch her face, then remembered Emilie. Sighing with unrequited desire, he dropped his hand. "Are you angry with me? I wish

I could say I am sorry for what happened, but I'm not.''

Even though Emilie had turned and called after her, Rose beamed. She didn't care if the whole world was watching. "No, I'm not angry. I'm only sorry it ended.''

Coleman started to speak, but Emilie called again. "Boil the crawfish," Rose instructed as Emilie grabbed her elbow and pulled her away. "Add some pepper and onions to the boil and eat them like any other kind of shellfish.''

They were halfway to the woods when Rose yanked her arm from Emilie's grip. "What is the matter with you?" she protested.

"The question is, my dear sister, what is the matter with you?" Emilie shouted. "Have you completely lost your mind?''

There were so many things to say, an explanation at least, but Rose resented Emilie's tone and her rude manner. Without speaking, Rose brushed past her and headed toward the stream. This time when she met the slow-moving coulee, Rose plunged straight through, emerging on the opposite bank wet up to her knees.

"You are crazy," she heard Emilie shout behind her, but Rose kept walking, marching toward the house.

It didn't take long before Emilie's long strides caught up with Rose. The house was in view when Emilie grabbed Rose's elbow and forced her around. Surprisingly, despite the emotions raging within her, Rose calmly demanded that Emilie release her arm.

"It's not your fault," Emilie said. "Lorenz was supposed to watch out for you so that man wouldn't take advantage. You see what happens when you're alone? Do you see how naive to his charms you are?"

His charms? Rose wanted to laugh. Coleman had a million attributes that were near and dear to her, but charming wasn't one of them. André perhaps had a debonair manner, but Coleman preferred being straightforward and honest. His simple declaration of love stole her heart faster than any handsome man's "charms."

"Emilie, nothing happened," Rose said. Then realizing that wasn't exactly true, she added, "At least, nothing I'm ashamed of."

She meant to ease her sister's worries, but Emilie's jaw dropped at her last statement. "Where is Lorenz?" Emilie insisted, making Rose cringe inside. Would they ever accept her as the mistress of her own life?

"Who is looking for me?"

Lorenz emerged from between stalks of corn in the field neighboring the house. Covered in dirt and sweat, Rose knew the last thing he needed that day was a conversation about Rose's virtues.

"How could you let her go to that Englishman's house unescorted?" Emilie demanded.

Lorenz pulled off his hat and wiped the sweat from his brow. Even his silky midnight locks were marred with dirt.

"Let the poor man get a bath and catch his breath," Rose inserted. "We can talk about this later when we're calm."

Lorenz stared at Rose, then Emilie. "Why are we not calm?" he asked. "What has happened?"

"Nothing," Rose said. "I fell asleep."

"She was in that man's bed," Emilie added.

When Lorenz's eyes met hers, Rose knew there could be no pretenses. He had trusted her, believed in her. She tilted her face and sent him a look begging for sympathy. After all, Lorenz understood unrequited love after waiting months for Emilie to accept his marriage proposals.

"I love him," she whispered. "I'm sorry if this causes you pain, but I do."

Emilie gasped, raising her hand to her mouth, but Lorenz's eyes exhibited neither censure nor disapproval. "Why were you in his bed, Pumpkin?"

Rose sighed, remembering the passionate moments they had shared. "We love each other, Lorenz, but we didn't do anything wrong. We're comfortable together. I fell asleep, that's all."

"That's all?" Emilie shouted. Turning to Lorenz, she unleashed a rash of reprimands. "You should have been with her. What was she doing at that awful man's house alone? You know you can't trust the English. Have you forgotten what they did to us?"

"Emilie, you don't understand—" Lorenz began.

"I understand that she thinks she's in love with the horrid man."

Lorenz looked back at Rose, his eyes forgiving. "Maybe she is."

Emilie shook her head. "I don't believe this. One rifle and he has you under his spell."

Lorenz attempted a rebuttal, but Emilie stormed

inside the house. Remorse consumed Rose. Lorenz wrapped an arm about her and gingerly hugged her, considering his filthy condition. He placed a kiss on her forehead.

"I'm sorry," Rose said, trying to keep from crying.

"Don't be," Lorenz said. "She and I had a fight this morning. She's more angry at me than you. But I suggest you stay away from Coleman for the time being. Your mother and Gabrielle are helping with supper at the big house. When they return, do not speak of him to them. Your mother would not be pleased to hear where you slept this afternoon."

Lorenz placed his hat on his head and adjusted the rim. "Where are you going?" Rose asked.

"To have a word with *L'Anglais,*" he said. "From now on, you are not to go over there without me, understood?"

Rose nodded, dropping her eyes to the ground as a lone tear trickled down her cheek. Lorenz placed a finger at her chin and raised her eyes to his. "You have taken on a mountain, Pumpkin."

Loving and marrying Coleman was preposterous. Unthinkable. But as much as Rose dreaded having to face her mother and sisters with the prospect, the thought of being without Coleman for the rest of her life was ten times as frightening.

She raised her chin on her own. "I'm willing to face the challenge."

Lorenz nodded solemnly. "It will be a challenge, *'ti monde,*" he said softly. "An enormous one."

With those words, Lorenz headed down the path to the area locals called *la prairie de L'Anglais,* his form disappearing in the twilight shadows of the oak and cypress trees.

Eat them like any other shellfish, Rose had said. Staring down at the bright red crustaceans, which didn't resemble any shellfish Coleman was accustomed to, he couldn't decide which limb to pull apart first. The crawfish's beady eyes stared at him accusingly, reminding him that his rash actions that afternoon had caused severe problems with Rose and her family. Not to mention that he literally ached for the flower, now that he had tasted its honey.

He wasn't sorry he kissed her; it had been the culmination of weeks of desire. He wasn't sorry for holding her close, having her head rest upon his chest. But if he'd hurt her, caused her pain because of her involvement with him, he'd never forgive himself.

He turned the crawfish over and disengaged the tail. He ate shrimp that way, perhaps the same rules applied. The tail was harder to peel because of its rock-hard shell, but after a few tries a small piece of red meat emerged.

Coleman popped it into his mouth, amazed that something so tiny could taste so good, especially since the pepper had produced a nice spicy aftertaste. But his heart wasn't in the supper. He pushed the rest of the crawfish aside, then in a fit of frustration stood and threw the empty pot across the room.

"You'll be reprimanded if you damage that pot," Lorenz said as he crossed the threshold. "And you don't want to insult the hand who feeds us."

Coleman pushed his hair off his forehead and waited for Lorenz's accusations. He didn't blame Lorenz for being angry; he would feel the same if he were in his shoes. Still, Coleman couldn't help wanting to preserve the precarious friendship that had developed between them and dreaded the confrontation that was to follow.

"It isn't what you think," Coleman began. "I kissed her, yes, but that's all that happened." He gripped the back of his chair for support as a flood of passion roared through him. "I would die before I'd do anything to harm her."

He expected an outburst. A fist through his teeth perhaps. Instead, Lorenz sighed, appearing more eager for bed than a confrontation.

"You're more emotional than the French," Lorenz said. "I hope you're not anticipating a duel."

"You're not mad?"

"I don't know yet. Perhaps"—Lorenz sighed, his fatigue evident—"Or maybe I'm too tired to be angry."

Now that Coleman had time to examine him, his neighbor looked as if he'd been dragged behind a cow. "What happened to you?" Coleman asked.

Lorenz pulled out a chair and fell into it. "I have finally figured out André's motives," Lorenz explained. "I always wondered why he never let me work in the fields, to farm as God intended me to. Why instead he sets me to manual jobs around the plantation while his slaves work his crops." Lorenz placed his elbows on the table and rubbed his filthy forehead. "If a slave is injured or takes sick, André loses a lot of money. But I am expendable. If a slave dies, he's lost his investment. But if I die, it's one less Acadian in the world.''

Lorenz looked up at Coleman frowning, wondering perhaps if he should trust him or not. Then his features softened. "But it doesn't matter," he finally said with a grim smile. "I have no other means of supporting my family. What choices do I have?"

In that moment, when no differences occurred between them, when it didn't matter what language they spoke at birth or what they ate for breakfast, Coleman understood Lorenz completely. The hopelessness of his situation, the endless reliance on other people's charity, the yearning for self-sufficiency burned in his eyes. He was a man, newly married, head of a household. And he was powerless.

Coleman reached into the cupboard and produced a half bottle of rum. He grabbed two pewter mugs and placed them on the table, then sat down. Silently, he poured, then saluted Lorenz, who returned the favor.

"To your health and prosperity," Coleman said in English. "And a farm of your own."

"A votre santé," Lorenz returned.

They tilted their heads back and drank their fill. Coleman poured another round.

"Emilie is a wonderful woman," Lorenz said, his eyes glazed with fatigue. "She wants a child. She wants a home. And I can't give her any of this. We sleep on the gallery for privacy, but it's beneath the window of the bedroom where the rest of the family sleeps. She complains I'm not romantic anymore. Besides not wanting to disturb the others, I'm afraid to expose certain parts of my body to the mosquitoes.''

Funny, Coleman thought, *how similar our lives are at present.* Two frustrated men fervent with desire.

"You will be in Attakapas soon," Coleman offered, wondering if it was the rum or the fact that Rose would be leaving that left a sharp pain in his chest. "You will make a home on Joseph's land grant and have a room of your own."

Lorenz stared at the liquid in his mug and shook his head. "Where are we to find money to build a house? How are we to make it through the winter?"

Coleman sat back in his chair, leaning a confident arm over the back. He had spent many a night contemplating such a scenario. "We'll make due."

Lorenz laughed, then knocked back the rest of his rum. "Why are you so optimistic, *L'Anglais?* You just spent most of your money on seed. What will you live on once we leave? There will be no one around to help you harvest those crops or to serve you scraps from the DeClouet house."

Did he detect a trace of regret in Lorenz's voice? Could it be remotely possible that Lorenz approved of him as a brother-in-law?

Coleman leaned forward and poured Lorenz another drink. "Hides," he said.

"Pardon?"

"I'll sell hides in the winter. Move them downriver to New Orleans with a smuggler friend I met in Natchez, a former French sea captain who runs goods up and down the river. I can make more money in hides than in farming."

Lorenz's eyes suddenly became focused. "How much more?"

"I tried it last winter when I was building this place," Coleman continued. "I traveled out here for weeks at a time to see if it could be done and made a good bit of money, enough to pay back my investment." Thinking back on his business partner, Coleman laughed. "I would have made more if Jean wasn't such a pirate."

"Jean Bouclaire?"

Coleman smiled at the mention of his friend's name, a man whose distrust of Coleman and the English rivaled Lorenz's. But somehow that barrier had fallen, more than likely because the two men had one important thing in common: They were both in love with a Gallant woman. Now that Coleman thought about it, it was a bond between him and Lorenz as well.

"Yes," Coleman answered. "Jean Bouclaire. Do you know that swindler?"

A new appreciation shone in Lorenz's eyes. "I'll be damned. He helped Emilie and me at St. Gabriel. Saved our hides, actually."

Coleman leaned in close. "Hide is the word here. The Attakapas Poste is south of Opelousas down Bayou Teche. We'll form a triangle with Bouclaire, bringing him hides from all of southwest Louisiana. If all goes well, we should be able to greet the spring well fed and comfortable."

Lorenz grew silent, studying Coleman intently. His countenance was devoid of all emotion, and Coleman

INTRODUCING BALLAD,
A BRAND NEW LINE OF HISTORICAL ROMANCES

As a lover of historical romance, you'll adore Ballad Romances. Written by today's most popular romance authors, every book in the Ballad line is not only an individual story, but part of a two to six book series as well. You can look forward to four new titles a month – each taking place at a different time and place in history.

But don't take our word for how wonderful these stories are! Accept our introductory shipment of 4 Ballad Romance novels – a $22.00 value – ABSOLUTELY FREE – and see for yourself!

Once you've experienced your first four Ballad Romances, we're sure you'll want to continue receiving these wonderful historical romance novels each month – without ever having to leave your home – using our convenient and inexpensive home subscription service. Here's what you get for joining:

- 4 BRAND NEW Ballad Romances delivered to your door each month
- 25% off the cover price of $5.50 with your home subscription
- a FREE monthly newsletter filled with author interviews, book previews, special offers, and more!
- No risks or obligations…you're free to cancel whenever you wish… no questions asked.

To start your membership, simply complete and return the card provided. You'll receive your Introductory Shipment of 4 FREE Ballad Romances. Then, each month, as long as your account is in good standing, you will receive the 4 newest Ballad Romances. Each shipment will be yours to examine for 10 days. If you decide to keep the books, you'll pay the preferred home subscriber's price of $16.50 – a savings of 25% off the cover price! (Plus $1.50 shipping and handling.) If you want us to stop sending books, just say the word… it's that simple.

If the certificate is missing below, write to:

Ballad Romances, c/o Zebra Home Subscription Service, Inc.,
P.O. Box 5214, Clifton, New Jersey 07015-5214

OR call TOLL FREE 1-888-345-BOOK (2665)

Visit our website at www.kensingtonbooks.com

4 FREE BOOKS are waiting for you! Just mail in the certificate below!

FREE BOOK CERTIFICATE

Yes! Please send me 4 Ballad Romances ABSOLUTELY FREE! After my introductory shipment, I will receive 4 new Ballad Romances each month to preview FREE for 10 days (as long as my account is in good standing). If I decide to keep the books, I will pay the money-saving preferred publisher's price of $16.50 plus $1.50 shipping and handling. That's 25% off the cover price. I may return the shipment within 10 days and owe nothing, and I may cancel my subscription at any time.

The 4 FREE books will be mine to keep in any case.

DN110A

Name _____

Address _____

City _____ State _____ Zip _____

Telephone ( ) _____

Signature _____

(If under 18, parent or guardian must sign.)

Orders subject to acceptance by Zebra Home Subscription Service. Terms and Prices subject to change.
Offer valid only in the U.S.

Get 4 Ballad
Historical Romance Novels
FREE!

PLACE
STAMP
HERE

BALLAD ROMANCES
Zebra Home Subscription Service, Inc.
P.O. Box 5214
Clifton NJ 07015-5214

$4 per time - FREE! No obligation to buy anything - ever!

had no chance of reading his thoughts. "Are you a religious man?" Lorenz finally asked.

"Why?" Coleman asked. "Do I not have a prayer of a chance with Rose?"

A slight grin grew out of the corners of Lorenz's lips. "What are you, a Protestant?"

"I'm a Methodist."

"That's a Protestant, right?"

Coleman hadn't meant to appear defensive, but he found himself folding his arms about his chest. "Yes, why?"

"How attached are you to this Methodist?"

Coleman frowned at the question. He never thought about religion much. "I'm not a church-going man. I was when my mother was alive, but . . . "

"Then it's not important?"

When had the conversation turned to his personal beliefs? They were discussing business, were they not? As if sensing his confusion, Lorenz leaned forward, his hands flat on the table, ready for a serious discussion.

"We were exiled from Canada because of our religion, did you know that?" Lorenz asked. "There were many other reasons, having the best farmland in the country being one of them, but we refused to speak their language, practice their religion, and swear allegiance to the Crown, even though we swore neutrality in the wars between England and France. We are a stubborn people that way. We don't give up certain things easily, even though we fed the English and minded their laws."

Coleman had heard the tales of the displaced Acadians, but most had been from the mouths of

Englishmen, stories that placed the blame on the Acadians. They had refused compliance, aided the French, incited the Indians to attack English soldiers. They were exiled for their impertinence and non-cooperation. Now that Coleman had met Acadians, however, he doubted such peace-loving, industrious people could have been considered such an enemy.

"We were exiled simply because we were French and Catholic," Lorenz said as if he read his mind. "Religion and family are two things we value above all else."

A force hit Coleman, as if Lorenz had finally landed a fist in his face. He knew what Lorenz was implying. And for the first time, Coleman actually believed marrying Rose was a possibility.

"You want me to become a Catholic?" Coleman said more than asked.

"It's one less obstacle," Lorenz explained. "But it's a giant one."

"Bigger than learning this horrid language where you talk through your nose and choke on your words?" Coleman said with a grin.

Grabbing the bottle and smiling, Lorenz emptied its contents between them. "I have to admit, it's a hell of a lot easier speaking to you in French. English gives me a headache."

Coleman accepted his mug and saluted again. "Wait until tomorrow morning."

Placing his mug on the table, his smile disappearing, Lorenz studied him again.

"Of course I will," Coleman answered his unspoken question. "Let's talk to the minister tonight."

"Tonight?" Lorenz asked. "It's time for dinner. And he's a priest, not a minister."

Coleman could feel Rose's arms about him, envision her lying next to him smelling of herbs and sunshine. Whatever it took, he had to have her.

He picked up the plate of crawfish he had deposited on the cupboard and placed it before Lorenz. "Hurry up and eat."

Chapter Ten

Seven pairs of eyes remained glued on Coleman as he and Lorenz waited for the priest at the home of Sostan Blanchard, a farmer taken to his bed with a cold. Since Sostan was the eldest of the household and prone to sickness, the priest had been called just in case. Coleman and Lorenz hadn't known the gravity of the situation until they arrived. Now they were faced with waiting in the common room with the rest of the relatives.

Lorenz didn't seem to mind. He sat grinning at his new shirt, admiring the lacy ruffles at his neck and the finer linen at his wrists. After Lorenz finished off the crawfish, Coleman had offered him a washtub and a clean set of clothes. In addition to borrowing his good shirt, Lorenz hadn't hesitated to try on Coleman's hip-length waistcoat, purchased on his last trip to New Orleans. The billowy sleeves emphasized Lorenz's muscular arms and the waistcoat's opening at the neck showed off the shirt's elegant ruffle. If only Emilie could see him now, Coleman thought. Lorenz wouldn't have time to consider mosquitoes.

On the other hand, Coleman still sported his work-shirt, only he too had washed up and added a waistcoat in preparation for meeting the priest. But what he wore was of little matter. The fact that the blond-haired, blue-eyed Englishman sat in the Blanchard house was reason enough for every Acadian present to stare in astonishment.

Not knowing where to look, since the entire family almost completely surrounded him, Coleman turned to the only spot in the house where no one sat glaring. To his surprise, a violin occupied the corner.

"Do you play?" he asked the man next to him.

The man appeared even more astonished that an Englishman was speaking French to him. He shook his head.

Coleman raised the instrument from the floor, noticing that a peg had been damaged, causing the G string to fall loose. He plucked the other three strings, testing their tautness and tune and finding them suitable for playing.

"Who's touching my violin?" shouted a hoarse voice from the bedroom, followed by a fit of coughing.

Coleman's fingers froze on the fingerboard, while an older woman threw back the curtains separating the two rooms. When she discovered the culprit, it was now eight pairs of eyes burning into him.

"Who is it?" demanded the voice Coleman assumed was Sostan. But the woman didn't speak. She simply stood there, mouth open and staring.

"Sorry," Coleman said in English, wondering why of all times he had switched back into his own language, his normally dormant English accent slipping into the tone. "I noticed it was broken," he added in French. "I can fix this."

"Who is that?" Sostan demanded. "Who can fix my violin?"

The woman finally shut her mouth and swallowed, but when she started to explain, no words emerged. The rest of the family offered no help.

Coleman rose, deciding an explanation was the best solution. What more harm could he possibly do? He was English and sitting inside the Blanchard house, that was insult enough.

When he reached the candlelight of the bedroom, he found Sostan propped up on pillows waiting for him to appear. The priest sat next to the bed, garbed in a long black robe and holding beads of a sort. A dish consisting of a potato ball smelling of pork sat on the bedside table. Despite the bond Coleman had felt with Rose and Lorenz, he suddenly realized how vastly different their two nationalities were and felt a sudden urge to bolt out the door.

"You're the Englishman," Sostan demanded.

"Oui, monsieur," Coleman said.

Sostan gazed at the object in his hands. "What are you doing with my violin?"

As if remembering why he had crossed the room and the enormous chasm between their worlds, Coleman looked down at the instrument, its string hanging sadly to the floor.

"I can fix this," he said. "I play myself and have extra strings."

Sostan lifted himself up, a gleam beginning in his eye. "Play me something."

Coleman wondered if he'd translated right. "You want me to play?" he repeated.

"*Oui,*" the older man said. "My fingers are too crooked for me to play anymore. Let's hear what you can do."

Coleman turned to the woman to gauge what he should do next, but she only frowned and shook her head. "Don't encourage him," she said.

"Go away old woman," Sostan said. To Coleman, he insisted, "*Jouez!* Play."

Feeling a prodding at his back, Coleman turned and found Lorenz stabbing him with the violin's bow, a sly smile on his face.

"You're enjoying this, aren't you?" Coleman asked him in English.

"Play," Lorenz answered in French. "I've heard so many stories about your supposedly famous playing abilities, but I'm beginning to doubt them."

A warm rush of pride flooded Coleman's veins. "Doubt no more," he said confidently and placed the violin at his chin.

Rose and Emilie spent the evening without a word passing between them, but toward bedtime Rose ventured out to the back gallery to try to break the silence.

"Emilie," she said, approaching her sister sitting on the stairs. "Let us not have this come between us."

Emilie said nothing as Rose sat down, but when they were side by side she turned and studied her hard. "How can you love this man?" she asked. "After everything that has happened to us."

Rose took Emilie's hand, always amazed how her fingers were dwarfed inside her sister's. Everything about Rose differed from her family, which made the rift between them that much more acute.

"I don't know, Emilie, I just do. I didn't choose him with my mind. I chose him with my heart. And I believe he has done the same."

"But he's . . ."

"He's English," Rose finished, so tired of hearing those words spoken. "If he were Acadian, there would be no objections, *oui?*"

"His father is an English soldier, Rose. Lorenz told me."

"Am I right?" Rose insisted.

Sighing, Emilie turned and stared off into the dark night. "Of course, there would be no objections if he were Acadian. But he's not."

Rose pulled her fingers away from Emilie. The words her sister spoke angered and disappointed her. "He's the same man, Emilie," Rose whispered, trying to keep her emotions under control. "You're condemning him because of his nationality just as they condemned us because of ours."

A rush of emotion shot through Emilie and she

stood up, turning emblazoned eyes on Rose. "Only he wasn't ripped from his home as we were."

Rose stood upon her step, making her at eye level with her sister. "Then let's get the neighbors together and exile Coleman from Opelousas. Will you then have no objections?"

"How can you say such a thing?" Emilie asked, her eyes burning. "There is no comparison."

"How can you?" Rose shot back. "He was born in Georgia. What does he know about Acadia? He's not to blame for our fate simply because he's English."

She hadn't meant to get angry, and it wasn't until Marianne and Gabrielle emerged on the gallery that Rose realized she was shouting.

"What is happening between you two?" Marianne asked.

No one spoke, as if they all knew the subject and dreaded speaking of it.

"I will not have this family quarreling," Marianne continued. Turning to Rose, she added, "Is there something you wish to tell me?"

Rose wanted so badly to confide in her mother, to share her newfound happiness with the woman who had wished it upon her since her birth. "No, Maman," Rose answered, as a tear escaped down her cheek. "I am sorry. We will not quarrel anymore."

Marianne approached Rose, cupping her face in her hands. Afraid to meet those inquisitive maternal eyes, knowing that a crying fit would soon follow, Rose kept her gaze on the buttons on Marianne's vest. Just when she knew she would have to face her mother and expose her thoughts and actions that day, she heard singing from the direction of the stream.

The four women turned toward the source and watched in amazement as a slightly drunk Lorenz appeared around the corner, dressed in fine linens and wearing a tricornered hat. When he realized his audience, Lorenz took off his hat and bowed.

"Me ladies," he said in English, trying to imitate an aristocratic accent.

"My God, you're drunk," Emilie stated.

Lorenz offered his charming smile. "No, my dear. Just a few glasses of wine."

"Where have you been?"

"At the Blanchards." Lorenz placed the hat back on his head, adjusting the crown so that its cockeyed position mirrored his disposition. "Coleman and I went in search of Father Felicien. We ended up staying for a while and Madame Blanchard offered us some wine."

"Why were you looking for—" Marianne asked, but Lorenz didn't hear her in his excitement.

"It was the most amazing thing," Lorenz said, looking at Rose. "You were right, Pumpkin. *L'Anglais* sure knows how to play that fiddle. It was magical. Absolutely magical. Sostan even asked him to play at the *bal de maison* tomorrow right."

"Coleman Thorpe at the house dance?" Emilie asked.

Gabrielle laughed. "It is magical, Emilie. I've never seen anyone play an instrument so fast in my life."

"What were you doing looking for the priest?" Marianne asked.

"Not for me," Lorenz answered. "For Coleman."

"Coleman's Catholic?" Gabrielle asked.

Lorenz turned his brown eyes to Rose and winked. "He will be soon."

Rose found it difficult to breathe. Coleman was changing his faith for the prospect of marrying her? She struggled to catch her breath, but before she had a chance to confirm what Lorenz had implied, Emilie asked the question for her. "He's converting to Catholicism?"

Lorenz rested a foot on the second step and leaned an elbow against his knee. "Not only that, but he's working with Jean Bouclaire in the hide trade. He wants us to join him this winter. It's a profitable venture that will give us an income until Joseph returns."

"He knows Jean Bouclaire?" Emilie asked.

"They met in Natchez," Gabrielle offered, a blush beginning on her cheeks. "Jean, uh, Captain Bouclaire used to translate for him."

"And Jean approves of this Englishman?" Emilie asked.

With lightning speed, Lorenz straightened, removed his hat, slid an arm about Emilie's waist, and drew her forward for a kiss. "You ask too many questions, *mon amour,*" Lorenz said when he allowed her a chance to breathe. "Why don't we go for a long walk in the woods so I can silence those inquisitive lips?"

A light sparkled in Emilie's eyes, a glimmer of hope that their romance was still alive, although she wasn't quite ready to give up the fight. "But—"

"But nothing," Lorenz said, taking her hand. "Jean

does business with the man. I help him in his fields. Isn't that confirmation enough? Besides, we're all forgetting one important detail. Rose approves of him."

While her family had debated the man she loved, Rose had felt herself turn invisible, as she had so many times before. When she heard Lorenz speak her name, she glanced up, amazed that someone finally considered her opinion to be of value.

Lorenz replaced his hat and tipped it toward Rose. She answered him with a warm appreciative smile. Then Lorenz led his wife into the darkness of the woods, Emilie's protestations echoing through the trees.

"Mon dieu," Gabrielle whispered, and Rose wondered if she disapproved of their lovemaking out-of-doors. "He's converting to Catholicism."

Suddenly, Rose remembered she was the center of attention and that so much had yet to be spoken between her and her mother. Marianne stood by her side, watching the couple disappear into the darkness, her arms folded sternly across her chest.

Rose thought to remain silent, but her heart was too full of everything that had transpired that day. She loved him, of that she was certain. Now she knew he loved her too, that he would go to great lengths to make her his. They had to discuss it. She couldn't live without knowing she would lie in his arms for the rest of her life.

"Please, Maman," Rose said softly. "Give Coleman a chance."

Marianne continued staring into the black night,

then turned and silently entered the house. As Rose's spirits descended, she felt Gabrielle's arms around her.

"Cheer up, *chère*," Gabrielle said. "At least she didn't say no."

Rose rested her head against her sister's cheek, realizing Gabrielle was right. It was a small sign, but an important one.

At least she didn't say no.

The sun inched its way toward dusk, but the scorching humid air continued to hang about the plantation like an invisible curtain of water. Rivulets of steam emerged from the ground where a light shower had provided some relief. As the sun burned his face, André slid his handkerchief inside his collar in a vain attempt to rid himself of perspiration.

André was tired of the endless heat, but more than that he was tired of Rose's games, tired of her excuses. He wanted an answer and he wanted one now.

As he crossed the threshold into the kitchen, Rose stood by the stove. She had removed her vest so that only her cotton blouse remained, its fabric plastered to her skin, revealing a petite but firm bosom. Instead of her usual braid, Rose had let her auburn hair fly free in the heat. The wild tendrils stood up every which way, no doubt from her constant brushing it away from her face; but they reflected something wild and untamed about her nature, something André found enchanting.

She was, in a word, astonishing. Unusually uninhibited and attractive. Seductive.

Despite his better judgment, André wanted to touch those breasts, to kiss those sweet lips.

Sensing his presence, Rose turned. Discreetly and without blushing, she picked up her vest and put it on, robbing André of a delicious view.

"May I help you?" Rose asked.

All desirous thoughts aside, André's anger returned. "I need an answer, mademoiselle," he said. "I am tired of waiting for you to make up your mind."

Rose's attention remained on the buttons of her vest. "You must talk to Lorenz," she said without looking up. "He is my guardian."

André erased the distance between them and tilted her chin up to meet his eyes. "But it's *your* decision," he demanded. "I need to know your answer on this."

He meant to intimidate her, to force her into agreeing, but Rose met his eyes forcibly.

"Then I will say no," she said confidently. "I mean you no disrespect, monsieur, but I wish to marry for love."

For a moment, André was too shocked by Rose's defiance to think clearly. Then the impact of her words set in. "For love?" he asked incredulously, then laughed. "You wish to marry for love?"

To her credit, Rose cowered only slightly. Her refusal to wilt under his laughter might have angered him further if he hadn't found her so attractive as a stronger woman. Perhaps there was another solution to this problem.

"My dear," André began, taking her hand and

inching closer. "I didn't realize that was what you wanted."

Rose's eyes grew large and she attempted to withdraw her hand, but André was faster. He slid an arm about her waist and pulled her against his chest, delivering a searing kiss on her lips.

She tasted of peaches and cream and smelled of lavender. How long had it been since he kissed a desirable woman, one who came free? For a moment, nothing mattered but continuing his time in heaven. He pulled his other arm about her to hold her close and savor the gratifying connection.

It wasn't long before Rose managed to pull away, but he made damn sure she worked for it. When she finally yanked herself from his embrace, she stumbled against the cupboard, causing the candle to fall into the kitchen curtains. Within seconds a fire began, spreading to the flour along the cupboard and exploding on to the pan of melted lard on the stove. Neither one had time to think. André grabbed Rose and pulled her from the building. When they glanced back, smoke was billowing from half of the kitchen.

Coleman and Lorenz saw the smoke at the same time they heard Marianne's distant screams. Coleman's heart constricted, knowing that most plantation fires begin in the kitchen and that Rose was destined to be there.

He dropped his hoe and ran for the barn, grabbing the horse without thinking of Lorenz. As he kicked the horse into action and headed to his neighbor's house, he heard Lorenz shouting after him. But he couldn't stop now. He had to find her. Had to know she was safe.

Coleman rode up to the plantation house and found most of the slaves, Marianne, and Emilie carrying buckets of water to and from the cistern. Trying to steady his breath, he dismounted and ran toward the kitchen, the heat searing his face. Flames reached toward the sky as part of the roof fell in. If Rose had been inside the kitchen, she was most likely lost.

Coleman wasn't ready to accept that fact. He searched the half of the kitchen not engulfed in flames and found no one, nothing. He ran through the water line searching the faces, scanning the area around them.

Where was she? Dear God, he couldn't have lost her. Not now. Was this his punishment for a kiss? Was he destined to lose everyone he loved?

Realizing Rose was nowhere to be found, Coleman leaned against the side of the barn, feeling as if a horse had backsided him in the chest. His breathing became labored and he sank to his knees. He closed his eyes imagining the worst, knowing his heart would not survive such abuse. He couldn't live without her. He wouldn't.

Suddenly, Coleman felt a hand on his arm. Afraid to look, afraid he might find sympathetic eyes revealing Rose had indeed perished in the fire, he shut his eyes tighter.

"Monsieur Thorpe."

The voice was familiar—like Rose's, only deeper—and there was no sadness in its tone.

Coleman looked over and found Marianne kneeling beside him. "She's fine. Part of her dress caught fire and she's in the big house for a burn."

Bolting upright to rush into the house, Marianne grabbed his arm again. "She's fine," Marianne insisted, hinting that his place was not inside the Creole home. "She'll be out shortly."

An enormous burst of air rushed out of Coleman, as if he had held his breath since arriving at the scene. He felt light-headed and exhausted. To his surprise, his cheeks were streaked with tears—perhaps from the fire, he wasn't sure—and he wiped them away. He glanced back at Marianne, who stood staring, and nodded.

"What do you want, Englishman?" André yelled in English as he approached the barn. "This is not the time to talk about your stupid pigs."

Coleman recovered, taking the bucket from Marianne's hands. "I'm here to help," he answered André in French and headed for the cistern.

Marianne watched the blond man with eyes the color of a winter sky rush to bring water to the fire that now burned out of control. The kitchen was lost, but Coleman and the slaves continued spreading the water while Marianne and Emilie filled buckets at the cistern. Lorenz came running minutes later. After finding that Rose was safe, he joined Coleman and the two worked together like brothers.

Was it possible, Marianne thought, watching the two men so close in age and stature, that people could be compatible despite such enormous differences? The way Coleman had reacted that afternoon, Marianne was certain he cared for Rose more than his own life. He would have charged the fires of hell had Rose been trapped inside.

Wasn't that exactly what she wanted for her youngest child? A man who would not only love her as passionately as Rose embraced life but who would protect her from the evils that she failed to see coming? Which Rose failed to see on a daily basis.

Oh, why does he have to be English? Marianne wondered. *Why does every step in this new territory bring such difficult problems and decisions? What a joy it would be to have Rose happy and in love. To have another man about to help ease Lorenz's burden. If only Coleman were Acadian.*

Finally, the fire was brought under control. The men collapsed onto the back gallery steps while the slaves were relieved to return to their cabins. Only André remained standing, studying Coleman unemotionally. If Marianne guessed right, André hated being in the Englishman's debt.

"You could just say thank you," Coleman offered, obviously feeling the weight of his gaze.

"Why are you here?" André asked. "And when did you learn French?"

Coleman sighed and beat the ash from his sleeves. "I'm your neighbor," he said. "Although you would hardly understand what that means. Where I come from, neighbors help each other out."

"Unless, of course, they're French," André returned with a sneer. "Then you English toss them out like dogs."

"I was not at Mobile," Coleman returned. "I do not know your story. But stealing your neighbor's land and animals hardly puts you in position for sainthood."

André's eyes burned with such intensity that Marianne feared a fight was imminent. "How dare you insinuate—"

"I know about Blanchard's fences being moved and Thibodeau's disappearing cattle," Coleman continued, unafraid of the Creole, unlike most of the Opelousas residents. "If it happens again, I will represent them and bring this matter to court."

"You?" André said with a laugh. "You can't hoe your way through a potato field."

Coleman found his hat and placed it on his head, unmoved by André's comments. "I'm not much of a farmer, no, but I'm a hell of an advocate. I spent three years at university studying law."

The blood drained from André's face as the men stared at each other. Tension filled the air and no one dared look away for fear of what might happen next. Marianne heard the door of the gallery open and close, but her eyes were riveted on the blond confident man who seemed to fear no one.

Just then a rooster ran between them, filling the yard with his crowing. Coleman looked down at the red-topped animal and laughed sarcastically. "He looks familiar."

André gritted his teeth. Then he turned toward a young slave boy. "Catch that rooster and bag it," he ordered. "It's a present for my neighbor." Looking back toward Coleman, he concluded, as if his final statement had been a hint that Coleman should leave. "That makes us even."

Coleman laughed again. "Hardly. But I graciously accept your token offering."

Turning toward Marianne, Coleman bowed discreetly, and she couldn't help but admire the self-assured Englishman. For a moment, before her logical mind interfered, she thought him the perfect husband for her Rose, the ideal candidate for son-in-law.

Then Coleman caught sight of Rose on the gallery and his confident stature disappeared, replaced by an uncertain countenance. *Funny, how love can bring the strongest people to their knees,* Marianne thought, watching the two lovers exchange guarded smiles. Marianne knew that feeling well. One look from Joseph used to melt her insides.

What would Joseph think of Rose and her Englishman?

When the slave boy brought the rooster to Coleman, he thanked the young man, mounted his horse, and rode away. But not before sending Rose a romantic glance and not before André realized what was transpiring between them.

Tonight was the *bal de maison*. If Marianne was correct in her premonition, the kitchen fire was an inconsequential prelude to bigger fires yet to come. André would never let a man best him, particularly if that man was English.

Things were going to heat up considerably.

Chapter Eleven

The entire contents of Sostan Blanchard's house had been emptied into the backyard in preparation for the house dance, but the effort had been in vain. No one ventured indoors, preferring the slight breeze and pesky mosquitoes to the muggy suffocating heat of the house.

Jean Bouclaire scanned the faces, most of them still strangers despite his increasing trips to the Opelousas Poste to trade. So many new claims, so many new fences stretching across the prairies. In time, farms and *vacheries*, or cattle ranches, would line the bayous all the way to the Attakapas. Smugglers like himself would soon become useless entrepreneurs.

Jean wasn't planning on running supplies to the outposts forever. The high markup on the goods he sold kept him deep in gold, as did the sale of the furs and hides on his return trips to New Orleans. But as soon as he acquired enough cash to pay off the Spanish officials who had confiscated his ship, he'd be sailing again, happy to have waves beneath his feet and heading for the tropical islands of the Caribbean.

Resting his eyes on the midnight hair that had consumed his nightly dreams, Jean was reminded how ironic life could be. Giving up smuggling meant giving up Gabrielle. Once his ship was retrieved, he'd be happier and more successful with a crew at his call and higher profits on the high seas. But he'd probably never see Gabrielle again.

Unless he could convince her to sail away with him.

As if she heard his thoughts, Gabrielle turned. Her deep-set ebony eyes brightened when she recognized him, her features ready to beam with excitement yet cautious that she might be seen. Discreetly, Gabrielle raised her skirt an inch and moved silently through the crowd until she joined him on the periphery of the action.

"Looking for someone?" Gabrielle asked with a coquettish tilt of her head.

It took everything in Jean's power to keep from grabbing the dark-haired witch who had cast a spell on his heart and kissing her madly. Instead, he leaned nonchalantly against the trunk of a nearby tree and pushed his hat off his forehead.

"Depends," he answered with equal audacity. "I met this enchanting woman in Natchez a few months back and have not been able to get her off my mind. Perhaps you know her?"

Gabrielle tucked a strand of silky hair behind an ear. "Was this the woman you so brazenly kissed that night on your boat?"

There it was again. That irresistible glow in her eyes, those tempting lips begging to be devoured. Gabrielle was the epitome of femininity yet she spoke with brutal honesty, forgoing decorum and heading right for a man's jugular. She was unlike any woman Jean had ever known. Her candid nature and wisdom made her more like a good friend than someone to be courted with flowers and poetry.

But he *had* kissed her that night. And friendship was not what Jean had in mind.

"If I remember, mademoiselle, we were on shore when you blessed me with your delicious lips."

Jean knew he crossed a line between flirtation and seduction, but the blush that followed was worth every word. Gabrielle turned toward the crowd, adjusting the hem of her vest at her waistline.

"I have offended you," Jean said.

Gabrielle didn't turn back, but her features softened. "No," she whispered.

"I meant no disrespect, Gabi. It was only a token of my genuine admiration and respect."

The blush darkened. "I know."

Jean's expectation returned. He longed to continue the flirtation. "Then may I hope for more?"

Gabrielle finally looked his way, offering a scant smile. "Did you retrieve your ship?"

The change in conversation felt like cold water being thrown in his face. "My ship?" Jean asked.

"You said you were hoping to raise enough money to . . ."

"No," Jean answered. "My obligations in New Orleans prevented me."

Jean hesitated to continue. Even though Gabrielle was aware of his illegitimate daughter and his support of her and her mother, he hated broaching the subject. Gabrielle had not censured him, as had so many of his friends from his social class, but he feared he tarnished their friendship with his scandal.

He had met Louise Delaronde at a garden party, drunk too much champagne, and followed the socialite to her father's *pied à terre*. When Louise found herself with child, she refused Jean's hand and his "meager Second Son income." Instead, she lured rich Count Delaronde to her bed and then to the altar.

Jean had only asked to be an uncle to the child, promising to keep Louise's secret. But Delphine Delaronde was born Jean's mirror image, a head full of black wavy hair and cheeks sporting dimples. It didn't take the count long to piece the puzzle together, rid Louise of her inheritance, and return to France and the endless women at court. Louise and Delphine remained in New Orleans, penniless and shunned by society, ironically left dependent on Jean's "meager" income.

If it hadn't been for Delphine, Jean would have left Louise to starve. Louise matured into a bitter vindictive woman who blamed all of her misfortunes on Jean.

But Delphine. Delphine was his life.

"How is your daughter?" Gabrielle asked, genuinely interested. "Is she well?"

Jean straightened, thinking of the young woman who consistently made him proud despite her compromising circumstances. "She is well, thank you. Although she wants me to stow her away on my ship and carry her off to exotic places."

At this Gabrielle laughed. "I don't blame her."

The way Gabrielle thrust out her chin and cocked her head when she laughed reminded him of Delphine. He wondered what life would be like with the two of them by his side. Was it possible to be happy, after all? To be surrounded by the women who loved him?

Did Gabrielle love him? She certainly gave that impression. As much as the thought seemed absurd— Gabrielle was a respectable young woman and he was a scandal-tainted smuggler who never rested too long on land—Jean couldn't help wishing it was true.

Without thinking, Jean reached up and placed a hand at Gabrielle's heated cheek. He imagined the three of them sailing away, laughing in the sun and the warm breezes blowing from the Antilles.

The words "Come with me" lingered on his tongue but he said nothing. Instead, Jean leaned forward and kissed the lips that had been haunting his nights for weeks.

Gabrielle knew she must push Jean away. Her mother stood pouring drinks for the visitors within a stone's throw. But she had relentlessly dreamed of this moment, relived the kiss Jean had left her with in Natchez, one large callused hand caressing her cheek while the other rested on her waist.

He smelled as he had that night on the Mississippi bank, of wood burning on a campfire, of leather and furs, of breezes on open waters. A large man with hands the size of melons, Jean seemed to envelop her, consume her with his presence.

Trying to regain some shred of logic, Gabrielle placed a hand on the front of his shirt. She meant to push him away, but the feel of his broad, rock-solid chest intoxicated her and her resistance failed. Jean must have sensed her relenting for he placed a hand on her lower back and pulled her closer into his embrace.

"No," Gabrielle said, turning her head to one side and catching her breath. "We mustn't."

Jean pulled back, his lips lingering on top of her hair. "I'm sorry, *mon amour,*" he whispered. "I have forgotten my manners."

Hearing voices approaching, Gabrielle stepped back and straightened the front of her skirt. "No," she whispered back. "You have forgotten we are not alone."

Jean sent her a sly smile that Gabrielle couldn't help returning. God help her, but the sight of the tall man in his billowing shirt and knee-high leather boots made her lose all common sense—if she ever had any in the first place. Emilie always said she had no right thinking the thoughts that she did, that sooner or later a woman daring to imagine such things would end up in trouble. Staring at the pirate before her, feeling a delicious shiver roll up and down

her spine, Gabrielle knew Emilie was right. And God
help her, she didn't care.

"Jean!" Lorenz called out. Reaching the pathway
where Gabrielle and Jean stood, Lorenz grabbed Jean
by the shoulders. "What are you doing here?"

Jean placed a friendly hand on Lorenz's shoulder.
"Business, my friend. Business with an old friend of
your sister's."

Lorenz stared at Gabrielle, puzzled.

"Not me," Gabrielle said. "I think he's referring
to Rose."

"That reminds me," Lorenz continued. "There's
an Englishman here who says he knows you."

"Coleman Thorpe."

Lorenz smiled, glad to hear that Coleman wasn't
lying about his friendship with Jean. "Then you know
him?"

"Of course, I know him," Jean said with a broad
smile. "I helped him make a fool of himself one day
in front of your mother-in-law and two sisters."

Lorenz shot Gabrielle another puzzled expression.

"I'll explain later," Gabrielle said. "Why don't we
join the party and go find this Englishman?"

Gabrielle moved to leave, but Jean caught her
elbow. "Coleman's here? At the Blanchard's house
party?"

Now it was Gabrielle's turn to smile. "He's the
featured entertainment."

Jean leaned his head back and laughed. "Imagine
that."

The threesome made their way down the path
toward a mass of candlelight, where Acadians from

miles around gathered in the hope of dancing. Emilie and Marianne were busy bringing chairs onto the lawn for the elderly to sit on while Rose helped with the cooking, her petite frame bent over a hot iron skillet.

Louisiana had been a good change for Rose, Gabrielle thought, in more ways than one. She had learned new styles of cooking from the Spaniards at Natchez and from the Creoles at André's plantation, and enjoyed perfecting their everyday cuisine. Happy to experiment, Rose created dishes with an endless array of Louisiana vegetables and wild meats accented by herbs, peppers, and spices. Gabrielle was even beginning to like the hot peppers Rose had acquired from the Spaniards, although those dishes usually required an extra glass of water to wash down the fire.

For weeks Rose had been exploring what she called a "gumbo," a thick soup that resembled a bouillabaisse filled with exotic ingredients like African okra and an Indian herb called *filé*. Gabrielle called it a *méli-mélange,* or hodgepodge soup, because usually what Rose put into a gumbo was whatever meat or seafood was available that day.

Rose had promised to serve a chicken-and-sausage gumbo around midnight, which probably accounted for the large crowd. It hadn't taken long for Opelousas to hear of Rose's culinary talents.

It hadn't taken residents long to hear of Coleman's performance that night, either. Gabrielle wondered if many came just out of curiosity. Coleman Thorpe had been the brunt of jokes for months. Maybe now the Opelousas Acadians wished to see the man they had spent weeks verbally lashing.

"Now what's he doing here?" Gabrielle heard Lorenz mutter. Before she had time to ask, André DeClouet sauntered past, a violin in one hand.

"He owns the place, haven't you heard?" Jean said sarcastically.

"Like hell he does," Lorenz answered.

André greeted Sostan, who appeared surprised to see him. Madame Blanchard offered him something to drink, but it was obvious the rich Creole was not welcome at their humble gathering. Gabrielle wondered if what Coleman had said about André stealing their land and cattle was true.

"I came to play for you," André announced. "I heard you were having a dance and thought I'd contribute."

A silence fell among the group and Sostan glanced at his wife nervously.

"You didn't know I could play the violin, did you?" André asked, turning toward Rose.

Marianne walked behind Rose and placed her arms about her shoulders protectively. It was a simple gesture, but a powerful one. Still, no one dared speak.

"That's very kind of you, André" came a voice from the rear of the crowd. When several people parted, Gabrielle recognized Coleman, two violins in his hands. "But they already have someone to play for them."

André frowned and put his hands on his hips. "When did you learn to speak French, *L'Anglais?*"

Coleman sent Rose a side glance, his eyes brightening at the sight of her. "I had a good teacher."

André's countenance hardened and he stared at Rose accusingly. Gabrielle could almost feel the anger burning in his eyes. *Poor Rose,* she thought, *to be caught in such an awkward position.* Thankfully, Coleman broke the silence.

"If you don't mind, André, the people are waiting for their music."

"Then they shall have it," André answered, riveting his blue eyes on Coleman. "But not from the likes of you."

Gabrielle could feel her insides tighten at the confrontation before her, but Coleman didn't appear the least threatened. He handed Sostan his repaired fiddle, then walked toward André, circling him while examining the Creole's instrument.

"I have an idea," Coleman said. "Why don't we let the people decide?"

André laughed. "Great idea, *L'Anglais.* Let's let the people decide."

Coleman placed the violin at his chin. "I'll go first and you follow. Then we'll ask our guests which they prefer."

André answered with a self-assured smirk as he placed his own fiddle next to his chin. "You do that."

Jean leaned back against the side of the Blanchard house, exchanging smiles with Lorenz. "This is some entertainment you got here."

"Only the best," Lorenz answered.

Emilie rushed over to where they were standing.

"Do something," she whispered to Lorenz. "He's going to make a fool of himself."

"I think André could use a lesson in manners," Lorenz said, fighting back a laugh.

Emilie stared at him. "I wasn't talking about André."

Jean leaned forward and patted Emilie on the back. "Don't worry, Emilie. The Englishman can take care of himself."

Gabrielle didn't know which was funnier—the shocked look on Emilie's face at seeing Jean again and realizing Coleman could best the man they all cowered before, or the large grin Rose was sporting on the other side of the crowd.

A hush fell when Coleman pulled his bow across his strings and an awkward tune emerged. It was a slow jig of some sort, an easy tune almost anyone could follow. And André did just that. He copied the tune effortlessly, and better. When he finished the easy ditty, he turned to Coleman triumphantly.

Again, Emilie turned toward Jean and Lorenz, her eyes wide. Again, both men returned her look with a knowing smile.

Before André could proclaim himself king, Coleman repeated the tune, only a bit faster and more melodically. André placed the violin back at his chin and performed what Coleman had just played. The last note had not left André's string before Coleman started up again, faster, better, and twice as long. André managed to keep up, but it was clear he was having difficulties.

When André finished the third round, Coleman

increased the tempo again, his bow flying across the strings. Gabrielle had heard him play at Natchez, but she had forgotten how incredible it was to watch him in action, his fingers moving in a blur across the fingerboard. And the music! The concert halls of Paris should be blessed with such a talent.

Poor André, Gabrielle thought. *He doesn't have a chance.*

To his credit, André struggled to follow. He missed several notes but managed to finish the round. When he reached the end of the song, his arms fell down at his waist and he exhaled loudly.

Coleman continued to play, his foot beating out a wild rhythm on the Louisiana mud and his fingers racing across the strings. He raised the tempo to a dizzying speed, his bow sawing across the instrument as if possessed. Coleman smiled at Rose, then moved the tempo even faster, if that was possible.

Someone in the crowd yelled in response and everyone began to clap to the beat. Jean grabbed Gabrielle around the waist and turned her around madly. Out of the corner of her eye, Gabrielle saw others dancing, including Lorenz and Emilie.

When Coleman finally finished his wild song, everyone cheered. Coleman wiped the sweat from his brow with his sleeve, then offered André his hand. André reluctantly accepted it.

"You're quite a violinist," Coleman said.

"And you're quite a surprise," André answered.

Something in the way André spoke sent shivers up Gabrielle's arms. She doubted this confrontation would be their last.

Thankfully, André accepted his defeat graciously, bowing politely to Sostan and his wife, then moving to leave. Coleman caught his arm.

"You don't have to go," he said, "We can both play. This doesn't have to be a competition."

For a moment, André appeared ready to acquiesce. For a moment, Gabrielle suspected there was a decent person beneath that arrogant exterior, a man wanting to dance and enjoy himself like the rest of them. But André straightened and walked silently through the crowd and into the darkness.

Sostan slapped Coleman on the back and motioned for the dance to begin. To his credit, Coleman started with an Acadian song, one he must have learned from Rose during their weeks at his farm. A collective awe rose from the crowd, then slowly everyone began to dance.

"I stand corrected," Jean said. Gabrielle turned to find a deep dimple appearing in his right cheek and his eyes twinkling with mischief. "I thought all Englishmen were idiots."

Before Gabrielle had time to respond, Jean led her into the circle of dancers and turned her round and round. When she passed Rose standing at the table, she found her sister beaming with pride.

And something else.

Was she mistaken or had her sister become an independent woman these past few weeks? For so long the family had treated Rose as a child, protecting her, guiding her. Now, Rose was leading them all into a new adventure, one with an Englishman who played like the devil.

What a strange place Louisiana is, Gabrielle thought, as Jean smiled down at her and turned her around the firelight. She was listening to her father's favorite song played by a blue-eyed Englishman while her sister cooked a gumbo on an open fire. Where aristocrats could be bested and fur trappers could become rich. Where pirates appeared in the night and stole kisses.

Gazing up into Jean's eyes glowing from the exertion and the pleasure of her company, Gabrielle knew everything was going to be all right. For the first time in years, Gabrielle felt hope.

Chapter Twelve

Hours had passed and still the Acadians wanted more. Coleman never thought he would tire of playing his beloved violin, but the evening was beginning to wear on him. All a person had to do was hum a song and he would repeat it. By midnight, Coleman was sure he had performed the favorite song of every person present.

On occasion Rose would join him, her angelic voice blanketing them all like a heavenly mist. While everyone danced, they would sneak a glance at each other, their eyes speaking what words could not.

Finally, Sostan announced dinner, and Rose and several other women began serving a thick soup. Thankful for the interruption, Coleman sat on a nearby bench, wiping the sweat from his neck and forehead with his handkerchief. When he felt a hand on his shoulder, he looked up to find Marianne handing him a glass of water.

"Merci," Coleman said, but Marianne didn't answer. To stop her from leaving, Coleman added, "Do you miss dancing?"

Marianne appeared confused, as if she wasn't sure whether to speak to the brazen Englishman who wanted to steal her daughter. Then she raised her chin and looked him straight in the eye.

"I miss my husband," she said flatly.

There was an unmistakable note of blame in her statement; he represented all that had caused her pain. At the same time, Coleman felt the fears and heartache of a lonely woman tired of the separation.

"I am sorry," Coleman said, knowing that his simple apology could not right the wrongs made by others of his nationality, but hoping that it might ease her suffering a little.

"I have written letters on your behalf," Coleman added. "Is there anything else I can do?"

Marianne smiled grimly. "You can stay away from Rose."

An intense pain struck his heart. They had come so far. He was finally beginning to have hope. "I can't do that," Coleman said. "I love her."

Marianne sat down on the bench next to him and sighed. "I know."

"How can I convince you I am worthy of her attentions?" Coleman asked passionately. "How can I convince you I would face death if it meant being near her?"

Marianne looked down into her lap. "I'm convinced."

"Then . . ."

Marianne turned her hazel eyes to his. "What if I were to let you court my daughter?" Marianne began. "Suppose the two of you married. What then?"

Coleman's thoughts went wild. He could imagine a lot of things. "I don't understand."

"Rose is uneducated. She's poor. Not to mention she speaks another language, practices another faith."

"I have learned French," Coleman insisted. "I am converting . . ."

"But what about your background?" Marianne answered. "You are an educated man, from an aristocratic family. How soon before you tire of Rose and her limitations? What will your family think of this marriage? How will your English friends treat her, a poor uneducated Acadian?"

So that was it. These were her worries. Coleman almost breathed a sigh of relief. Marianne offered valid reasons for objecting, but they were groundless.

"I assure you, madame, that despite my years at university I stand in awe of your daughter's wisdom," Coleman began. "I shall never tire of Rose. Never."

"As for my friends and family," he continued. "My mother is deceased, my father and I are not on speaking terms, and I do not consider any person a friend who would belittle my Rose."

Marianne said nothing, staring off into the darkness of the nearby woods.

"I have not convinced you," Coleman said.

When she finally looked back at him, Coleman felt

his spirits drop. "I'm sorry, Mister Thorpe," she said quietly. "I cannot agree to this."

Marianne rose, but Coleman grabbed her hand. "Please," he said. "Do not say no. At least say you'll consider it."

Marianne withdrew her hand but she remained at his side. Finally, she nodded. "I will think about it," she said. "But I pray you will too."

"My only prayers are that you will agree to end my suffering," Coleman said. He hadn't meant to sound so melodramatic, to let his emotions emerge through his words, but he couldn't bear the thought of living his life without Rose.

Again, Marianne nodded, then returned to her duties.

Coleman felt the earth collapse beneath his feet. He had sworn to himself that he would be grateful for any moments shared with Rose, knowing the difficulties they would have to overcome. But his patience was wearing thin. Looking over to the petite angel who had stolen his heart, he knew he would never be satisfied with anything but a lifetime married to Rose.

Rose sent him a sympathetic smile. She must have seen him speaking to her mother, must have known the conversation ended in defeat, for she placed her finger at her chin and raised it, signaling for him to keep his chin up. Despite everything that had just transpired, Coleman couldn't help but smile back, even though his heart was splitting.

"I hope you were more tactful this time."

Jean sat on the other end of the bench, stretching

his long legs in front of him while enjoying a bowl of Rose's gumbo and grinning slyly. Jean had witnessed Coleman's wild declaration of love to Rose in Natchez after Coleman had paid him to translate.

"I am forever grateful that you did not translate my embarrassing exclamation that day," Coleman said to his old friend. "Although I think they are on to me."

Jean laughed. "I can't blame you, my friend. The Gallant women are charming creatures."

Coleman was beginning to feel better. It was nice talking to someone who understood. "I saw you dancing with Gabrielle."

Jean offered a fake expression of surprise. "Who?" When Coleman laughed and began to respond, Jean quickly changed the subject. "No wonder you're in love with Rose. The woman really knows how to cook."

Coleman smiled glumly. "We'll have you over for dinner."

Now it was Jean's turn to laugh, then he patted Coleman on the back. "Come on. The next bowl of gumbo is on me."

"How generous of you," Coleman said, following him to the table where the gumbo was being served.

"It's the least I can do after your duet with André," Jean said with a grin. "I don't know when I've been entertained so well."

"Stick around," Coleman answered. "I'm sure there's more to come."

When Coleman and Jean approached the table,

Rose brightened. "What may I do for you gentlemen?"

Jean leaned in conspiratorially toward Rose. "I have heard the way to a man's heart is through his stomach," he said with a glance back at Coleman, who rolled his eyes. "Is that what's happening here?"

Rose leaned forward so that only Jean and Coleman could hear. "If that is the case, monsieur, then you must recommend to Coleman that he start cooking for my mother."

A burst of laughter emerged from Coleman, despite her mother's defeatist words. "If that is the case, mademoiselle," Coleman answered with a broad grin, "your mother would never agree, since I have trouble boiling water."

Reaching down to pour him a bowl of gumbo, Rose returned the smile. "No, I don't suppose that's such a good idea."

Coleman took one bite of the deep brown soup and groaned with pleasure. In addition to the tasty chunks of chicken and sausage, there were tidbits of onions, celery, and okra swimming in a dark roux. "This is delicious."

"Mademoiselle," Jean concurred, handing her his empty bowl to be refilled, "this is the finest gumbo I have ever tasted and I have dined with some of the finest families in New Orleans."

Rose bowed to them both. *"Merci."*

"But I must say, I have never tasted one quite so spicy."

"Rose gets a little carried away with the peppers," Emilie said, bringing them both a half loaf of bread.

"Peppers?" Jean asked.

"Rosarita in Natchez said that spice in food causes perspiration," Rose explained. "When you perspire, your body cools. This is important in Louisiana, no?"

"So these peppers, this spice is not a culinary trait of Canadians?" Coleman asked.

Emilie laughed. "The only perspiration we caused in Canada was rushing to keep the fires going so we wouldn't freeze."

The gumbo went down smoothly, easing Coleman's hunger, but the spice left an enticing afterbite. Coleman quickly finished off his glass of water.

"Maman," Emilie called out. "These men need more water."

Marianne brought the water pitcher to the table, followed by Gabrielle and Lorenz, who were practicing a jig, laughing all the way.

"What brings you to Opelousas, Jean?" Marianne asked him as she refilled their glasses.

The question caught him in midbite and he almost choked. "I completely forgot." Jean turned toward Coleman, pulling a letter from the top of his boot. "I am here to deliver a letter."

Coleman placed the bowl on the table and accepted the letter.

"Not bad news, I hope," Rose said.

Coleman spied the return address and shot a glance toward Marianne. "It's from my cousins in Georgia."

Marianne frowned, puzzled why he had sought her out in that announcement, so Coleman wasted no time opening the letter. He scanned the contents and quickly found what he was hoping for. Despite his better judgment, he reached for Marianne's arm and squeezed.

"This is good news," he said enthusiastically. "Very good news."

Marianne stared at his hand gripping her arm, so he released her; but he couldn't contain his excitement.

"It's from my cousins," he began. "I wrote to them about Joseph, explaining that he might be traveling through Georgia on his way to Louisiana. They have seen him. They are writing to tell me he's well."

Marianne appeared as if she might faint, so Coleman took her by the arm and gently led her to a nearby chair. As soon as she sat down, it was her turn to grab his hand.

"Read it," she demanded.

Coleman bent to one knee before her while the rest of the family and Jean gathered around. He began, trying his best to translate the English.

Dearest Coleman,

We have received your letter regarding the Frenchman and it couldn't have come at a better time. A person fitting your description was indeed visiting our town, traveling to the Louisiana Territory. Because he kept to himself and spoke as a stranger, we avoided him and offered no assistance. When your letter came, we sought him out and found him ill in a neighbor's barn.

"I thought you said he was well," Emilie insisted. Coleman resumed reading the letter.

*We know him to be the man you spoke of, for his
tale was a 'Gallant' one indeed. He said he had taken
a ship to Maryland to reunite with his Acadian family
only to find them gone. He refused medicine and rest,
insisting he must continue traveling to Louisiana in
search of them. We were humbled by his tale.*

Emilie covered her mouth, the tears pouring down
her face, and turned away. Lorenz encircled her
shoulders and held her tight.

"Go on," Marianne urged him.

*Thankfully he fell into a deep slumber and we were
able to call for a doctor. The physician convinced him
to spend at least a week of bed rest at our house while
Mother forced him to eat everything she put in front
of him. (You must remember how horribly insistent
Mother can be.)*

*Our Frenchman rallied nicely. We all hoped he
would stay longer, but he wouldn't hear of it. We were
quite entertained with stories of his homeland. Did
your friend tell you they have tides in Nova Scotia
upward of forty feet?*

Coleman paused to glance up at Rose, who smiled
in the midst of her own tears. Then he continued.

*Alas, he chose to leave. We sent him on his way
with provisions, a rifle, ammunition, and a letter of
introduction to families we know along his route. He
should be halfway to Louisiana by now.*

As for your offer to compensate, we only ask for an

explanation. Could it be, Coleman dear, that you are finally finding happiness at last?

A silence so heavy fell about the group that Coleman swore he could feel its weight about his shoulders. He stood and watched as the awestruck family came slowly to life. Gabrielle knelt down and hugged her mother while Marianne stared off silently. Emilie continued to cry, but there was a smile beneath her tears. Lorenz, too, seemed overcome with emotions.

Before he could turn and find Rose, Coleman felt her fingers slip into his. "Thank you," she whispered.

Coleman grasped her hand, pulling her gently to his side. He could feel the silky strands of her hair against his cheek and smell the lingering effects of the herbal soap she used in her hair.

"It was purely selfish," he whispered back.

Rose lifted her chin, her perfectly round eyes enveloping him in their gaze. If they were not surrounded by family and dozens of people, Coleman would have wasted no time pulling her to his chest and tasting those sweet lips.

"Liar," she said softly. "You would have done it anyway."

They stared at each other for what seemed like minutes, although Coleman doubted the family would have allowed such intimacy to pass between them without protest. Still, for what seemed an eternity, the world with all its objections disappeared.

"Coleman," Sostan shouted, tearing Coleman from his thoughts. "Time for more music."

Coleman inhaled a deep breath in an effort to

regain his composure. When he realized others were watching them, he discreetly released Rose's hand, feeling the warm glow leave his body as he did so.

Gabrielle and Jean helped Marianne to her feet, but it was clear she was still reeling from the news. She glanced at Coleman as if unsure of what to think of him now. Emilie, too, looked at him with new eyes, something between distrust and appreciation.

Feeling uncomfortable, Coleman grabbed his violin. Then he thought of the letter.

"Perhaps you would like to keep this," he said to Marianne.

Marianne accepted his gift gingerly, then held it reverently to her breast. "Thank you," she said in English.

Sostan called out again so Coleman nodded and moved to leave.

"Coleman," Marianne said, stopping him.

Glancing back on the woman who would determine his fate, either a lifetime of happiness or days of loneliness and despair, Coleman saw a new sparkle in Marianne's eyes.

"You have my permission," she said.

A wild smile spread about Coleman's face like a brush fire in August. Without thinking, he grabbed Marianne's hand and shook it several times.

"Merci," he said enthusiastically. *"Merci."*

"All right," Marianne said, laughing along with the others. "You can let go of my hand now."

Coleman dropped Marianne's hand, but he did something even more shocking. He turned and grabbed Rose by the waist, raising her skyward and turning her around and around. She squealed with delight, taking the opportunity to throw her arms about his neck and press her cheek to his. When he finally placed her feet back on the ground, he left her with a kiss on her right cheek. *"Je t'aime,"* he whispered.

"I love you, too," she whispered back to him in English.

Realizing he had overstepped the boundary of gentlemanly behavior, Coleman put some distance between them and cleared his throat. He felt a hard slap on the back.

"Show some enthusiasm," Jean said jokingly.

Coleman laughed and glanced back toward the rest of the family, who were laughing too. Lorenz offered his hand. "Welcome to the family, *L'Anglais,*" he said.

Coleman gratefully accepted his handshake, remembering the day in Henri's store when Lorenz had refused his.

"Will you come to dinner tomorrow?" Marianne asked.

Again, the broad smile returned, his happiness so intense he had no control of his emotions. "I think I can arrange that," he said.

"Bon," Marianne answered, taking his elbow and turning him around to face Sostan, who was waving at him. "But for now, you have work to do."

Coleman sighed. "And I thought the Irish were demanding."

"We love to dance," Lorenz said, pulling Emilie close. "So play something lively."

"Yes, monsieur," Coleman said to Lorenz and

bowed. "The way I'm feeling tonight, I shall play till the sun rises."

Coleman winked at Rose and joined Sostan on the other side of the crowd. He placed the fiddle at his chin and launched into a wild tune, the bow igniting the strings beneath it. As he met Rose's eyes across the dozens of couples dancing between them, he smiled. God had finally stopped laughing and taken pity on his soul. And tonight he would serenade the heavens in thanks.

"Is that the man?" Gerard Soileau asked.

From the cover of the nearby woods, André watched as Coleman performed a soft ballad while Rose sang about unrequited love. Every so often, the two exchanged intimate glances. The sight enraged him.

"What do you know of him?" he asked the boat captain tersely.

"I've seen him before," Gerard answered. "Upriver, at Natchez. He's the son of Richard Thorpe."

Rose looked at Coleman and beamed. How could she dismiss his advances? André thought. How could she reject his hand for that bastard Englishman who didn't know the difference between indigo and tobacco?

"He must have seduced her."

"What?" Gerard asked.

"Nothing," André answered angrily. "Are you sure that's him?"

While the boat captain studied Coleman further, André watched an enchanting smile grace Rose's lips as the crowd clapped their approval at the end of the song. He remembered those lips and their heavenly taste. Despite her plainness, Rose glowed with an inner radiance, burned with a fiery passion. Watching her curtsy and bow to the crowd, André felt the now-familiar tightness in his breeches.

"He must have seduced her," André repeated. "I chose her because she was plain and naive, a woman who would agree to a marriage simply for money. He's doing this to best me."

The captain said nothing and stared. André immediately regretted his outburst. "Just tell me what you know," he demanded.

"He's the son of Richard Thorpe," the man repeated.

"What does that mean?"

André was answered with an outstretched palm. He sighed and placed two silver coins in the man's hand.

"Richard Thorpe's a British soldier," Gerard answered.

Two piastres for that news? "Is that it?"

The man replaced his hat on his head. "He's fluent in French, worked in the French and English wars."

André's patience had expired. He was ready to strangle the man. "I paid you for real information."

"And you got it," Gerard replied. "Richard Thorpe is a spy. Word has it he was sent to the Louisiana Territory to capture the Mississippi for the English." With added emphasis, Gerard leaned closer. "Your man's the son of one of the most notorious English spies on the continent."

For the first time in weeks, André felt better. In a

short time the damned Englishman would be only a memory in the Opelousas Poste.

And Rose and five thousand piastres would finally be his.

Chapter Thirteen

"Forty-foot tides in Nova Scotia?" Coleman asked, passing the *sauce piquante*. "Is that unusual?"

"I don't know your English measurement," Lorenz answered, handing him a bowl of cooked rice. "But whole rivers disappeared every day when the tide went out."

"That's amazing," Jean added, leaning back in his chair and hanging a lazy arm over its back.

"Ships had to be careful coming into Minas Basin," Gabrielle interjected. "Or else they were grounded in low tide and it was a long walk to shore."

Rose watched as Gabrielle and Jean exchanged guarded glances, realizing they were like two ships grounded in the Louisiana interior. She wondered what would become of their affections for each other.

He was a ship's captain destined to return to sea; she wanted to follow him but was anchored by her familial obligations.

As quick as the thought entered her mind, Rose dismissed it. She didn't want to think of conflicts and obstructions to happiness; her summer had been consumed with those. Her entire family was finally breaking bread with the man she loved, and Gabrielle and Jean had been reunited. All was right in the world.

"This is delicious," Coleman said, bringing her attention back to his haunting blue eyes. "I don't know how you do it."

"Sauces, my dear man," she answered with a bright smile. "It's what separates the English from the French and the poorly fed from those who dine well. Of course, I have added a lot of my Louisiana favorites like tomatoes, green peppers, and onions."

Coleman raised his fork and rolled his eyes as the delectable combination tantalized his senses. "Whatever you're doing, please don't stop."

"What I want to know is what is the meat you added to this?" Emilie asked.

Rose hesitated, thinking of the alligator Jean had delivered that morning. Some things were best left unspoken. She glanced at Jean but he refused to meet her eyes, a smile lingering beneath his thick mustache as he took another bite. "Let's just say it was a special Louisiana creature," Rose said.

Everyone paused, contemplating the comment, but Jean continued to eat, his grin erupting into a laugh.

"A bayou creature whose hide makes a great pair of shoes."

Gasps and laughter followed, but Coleman became silent, his fork stilled halfway to his mouth.

"Lesson number two, *L'Anglais*," Lorenz said, patting him on the back and laughing. "The French eat anything."

Coleman gingerly finished the bite, but it was obvious the image had tarnished his pleasure. "I'd like to give an *English* lesson if I may," he said.

Everyone riveted their eyes on Coleman and Rose felt her heart thumping in her chest. They were all getting along so well. She prayed he wouldn't push her family into waters they were not ready to swim.

"I'm not English," Coleman said.

Jean put his fork down and rested his elbow on the table as he leaned toward Coleman. "What?"

"My father is English," Coleman explained. "But I was born on this continent and I consider myself an American."

"You're still English," Jean said.

"I *speak* English," Coleman insisted, "just as you speak French. But you're no more French than I am."

When Jean appeared to protest, Coleman placed his own fork down. "You've been here many years, Jean. You would find Paris as foreign as I would find London. We live in swamps and deal with Indians." Pointing to Jean's empty plate, he added, "What would your family say if you brought home an alligator to the chateau?"

Jean started to object, then thought better of it.

"No one in my family would ever *catch* their supper. It's beneath them."

Coleman smiled. "My point exactly."

"That doesn't mean we're not French," Emilie inserted.

"Then why do you call yourselves Acadian?" Coleman asked.

Marianne rose and refilled the glasses with wine. "Our ancestors settled Canada and called our land *L'Acadie*," she explained. "We're French, and we serve the Mother Country, but we are also independently Acadians."

"My ancestors founded America," Coleman said. "I'm English but I consider myself independently American."

"That's too hard," Lorenz said with a grin. "What am I going to call you now? *L'Americain*?"

"How about Coleman?" Rose offered.

"And what of your children?" Gabrielle asked. "What will you call them?"

Gabrielle instantly regretted her inappropriate choice of subject matter, and stared into her lap. Emilie's eyes grew wide as she stared at her sister and Jean cleared his throat. Rose knew she was expected to be shocked at the mention of something so intimate, especially since they were not yet formally engaged, but she found herself enjoying the thought of their children. Better yet were the images of the acts that would lead up to their births.

Rose glanced up at Coleman, trying hard to conceal the fervent musings flashing through her mind like the wild lightning storms that rumbled through Opelousas every afternoon. She thought of that day in his cabin, when his rough hands had explored every inch of her body, when his lips had ignited sparks on her skin. She thought of how close they had come to lovemaking and how much she wished they had.

Yes, she wanted children. She wanted a lot of things. And she wanted Coleman to show her the way.

Coleman must have read her mind, for when their eyes met he sent her a seductive smile that sent a shiver clear to her toes. Deep recesses inside her body pulsated with the prospect of what was to come. Her blood raced, and she wondered how soon her mother would consent to a marriage. Finally the blush appeared, but it had nothing to do with Gabrielle's indelicate question.

"What will we call our children?" Coleman repeated with a smile. "We will call them 'Cajuns.'"

The awkwardness disappeared, replaced by confusion. Everyone stared first at Coleman, then at each other. Coleman turned startled eyes to Rose. "I have said it wrong?"

"What have you said?" she asked.

"It was what I heard you call each other," Coleman answered. "You called Lorenz that name the day the pigs got loose."

Rose recalled the many nicknames she gave Lorenz, but none sounded like "Cajun." Then a strange thought came to her.

"Are you referring to 'Cad-jin'?" she asked, pronouncing each syllable slowly for him to digest. "Our nickname for Acadian?"

Coleman's eyes brightened. "Yes, that's it. Cajun."

Rose fought back a smile, not wishing to ridicule his poor pronunciation of her native language. Coleman had worked so hard trying to master the odd phrases and intonations that didn't exist in English. But Cajun? The word sounded so odd.

Lorenz, on the other hand, wasn't so considerate. He burst out laughing. "You may be an American, but your French is atrocious."

"It's better than your blasted English," Coleman returned.

"What do I care about English?" Lorenz said. "I'm not in Nova Scotia anymore. French is what's spoken here."

Coleman studied his wine for a moment. "You never know. It may come in handy."

Again, Lorenz laughed. "How?"

Coleman tossed back the last sips of his wine, then leaned back in his chair. "It's a changing world, a more enlightened age. A continent of many nations. Who knows what will happen?"

"There you go again with that American talk," Jean said, shaking his head. "A person would think you'd want us all to throw off our ties to Europe and be called Americans."

"Why not?" Coleman answered with a shrug. "When I was at university in Virginia, there was tension between the colonists and England, words spoken that could be taken as traitorous. But it made sense to me." Coleman leaned forward, his eyes bright with the possibilities. "It's a new world, Jean. We're not Europeans, we shouldn't be treated as such.

Why should we continually pay for Europe's problems, Europe's wars?"

Glancing at Marianne, he added, "Why should we suffer the *consequences* of those wars, be the victims caught in the crossfire of arguments we have no part of?"

Lorenz threaded his hands through the thick black hair some claimed was the result of a Micmac Indian ancestor. "It's all well and good, my friend, but you're talking treason."

"All I'm saying is we should be prepared for anything. Who knows where we'll be in ten years?"

Marianne rose and began clearing the table while Lorenz and Coleman continued debating the politics of colonial government. Before Rose joined her mother and Emilie, she noticed Jean sending Gabrielle a concerned gaze. Where would *they* be in ten years? Rose wondered.

The conversation would have lasted long into the night had not Marianne shooed the men out the door. Jean and Coleman headed for the neighboring cabin discussing hide tariffs while Emilie and Lorenz talked of a new farming technique Henri was implementing and Gabrielle hummed a slow tune about lovers separated at sea. The house was abuzz with laughter, activity, and ideas. And free from the anxiety that had clouded their days.

Rose felt her mother's arms about her. "It's nice having male company about the house. I had always wished this for you."

"I'll bet you did not wish for English-speaking company," Rose said good-naturedly as she wound her arm about her mother's waist.

"I approve of him," Marianne said. "And I approve of Jean."

At the mention of his name, Gabrielle stopped singing and gazed shyly at her mother. "Just be careful what you wish for," Marianne added to both of them. "Unfortunately, love is not as easy as we first imagine it to be. It can also be quite painful."

Later that night, her mother's words haunted Rose's dreams. She stood on the beach at Grand Pré, her arms wound protectively around her mother's waist while relishing the warm sun tanning their faces. Her father was there, smiling at them as he cast his net into the sea.

"I adore your father," Marianne said, her eyes alight with happiness. "I have loved him since the moment I first saw him."

Rose wanted to say she felt the same about Coleman, but her mother's eyes darkened. Rose turned back toward the water only to find Joseph onboard a ship, the massive tide rushing out and carrying him away as her mother's screams echoed in her ears. Rose hugged her mother tightly, trying to calm her tears. When she looked back toward her father, it was Coleman standing at the boat's railing, an older man standing next to him, an angry expression on his face. As the boat drifted away, the older man pulled Coleman from the railing and the ship disappeared on the horizon.

Bolting up in bed, Rose placed a hand on her breast in an attempt to steady her breath. It had been years since she recalled that beach, thought of those horrific days when the ships carried them all away. She had remembered so little about Acadia, save for the smell of her father's tobacco, the sound of his laugh, the way the trees turned to vibrant colors in autumn. But when she least expected it, the horrors of *le grand dérangement* emerged from the darkened neglected corners of her mind, threatening to strangle her at a moment's notice.

Rose reached up to brush the hair from her face and found tears streaking her cheeks. She needed to wash herself, get some fresh air.

Quietly she stole from the room and the house, treading the moonlit path down to the creek. The cool mud felt good beneath her feet, the night air a refreshing kiss against her perspiration-soaked chemise. Her heart still thundered in her chest and her emotions remained raw from the vivid dream. When she reached the bank, she knelt and brought the chilled water to her burning cheeks, patting her forehead in an effort to ease the painful memory and keep the tears from returning.

She felt like crying, and she wasn't sure why. Everything she had wanted was finally coming to fruition. She and Coleman were to marry, what else did she have to fear?

Rose saw her reflection shining in the water and the moonlight pouring through the trees. Although she lacked the dark hair of Gabrielle and her father and the auburn tresses of her mother and Emilie,

Rose still had the trademark attributes of the French. Brown hair, brown eyes, a petite frame, and a prominent nose—so vastly different from Coleman and his world of stocky fair-skinned people. Until that moment, she had never considered their differences, had never thought that anything save her mother's approval would be an obstacle to their happiness. But as she stared at the small oval face in the slow-moving stream, Rose wondered if their love would survive the hurdles of the long road ahead.

She had yet to meet his family, his friends. What would they think of a well-bred, educated Englishman calling himself an American and marrying an ignorant French refugee? What if the English conquered the Mississippi and assumed the territory as they had in Nova Scotia? What if Coleman wished for more? If he did not pursue his aspirations, would she be the cause?

Coleman was right; it was a changing world. And it was that uncertainty that brought tears to her eyes.

Suddenly, footsteps sounded from the opposite bank. Before Rose could rise and move to the safety of the nearby bushes, a figure approached, bounding determinedly down the path, eyes downcast. The figure reached the water, looked up, and spotted Rose immediately. In the darkness, where a soft white light fell from the moon and shadows provided the only variation on black, two brilliant blue eyes found hers.

"Rose?" Coleman asked, clearly shocked to find her at the stream. "What are you doing here?"

"I couldn't sleep," Rose answered guiltily until she

realized that he, too, was visiting the stream in the middle of the night. "Why are you?"

Coleman ran his fingers through his hair nervously. "I thought of taking a bath."

"At this hour?"

He smiled grimly. "It's what men do when their nights are invaded by images of a beautiful woman."

Rose found herself smiling despite the fear that still clutched her heart. She had heard Lorenz mentioning cold baths when the young couple lacked privacy. So now Coleman ached for her?

She wanted to touch him, wanted to convince him her desires were just as strong, that so many of her nights had been interrupted with thoughts of him, but she was reminded of the dream, reminded of the countless obstacles that lay ahead.

"Coleman," she said softly, "do you think we're doing the right thing?"

His smile disappeared and he strode across the stream not caring that he marred his breeches. Before she had time to think, his hand was on her waist pulling her into his embrace. His other hand cupped her cheek while vivid pools of blue studied her, gazing deep into her soul.

"Why are you asking this?" he said so passionately, Rose could feel his trepidation. "Has your mother changed her mind?"

Rose leaned forward to avoid his insistent eyes, her forehead resting against his cheek. "No, my mother approves."

Coleman pulled her back, forcing her to look at him. "Then why?"

His eyes burned with such a passion Rose wondered how she could ever doubt such a man. "I had a terrible dream. It made me wonder if we are making a mistake."

"Don't," Coleman said, holding her firmly by the shoulders. "The only mistake we could make is not allowing ourselves to be happy."

"But what about your father? What about . . ."

"My father?" Coleman asked, stepping back. "Why would you wonder about him?"

The eyes that had spilled forth love only seconds before grew ominously cold. Rose felt a chill and shivered. "You never speak of him."

"Why should I?" Coleman answered harshly.

A cloud fell about him, concealing the Coleman she knew and loved. In his place was a man with a troubled past, a man filled with anger and hurt. Rose's fears intensified.

As if sensing her anxiety, Coleman softened and pulled her back to his chest. He stroked her hair gently and closed his eyes. "I'm sorry, my dear. There are some memories I'd rather not relive."

"But you have to face them. Your father has to know about me."

Coleman ran his hand up her back while breathing in the scent of her hair. "We are estranged. But if it makes you more comfortable, I will write him and tell him about our marriage."

Rose thought to object further, to demand an explanation, to know why Coleman and his father had argued, but Coleman quickly placed both hands on her cheeks and kissed her. It wasn't a soft introductory kiss like the first time in his cabin. This time, Rose felt his hunger instantly, his lips pressed hot against hers, his tongue gently probing inside as a deep groan emerged from the back of his throat.

Rose gave up the fight. The images of Grand Pré disappeared, replaced by a warm solid chest and the searing lips of the man she loved. When he placed his hands at her back and pulled her closer, she wound her hands about his neck and threaded her fingers into the long blond locks falling about his shoulders.

While his tongue explored the reaches of her mouth, dancing delicately with her own, Coleman's hands roamed her body. With only a chemise between her skin and his demanding hands, Rose gasped as his fingers trailed down her back to the tops of her thighs, over the curves of her bottom and up her sides to her breasts, aching for his touch.

Coleman's lips left hers and descended her neckline, gently biting the soft skin of her neck and earlobe. At the same time, his hand cupped her right breast, circling his thumb around a taut nipple.

A wave of sensations rolled over her and she released a long passionate sigh. She arched her back to give him more room at her breast, and let her own hands explore his broad shoulders and strong back, kissing his nape when she had the opportunity.

Coleman ran his fingers through her loose hair and sighed as he paused his kisses and gazed into her eyes. "Shall I stop?" he asked with an expression that begged her to refuse.

She didn't disappoint him. "No," she whispered heatedly, meeting his lips once again.

Coleman took her lower lip between his teeth and sucked gently while his tongue savored and explored. Again his hands found her breasts and Rose felt her legs buckling beneath her.

Before she realized what was happening, Coleman was on his knees, pulling her waist forward and burying his face in her chest. "I love you," he whispered so passionately Rose knew she would never doubt him again. He glanced up, his azure eyes burning with desire. "I swear I will never let anything come between us. Nothing, Rose. Never."

She wove her fingers into his hair once more as he nestled his face between her breasts. They felt so right together, as if their souls were two interlocking pieces waiting to be joined.

Coleman's hand reached under her chemise and began a slow teasing ascent along her leg and thigh. As he cupped her bottom and moaned, Rose felt a burning begin in the innermost reaches of her femininity. It was time, Rose surmised. Time to cast away fears and embrace the happiness due them.

As she turned her head to rub her cheek against his hair, Rose spotted the towel Coleman had brought for his bath and then discarded when he had crossed the stream. Rose broke away from his embrace, picked up the towel, and headed for a clearing on the bank. Finding a dry area covered with leaves and soft grasses, she spread the towel on the ground and sat down.

Coleman took no time understanding her intentions. He pulled off his shirt, revealing ripples of muscles across a broad tanned chest. A long line of hair, as blond as the locks atop his head, stretched down to his navel, disappearing beneath his breeches as if inviting her to discover its end.

Coleman placed his shirt at her head and Rose leaned back while Coleman stretched out alongside her. Within seconds his lips returned to hers and his hands resumed their wild exploration. He released the buttons of her chemise until he had ample room to slip a hand inside, then alternated between caressing her breast and squeezing the nipple between his thumb and fingers while his lips again descended her neck.

Pausing at her shoulders, Coleman drew her chemise down to her waist. For a moment, he stared at the sight before him, his blue eyes dazzling with appreciation in the moonlight. "I love you so very much," he whispered, then bent his head to her breast.

Rose gasped when his lips found her nipple and gently sucked. By their own command her hips arched, aching for their joining. Coleman began to nip at her enlarged nub with his teeth while his hand reached under her chemise and moved up her inner thigh.

Feeling a heat travel up her body like lightning searing a tree, Rose parted her legs, inviting him in. Coleman gingerly slipped a finger inside, then withdrew it and softly explored its entrance before inserting it once again.

The combination of his pulsating movements with the magic of his tongue consumed Rose with waves of pleasure. Her breath came in short ragged bursts and a tension built deep inside her, waiting to explode. As he inserted his finger yet again, his thumb slipped forward to caress a tender spot nearby. His touch ignited the fuse and a swell of ecstasy overtook her, filling her with sensations that rocked her body with gratification.

Coleman left her breast to meet her eyes. He smiled, watching her attempt to take a steady breath when the waves subsided.

"What just happened?" she asked, her voice no more than a whisper.

Coleman raised a hand and caressed her face. "A prelude of what's to come."

Rose knew what lay ahead and her skin tingled thinking what might transpire. Despite the rapture he had just delivered, her body yearned for something more, something deeper.

Coleman wrapped his hands about her drawing her close, then kissed her passionately. When he pulled away and stared into her eyes, his cerulean irises burning with desire, he began to unbutton his breeches.

Rose couldn't help herself; she was too curious. She slid her hands down the length of his back and pushed his breeches down over his hips, relishing in the tight curves of his firm bottom. Coleman moaned and quickly freed himself of his clothing. When he pulled the bottom half of her chemise up to her waist, kissing her skin as it became exposed, Rose felt the waves returning, the now-familiar passion building once again.

Coleman gently parted her legs and moved on top

of her, all the while his hands caressed her legs, her thighs, the curves of her side and breasts. She caught a glimpse of his manhood before it came to rest at her entrance and began to doubt if such a coupling could occur.

"It's so large," she whispered. "Do you think it's possible?"

Coleman covered her face with kisses. "Trust me," he whispered. "We'll take it slowly."

When he entered, her body screamed the same questions. But Coleman moved gently, slowly inside, allowing her body time to adjust to the intrusion. He rotated his hips allowing himself entrance in a circular, easy motion that reminded Rose of the way her mother removed tight corks from wine bottles. And the deeper he delved, the less her body revolted.

She realized he had accomplished his task when Coleman began to gently move in and out, his hands planted on either side of her head. When she looked up at him, his eyes glazed with unrequited passion, she knew it was taking everything in his power not to plunge ahead and release his pent-up passion.

When he thrust inside her again, Rose felt the sensations returning, only this time more intense as if they resonated from a deeper part of her soul. She closed her eyes and arched her back, encouraging him to push deeper as the waves of pleasure washed over her.

And he did. He reached under her, grabbing her bottom and pushing farther inside, the tempo increasing. Like the air bursting forth when a wine cork is released, Rose's body exploded with bliss. She felt her skin burn with the excitement and her insides pulsate in fevered waves. Coleman instantly followed suit, yelling out while his own body shook with rapture.

They held each other for several minutes, their bodies still joined, Coleman continuing to kiss her while Rose savored the length of his back. Finally he moved aside, pulling her onto his chest.

"Are you all right?" he asked. "I was so afraid I was going to hurt you."

Rose placed a hand on his chest and rested her chin there, still reeling from the ecstasy. "I'm not as fragile as I appear."

Reaching up to caress her cheeks, Coleman's eyes reflected a deep appreciation. "You're remarkable," he said. "I can't imagine loving anyone more."

Rose answered with a sly smile. "Perhaps you'll change your mind when we have our 'Cajun' children?"

Coleman's eyes darkened as they had when she had spoken of his father. "What have I said?" she asked.

"My mother died in childbirth." The words were spoken so simply yet with such injury that Rose could feel his pain deep within her own heart.

"Don't worry," she whispered, stroking the blond curls from his forehead. "We have never lost a Gallant woman bringing life into this world. I will be fine."

Coleman's eyes filled with worry as his hands roamed her body. "But you are so petite."

"As I said, I am not breakable simply because I am small. I will be fine."

Her words failed to lift the ominous mood that had

descended upon them, so Rose stood, letting her
chemise drop to the ground. She offered him her
hand. Coleman placed an arm behind his head and
smiled at her naked form. "What now?"

Rose answered with a mischievous smile. "A bath."

In an instant Coleman rose from their makeshift
bed and lifted her into his arms. He carried her into
the stream and fell backward, plunging them both
into the cool, shallow waters. She landed safely on
top of him, giggling as the water hit her sweaty skin—
until Coleman silenced her with a kiss.

"Not too loud, my dear. We don't want to wake
your family."

"Heavens, no," Rose answered, returning his kiss.

Instantly, his hands enveloped her body, pulling
her into his lap. As he deepened the kiss and his hands
found her breasts, Rose could feel his manhood newly
aroused at her hips. She wrapped her legs around
his waist and raised herself to initiate their joining.
For the second time that night, Coleman escorted
her to heaven.

There were no birds to announce the coming of
dawn, nor did the darkness wane, but Coleman and
Rose sensed that morning was near. They dressed
and held each other one last time before Rose moved
away, ready to return home.

"Convince your mother to let us marry soon," Coleman said. "We cannot chance this again."

Rose thought of the nights ahead without him,

feeling an emptiness invade her soul. "I will do my best."

Suddenly, she was reminded of the reason for her trip to the stream that night. "But you must tell me."

Coleman reached up and brushed aside a strand of hair still damp from their bath. "Tell you what, my love?"

"Of your father."

A silence as intense as the deep night surrounded them. The light in his eyes extinguished. But as quick as his mood changed, Coleman brightened and attempted a smile.

"I will tell you tomorrow at the dance."

"Tonight," Rose reminded him.

"Yes, tonight," Coleman assured her. "Tonight you will know everything."

Rose hurried down the path toward home, her skin still tingling from their lovemaking. Everything was going to be fine. After all that had passed between them, what could possibly tear them apart now?

Chapter Fourteen

Despite his entrance into heaven the night before, the following morning brought a series of irritating problems for Coleman. When Jean attempted to help out by feeding the pigs, he left the gate ajar and the entire herd had sought out the newly planted fields. By the time the pigs had been rounded up and put into their pen, a nasty rain had started, giving birth to new leaks inside the cabin. Coleman spent the entire afternoon on the cabin's roof repairing shingles while lightning danced around his head. To top it all, Jean woke in a nasty mood that only intensified by day's end.

As Coleman dressed, removing one shirt to try another, Jean picked up the original linen shirt and waistcoat and threw them into his arms. "These will do," he said impatiently. "If you do not finish your dress, it will soon be St. Martin's Summer."

"We have plenty of time," Coleman replied, pulling on the shirt and buttoning his collar. "I am going to ask Marianne if I may set a wedding date. I want to look my best."

Jean reached over and tied Coleman's caravat, wrapping the rectangular piece of material around his neck and tying it in a bow. "What's your hurry?" he said with a twinkle in his eye, the first sign of humor he'd showed that day.

The memory of Rose and their lovemaking at the stream only hours before caused a tightness in his breeches and Coleman pulled his waistcoat over his shirt in an effort to regain his composure. "I'd say my rush to the altar is about as fierce as your resistance to leave."

Admitting that he loved Gabrielle was not something Jean was ready to do, even though Lorenz and Coleman were certain of his intentions. Gabrielle remained the only subject in Jean's conversations. If he wasn't inquiring about her childhood or her preference in clothes, he was commenting on the brilliance of her deep-set eyes or the richness of her ebony hair.

"I plan to leave tomorrow morning," Jean explained. "Am I wrong in desiring one last dance with a dark-haired beauty?"

"Absolutely not," Coleman replied, fastening the ties at his knees. "But why not ask that beautiful woman to spend the rest of your—"

"It's getting late," Jean interrupted, which wasn't

a surprise. Jean always changed the subject when it came to marriage. Grabbing his hat, he left the cabin with Coleman bringing up the rear, violin tucked safely under one arm.

"Is my hair in place?" Coleman asked.

Jean rolled his eyes heavenward. "You're the epitome of perfection. Now let's go."

They traveled the road to avoid the stream, which had risen considerably since the afternoon storm. As they passed the DeClouet plantation, Coleman found the house unusually silent. Gone were the chatting women with their endless commands and the hordes of slaves performing services for their mistresses. Also absent was André with his familiar sneers and accusations whenever Coleman passed by.

"Beware of that man," Jean said softly. "I do not trust him as far as I can spit. And you know I can't spit very far."

A foreboding invaded Coleman's senses, one he had trouble shaking. He attributed it to Jean's foul mood. "You've a strange way with words, Jean."

"And you choose strange lovers and enemies."

"I should have stayed with my own kind, is that what you're suggesting?" This was not the conversation Coleman had wished for on the way to ask for his true love's hand.

"It offers a life with less conflict."

Coleman hardly believed Jean based his choices in life on the easier course of action. He was, after all, a smuggler, always running from the law. His comment sparked a thought, one Coleman hoped wasn't the reason that Jean kept avoiding marriage.

"Is that why you haven't asked for Gabrielle's hand?" Coleman asked him. "Because of the difference between your social classes?"

Intense black eyes ignited when they turned his way. "I don't care a damn for my social class," Jean said heatedly. "I came into this world a second son with no inheritance, no title, and definitely no affection from my arrogant family whose only concern is marrying their children off to equally arrogant members of the aristocracy. I came to Louisiana to be rid of the lot of them *and* my suffocating social class."

"Then why?"

The fury abating, Jean still boiled with an inner turmoil. "Because I am not good enough for most women, let alone someone as special as Gabrielle." When Coleman began to argue the point, Jean held up his hand. "You forget, I am a sea captain and a smuggler. I support an illegitimate daughter and her mother, whose only aim in life is to see me ruined. What kind of life would I offer Gabrielle? She deserves more than the likes of me."

They approached the overseer's house in silence until the voices of the Gallant women could be heard inside. As if knowing there was unfinished business between them, they both halted before the porch steps.

"You underestimate both yourself and Gabrielle," Coleman finally said.

After a moment's pause, Jean began to speak, but was interrupted by Marianne appearing on the porch, her arms folded sternly, her eyes narrowed toward

Coleman. Coleman bowed politely, praying she had not become privy to what had happened at the stream that morning. Still, if their lovemaking was the cause of her stern countenance, he assured himself, she would insist they marry. It was a thought he had considered hours before when he had crossed that barrier reserved for married couples. He would have weathered a thousand tongue lashings to be wed to his darling. But now that he faced the lion's den, he dreaded what was to come. The foreboding that had begun at the DeClouet house intensified.

"Monsieur Thorpe," she began, causing Coleman to wince at the use of his formal name. "May I see you inside alone, please?"

Coleman glanced back at Jean for support, but Gabrielle had left the house and Jean's attention had shifted. Marianne opened the front door and waited. Coleman took the stairs in one step, removed his hat, and crossed the threshold, placing his violin on a chair. When his eyes adjusted to the dim light, he realized only Rose stood in the main room. She was dressed in a brightly colored striped skirt, a white cotton blouse, and a rich blue vest he had never seen before. In her hair were flowers, woven in a braid atop her head like a crown.

Despite the ominous feeling permeating the room, Coleman soaked in the sight of her and felt stronger. She smiled tentatively and he grinned confidently back, as if to convey that all would be well.

Surprisingly, although Marianne remained grim, she took her daughter's hand and then Coleman's, standing between them like a preacher.

"It's not easy giving a daughter away," Marianne said softly. "It's a mother's greatest wish to see her daughter happily wed, but it's a moment of dread as well. You spend your life watching over her, preparing her for life, keeping her safe from harm. To relinquish such a duty and hope that you are making the right decision is the hardest thing a mother has to do."

She sighed deeply, then continued. "Rose is my youngest. She is my baby and the child I worry about the most. Perhaps someday when you have children, you will understand the fear a parent carries for her child."

Coleman knew he must remain silent out of respect for Marianne, but he couldn't control himself. He had to convince her, had to make her realize. "I do understand," he said passionately. "She will want for nothing, will never see harm as long as I draw breath. I swear it."

Marianne squeezed his hand. "I know. That is why I have consented to you marrying my Rose."

They exchanged guarded looks. Coleman was afraid to let the happiness overtake him for fear it might disappear as quickly as it had come.

Marianne stepped back and placed Rose's soft hand in his. "I believe you should be married right away," Marianne added, and this time Coleman allowed the smile to spread upon his face. Rose answered him in kind, threading her fingers inside his. "I've seen the way you look at each other, and I realized it would do none of us any good keeping you apart any longer."

His breath caught in his chest as he slowly absorbed

the details of that moment: the way the dusky light reflected highlights of gold in Rose's hair, the freckles gracing her nose, the love spilling forth from her eyes. It was a moment he would remember forever.

"Oh, go ahead and kiss her," he heard Jean yell from the porch window, answered by laughter from the rest of the Gallant family who, no doubt, had heard every word.

Coleman wasted no time taking that advice. He placed a gentle hand at Rose's waist and pulled her close, savoring the sweetness of her lips. They lingered longer than was warranted but not so long as to be reprimanded. When he finally released her, he pulled her close to his side to breathe in the heavenly scent of the woman who was to become his wife.

"I love your daughter more than life itself," he told Marianne, his eyes never leaving Rose's face. "You can't imagine how much."

To their surprise, Marianne laughed, although she wiped tears from her eyes. "I can imagine plenty," she said. "I have stood in those shoes."

Coleman turned to his future mother-in-law, a woman whose eyes betrayed years of anguish, loneliness, and hope. With all his heart, he wished Joseph Gallant safe and Godspeed. As if she had read his thoughts, Marianne reached up and placed a maternal hand on Coleman's face, then kissed his cheek. Coleman leaned into her embrace and found her affection sincere, not at all like the empty hugs his mother's family bestowed on him at holidays. Now that he thought of it, he couldn't remember a time when his mother had been loving and affectionate, despite Coleman's repeated pleas for her attention.

For an instant, the foreboding returned. It had been years since he had allowed himself memories of his mother. Why now?

Shaking off the premonition, he focused on his new relations. "I'll do everything in my power to bring him home to you," he whispered to Marianne before she released him. In some deep recess of his heart, Coleman vowed to move mountains to make her happy again.

Marianne answered him with an appreciative smile, then moved back for the handshakes and hugs that were to come. Now that the grand announcement had been made, the family entered the house, offering congratulations all around. Only Emilie stood apart, arms folded defiantly across her chest and a painful expression on her face.

"What about Papa?" Emilie asked. "Will you not wait for him?"

Marianne approached her daughter and placed an arm about her stiff shoulders. "I had a vision last night," she told Emilie, although everyone stopped talking to listen. "We were all together again, your father and all of us, standing beside a bayou and a tree I have not seen before." She brushed the hair from Emilie's face. "We were all there," she emphasized. "Coleman included."

"Why must they marry so soon?" Emilie insisted, her eyes still reflecting a distrust of the Englishman marrying her beloved sister. "Why can't we wait until Papa arrives?"

Because we can't contain our desire any longer and Marianne knows it, Coleman thought. But when she looked at first Coleman, then Rose, he doubted that was the reason.

"Because I saw it that way" was all she said. "So they will marry as soon as Father Felicien allows it."

"I have one more lesson," Coleman assured Marianne.

"You're a fast learner," Lorenz said with a laugh. "My catechism took longer than that."

Emilie began to brighten, although she still regarded Coleman suspiciously. "Heathens always take longer, my dear."

The walk to the neighboring house where the *bal de maison* was to be held was infinitely happier. Gone was Jean's unhappy mood and Marianne's distress over losing her youngest daughter. Several times Coleman assured her she had made the right decision, and several times she had responded with an affectionate pat on his arm, a squeeze of his hand. Emilie had yet to come around, but she was the oldest and the one her father had left in charge. Relinquishing Rose was as hard for her as it had been for Marianne. By the time they were halfway to the house, her features softened and she began to tease the new couple along with the rest of the family.

Coleman felt a wave of contentment wash over him. How long had it been since he was surrounded by a loving family? Since Georgia, which was several years ago. His father's family had immigrated to the colonies before his birth, establishing a large plantation near the coast. For reasons unknown to Coleman, his mother was sent to Virginia to spend time with an aunt and had married his father while he studied at William and Mary. Coleman had only met his mother's Virginia family on occasion. They were cold distant people who loved to remind his father that he had married a woman of a higher station.

Well, that was one thing he and his father had in common. Neither cared about money and class when it came to matters of the heart. But then his parents' marriage had turned tragic.

"What is it?" Rose whispered, waking him from his memories.

Coleman shook his head to clear the past's painful images from his present happiness. "Nothing," he said, taking the opportunity to steal a kiss.

Beaming from the contact, Rose snaked her arm through his elbow and pulled herself close to his side. "Happy?" she asked.

"Amazingly so."

The family came to the small house that was now empty of all furniture but filled with anxious people, awaiting the chance to dance. Before they followed the others into the house, Rose tugged on Coleman's arm.

"You haven't forgotten your promise?" she asked.

"My promise?"

Rose leaned against him, her eyes chastising him for not remembering. It took everything in his power not to kiss her madly on the threshold of a stranger's house.

"You promised to tell me about your father."

Like the south Louisiana rain that appeared out of nowhere, blanketing the sky and shutting out the sun, a curtain fell upon his heart. Coleman couldn't explain the sensation, but it seeped into his soul and he felt his throat constrict.

"Coleman?" Rose's eyes dimmed as she studied him. "What is it you're not telling me?"

"I'll tell you what he's not telling you," Coleman heard André shout from inside the house. When he turned he found every person staring at him accusingly, except for his newfound family who looked puzzled.

André approached them, parting the crowd like Moses at the Red Sea. Coleman had a dreadful feeling that whatever André "knew," he had already imparted this information to the Acadians. The Creole said nothing until he reached the threshold, then turned his eyes toward Rose.

"His father is an English spy," André explained. "He was sent to the Louisiana Territory to spy on the French in the hope of winning the Mississippi for the English. While you were at Natchez, my dear, Mister Thorpe was busy spying on the government to be rid of you."

Rose's eyes grew enormous before turning to Coleman for confirmation. And he wanted so badly to deny it. The truth was, his father, well learned in the French language, was indeed an English soldier sent to the territory to try and win the river for the English colonies. Conquering the Mississippi for the English would dissolve the link between Louisiana and French

Canada and prevent the French from acquiring new western territories.

In a sense, his father did wish to rid the territory of the French. In a sense, he was no better than the soldiers at Grand Pré.

"Ask him if it's true, Rose," André demanded.

Rose never spoke, but her eyes silently asked the question. Coleman closed his own to shut out the image, feeling his world, so briefly joyous, crumble beneath his feet. When he opened them again, her eyes were filled with tears.

"I'm not my father," he insisted, reaching for her arm. But Rose pulled away, stepping backward down the porch steps. "Rose," Coleman shouted. "I can explain."

"Yes," André said to his rear. "Why don't you explain? Or perhaps you don't wish for us to know that you, too, are a spy, sent to the Opelousas Poste to rid the area of poor, naive French-speaking citizens."

The fear that had been building inside him all day turned into fury. He grabbed André by the front of his shirt and threw him against the side of the house. "You bastard," he shouted. "You have no idea who my father is or who I am. All you will ever care about is yourself."

André attempted to push off his arms, but Coleman slid a hand about the Creole's neck, cutting off his air. He could feel a burning in the back of his eyes and a pounding in his temple. He had come so close, realized happiness so sweetly. Now André threatened it all by reminding him and everyone he cared for that his father was a bastard.

"Coleman, let him go."

Lorenz's voice was quiet but firm, as he pulled Coleman's hands from André's throat.

"Come on, old boy," Jean said, grabbing him from behind. "He's not worth a trip to prison."

Suddenly, as if on their own accord, Coleman's hands released André and he fell to the floor coughing. Staring down at his nemesis, Coleman continued shouting, "I'm not my father. As if it matters anyway. Spain owns this territory now, you idiot."

Jean's large hands gripped his shoulders and led him backward. Coleman could hear Lorenz offering comforting words, but the anger still flowed furiously through his veins and nothing was comprehensible. When André regained his composure and stood, glaring menacingly at Coleman, Lorenz stepped in between. As the fog began to clear, Coleman realized his new family was standing up for him.

"Have you not heard what I just said?" André asked. "The man is a spy."

"Nonsense," Jean said. "I know both Coleman and his father, and the two are as different as you and me. Besides, Coleman has not spoken to his father in months. He's been disinherited."

"It's a front," André insisted. "Don't you see? He's pulled the covers over all of our eyes. Tried to make us believe he's our friend."

With a hard shove, Lorenz threw the Creole back against the side of the house. "We made him our friend, you self-centered bastard. The only enemy here is you. You established a kingdom and expected us to be your slaves. The only person who is deceitful is you, stealing everyone's livestock and property.''

The crowd began to turn; Coleman could feel it. It was one thing to have the son of an English spy in your presence and yet another to finally stand up to the man responsible for the loss of your stock and your land—of your livelihood.

"You've stolen my cattle a number of times," one man shouted. "I've seen them later, marked with your brand."

"Then they must be mine, you fool," André shouted back. "This is beside the point."

"It's precisely the point," Sostan added. "You have moved my fences so many times I have lost my spring. Now you're disputing my rights to the bayou when you know damn well that land is mine."

A collective agreement rose through the crowd. André shot Coleman a deadly look, then turned toward Marianne. "Are you going to allow this? Are you going to let that man marry Rose?"

Coleman's body shook, but he wasn't sure whether it was from anger or the fear of losing everything dear to him. He dreaded meeting Marianne's eyes, knowing that censure and disgust would likely be awaiting him. But he had to know her answer.

"He's part of the family now," she said softly.

André's face nearly burst with frustration. "Are you that foolish that you don't see what he is?"

"There's something you should know about Acadians, Monsieur DeClouet," Marianne said. "Once we make a friend, we are friends for life. Hurt us once and you are our enemy forever."

"And this includes Englishmen, the same people who expelled you from your homeland?"

Marianne paused and Coleman wondered how the Acadians would react to this comparison. Certainly his talents at the fiddle weren't enough to overcome such a history.

"You're mistaken," Marianne said with finality. "My future son-in-law is an American."

André's face burned crimson with anger. "I want you out," he shouted to them. "I want you off my property tonight."

"We'll do you one better," Lorenz suggested. "Give us our wages and we'll be on our way."

"I'll pay you nothing." André retrieved his hat from the floor and brushed it off.

"You promised us enough wages to get us to Attaka-pas," Emilie said.

Placing his hat on his head and pushing his way through the crowd, André offered one last comment. "Sue me."

Now that the source of the conflict had left, Coleman's anger dissipated and he dropped to one knee to catch his breath. He had a lot of explaining to do, but where to begin? Yes, Richard Thorpe was everything André had accused him of, including being a failure as a husband and father. But the confrontation had given rise to an emotion Coleman had never expected. As furious as he was at his father, Coleman had wanted to beat André senseless in his father's defense. Where had that sudden sense of pride come from?

As she had at the previous *bal de maison,* Marianne

stood before him and offered him a glass of water. Accepting Lorenz's outstretched hand, Coleman rose to face his jury.

Emilie still distrusted him; André's remarks had only confirmed her fears. She stood glaring at him, her arms folded tightly over her chest. The others didn't mirror her suspicion. They just stared uncomfortably at the floorboards.

"Drink up," he heard Marianne say. When he gathered enough courage to glance her way, he was surprised to find her calm and accepting.

"I knew about your father," she said as if to answer his unspoken questions. "I inquired about you in Natchez after that wild display you showed us."

At any other moment Coleman would have felt embarrassed for his passionate exclamation that afternoon, but tonight it gave him strength.

"The Spanish commandant at Natchez told us about your father," Marianne continued. "He explained who he was, that he worked for the English Crown. I have known all along."

Coleman took an unsteady sip of water, but it did little to quench his thirst. "I would have told you, thought to tell you." He swallowed hard. "My father and I have not been on good terms for years. It's been painful to speak of him."

He tried to string his words together in a coherent fashion, but they emerged as they always had, awash in a sea of emotion. "My mother died in childbirth. She and my brother bled to death in my arms. He could have saved them. He left us alone on our plantation when she was at her time. I was only sixteen. No doctor. No midwife.''

Through his fury, Coleman felt Marianne's hand on his arm. "You have to understand," he said. "He left us alone so he could do his duty to his country. I abhor my father and everything he represents.''

For the first time that night, Marianne appeared shocked. She raised a finger to his lips. "Don't. Don't ever speak of your father that way. And definitely do not say those things thinking I will be pleased. He is your father no matter what he has done and only God can judge his actions.''

Coleman shook his head, remembering the harsh words he had exchanged with his father the last time he had left Natchez. The day he had called his father a murderer.

"Coleman," Marianne whispered, bringing his eyes toward hers. "You must make peace with your father. If you are ever to hope for a lifetime of happiness with Rose, you cannot carry this pain with you. And your father has a right to know that he's about to inherit a French daughter-in-law. You have managed to win me over; now you must face your own family and friends. That is the price you pay for marrying someone outside of your faith and country. Rose deserves that much.''

Rose. Dear, sweet, beautiful Rose. The constant light in his dark existence, the hope that had brought him through this long summer.

"You're right," Coleman said. "I will do it for Rose.''

"And for yourself," Marianne added.

Coleman nodded, thankful for the maternal hand on his arm. Thankful to share the pain so long buried inside him.

He glanced around to find Rose, to feel the soft confident hand in his. He needed to hold her, to know that she still cared. But the more faces he encountered, the less certain he became.

A panic grew inside him as Coleman scanned the crowd and found her absent. When he turned toward Lorenz, he found him busy searching the faces, his eyes filled with fear. Coleman grabbed Jean's arm. "Where is she?" he asked heatedly.

It took the three men only seconds to bolt into action. They headed into the dark night, calling Rose's name and leaving Emilie standing on the porch, her questions unanswered.

Chapter Fifteen

"Are you sure there is nothing I can get you?" asked Jacques Guillaume Courtableau, the Opelousas commandant. "Is there someone I can fetch to bring you home?"

Rose shook her head as Madame Courtableau brought in a fresh pot of tea and poured her a cup. She wasn't sure why she was sitting by the commandant's hearth or how she had managed to walk as far as his house in the darkness. She only remembered André's hateful words, followed by Coleman's refusal to dispute them. After all she and Coleman had managed to overcome that summer, after years of always being the optimist in the face of constant disappointments, Rose's strength had left her. She had bolted from the *bal de maison* and headed down the road, not caring where she was headed or why.

"Your family is sure to be worried," Courtableau insisted.

"If you give me a moment, monsieur, I will return to my family," Rose said. "I need time to be alone, time to think."

"I will give you time to finish your tea," he answered. "Then I will escort you home."

Rose nodded. The commandant patted her arm, then led his wife into another room. Rose placed the tea at her feet and stared at the glowing embers in the fireplace before her.

She felt betrayed, although she wasn't sure who to blame. Coleman had kept his father's identity a secret, had refused to explain his background. Now that they were doomed to part and her heart was broken, was he the reason?

Thinking back on the night before, when Coleman had fallen to his knees and sworn that nothing would come between them, Rose had trouble believing he would deceive her. But what did it matter now? Her mother would never allow such a marriage. Even if he was sincere.

Rose leaned back in the overstuffed chair and watched a log burst into flames, sending a trail of sparks up the chimney. Her head ached. She didn't want to think. She wanted her heart to lead her. But a nagging voice in the back of her mind reminded her that it was her heart that had gotten her into this mess. Her heart that was now breaking into a million pieces.

The flame shifted with a draft of wind, and Rose heard voices at the front door. Before she could comprehend who had entered, Coleman was kneeling before her, grabbing her hands and raising them to his lips.

"Thank God, you're all right," he said, pressing her palms against his cheeks. "We searched everywhere."

Staring down into the pools of blue that had haunted her sleep since Natchez, Rose wanted to let her heart decide, but the voice suggested otherwise. She tried to pull her hands free. "Your father . . ."

Coleman held her hands tightly. "He's a soldier for the English Crown, yes, but that doesn't mean that I am nor does it mean I share his views. This will not separate us. I swore to you before and I swear to you now, Rose, nothing will come between us."

She wanted to believe him. Her heart ached to believe him. "But my mother," Rose began, "and your family?"

Coleman began to explain until another gust of wind interrupted. "Thank God," Rose heard Lorenz exclaim as he entered the room, followed by Jean. "We have been looking everywhere for you."

A tiny spark ignited in Rose's heart. "We?" she asked Coleman.

He wrapped his fingers tightly over hers and pressed them against his lips. "Your family stood up for me," he said. "Your mother has not changed her mind."

Was she hearing correctly? Her mother had not reversed her opinion of him, despite André's accusations?

She glanced up at Lorenz, who nodded and smiled. "We let that arrogant Creole know he couldn't speak to our family like that."

Coleman's eyes glistened in the firelight with a mixture of gratitude and awe. Rose knew exactly how he felt. Her family, brutally exiled from their home and separated from their father, had welcomed an Englishman into their house, had overcome their prejudices for the sake of her happiness. They had faced their landlord and source of income in defense of the man she loved.

A grateful tear slid down Rose's face. There were still things to discuss; she had much to learn of his family. But all was not lost.

"Are you the Englishman who lives by the DeClouet place?"

Still holding Rose's hands, Coleman cringed at the commandant's question. "Yes," he said soberly. "I am the Englishman."

"I have a letter for you," the commandant said. "It came this afternoon. The man delivering it said it was urgent."

Coleman stood, taking Rose with him. They both stared down at the elegant script gracing the envelope the commandant handed him.

"Is it your Georgia family?" Rose asked.

Coleman turned the letter over and flinched. "It's from my father's solicitor."

Rose didn't know what a solicitor was, but Coleman's tone held a trace of anxiety. When he ripped open the wax seal and removed the letter, small papers fluttered to the floor. Rose reached down and retrieved what turned out to be money, more money than she had seen in her lifetime.

"What is it?" Jean asked in a similar voice.

Something was wrong, she could feel it.

Coleman's eyes grew dark and he fell into the chair opposite hers, the letter dangling in his hand. Now it was Rose's turn to kneel before him, threading her fingers through his free hand and placing the money by his side. She tried to read the letter, but its English words flowed together into an incomprehensible blur.

"It's ironic," Coleman said softly.

"What is, my love?"

"That I would get this letter tonight of all nights."

Jean reached down and retrieved the letter from his hands. He stood silently by the firelight absorbing its details.

"What is it?" Lorenz asked.

Jean turned back toward the group with a sad expression.

Rose's heart faltered. "Is it my father?" she asked, dreading the words that were to follow.

"No," Coleman whispered. "It's mine."

Rose gripped his hand, waiting for an explanation, but none came. Coleman appeared too shocked to answer.

"His father is ill," Jean answered for him. "His solicitor has asked him to come to New Orleans directly. There isn't much time."

Finally coming to life, Coleman turned toward his friend. "May I leave with you?"

Jean folded the letter and returned it to Coleman.

"We will leave immediately, my friend. My boat is filled with provisions, so there is no need to return to your cabin."

Coleman nodded and rose, placing his hat on his head. "Have your family stay at my place," he told Lorenz, handing him several bills from the money that was sent. "This will help you acquire transportation to the Attakapas, should you wish to leave, and food."

"And forsake the crops we just planted?" Lorenz handed him back the money. "You'll need this more than we will. We will take care of your farm and wait for your return."

Coleman folded the bills and shoved them into Lorenz's front vest pocket. "I am well taken care of. But thank you for seeing to my farm."

It had all happened so fast Rose thought she might scream from frustration. Coleman leaving? Now?

"I'm coming with you," she demanded.

Gently placing a hand on her face and brushing his thumb against the rise of her cheek, Coleman shook his head. "It's impossible, *mon amour.*"

"No," she insisted. "I'm coming with you."

"Rose, I appreciate your concern but we can't travel together," Coleman said. "We aren't married."

Nothing he could say would deter her. He wasn't leaving without her. "I don't care. I want to go with you."

"He's right, Rose," Jean added. "We will be traveling for days. It's not proper for a young lady to be seen with two bachelor gentlemen."

She continued to shake her head. There would be

no discussion on the matter. She was going and that was that. But Coleman would not budge.

"I will not tarnish your reputation for my comfort," he said firmly. "We will marry when I return."

It made sense, but Rose didn't wish to be rational. Something in the back of her mind refused to let him leave the room without her. She had to accompany him. Was there no one who agreed?

"She's right," she heard Lorenz say. "She must go with you."

Rose turned toward her brother-in-law, who answered with a slight smile, but Coleman had yet to be convinced. "You shouldn't be alone right now," Lorenz continued. "If you are to become an orphan, you need family around you."

Sadness filled Lorenz's eyes. He had stood in Coleman's shoes once. He had watched his mother die in his arms and then buried his father at sea. In his darkest hour of grief, Emilie had been there for him, reminding him that his family, although not related by blood, still existed.

Coleman seemed to understand his meaning, but he shook his head. "We're not married. I will not subject Rose to scandal."

"I can marry you."

Rose had forgotten the commandant stood in the same room. After acknowledging his presence, she turned to Lorenz for approval. Lorenz smiled grimly.

"Your mother will kill me," he said. "But you must go."

Turning toward Courtableau, he added, "I am her

guardian in absence of her mother. I will serve as witness."

"As will I," Jean said proudly.

Surprisingly, Coleman was the last person to convince. "If anything happens to you . . ."

"Something has already happened to me," Rose answered. "You have. I will not let you face this alone."

His eyes studied her for several moments before he nodded, but it was clear he had misgivings. Rose prayed it was a result of his overprotective nature and not a reluctance to introduce his French wife to his aristocratic family.

She shook off the premonition when the commandant stood them before the hearth and read their vows. After repeating the pledges, the couple signed a formal paper and Jean and Lorenz witnessed it.

Madame Courtableau offered a round of drinks to celebrate the occasion, but there was no time. Before the ink had dried on the paper, Coleman and Rose Thorpe were on their way to New Orleans.

A heavy mist hung over the Mississippi as the ship glided to the empty pier. The trip down the bayou to Plaquemine, then downriver to New Orleans had taken less than half the time of the trip to Opelousas, but the days of traveling nonstop had left Rose bone weary and lethargic. She longed for a hot bath and a real bed, one made of cloth that didn't roll with each passing wave. What she would give for clean clothes, at the very least a freshly laundered chemise.

"There's a coach on the levee," Jean said as the vessel landed at the dock, jolting Rose awake. "Shall I signal it?"

"By all means," Coleman answered.

Wrapping his arms about Rose, Coleman pulled her close. "Are you still with us, my dear?"

"*Oui*, my husband," Rose said. "Where would I have gone?"

Jean laughed as he threw a line to a man on the pier. "Rose, I must admit you have been one of the finest passengers I have ever transported. Definitely the most agreeable woman."

"You have yet to travel with my sister," Rose reminded him, hoping he would get the hint.

Jean's eyes twinkled in the moonlight as he offered her his hand. "Point taken," he said as she stepped onto the pier. "But until then you hold the title of queen of my humble vessel."

He kissed her hand gallantly, then handed her to a coachman who helped her into his buggy. While Rose settled into the seat, Coleman and Jean made their good-byes.

Through the darkness of the predawn morning, Rose made out Coleman's form as he walked to the rig. Sighing heavily, he took his seat across from her. Rose knew her husband was twice as exhausted; he had refused to sleep for days.

"A few more minutes, my love, and a warm bed awaits us."

And what else? Rose wondered as the buggy rolled through the humid fog of the sleeping city. What would his family's reaction be when they learned of

Coleman's marriage to a poor exiled Acadian? In addition to the many objections they might raise, how would they even communicate?

The rhythm of the carriage wheels nearly lolled Rose to sleep. Through the darkness and the fatigue, she could barely make out the passing houses surrounded by smaller structures and rectangular gardens. Somewhere she smelled oranges, then a stable. In the distance, a dog howled.

"Rose?" she heard Coleman whisper. "We're here."

As they got out of the buggy, Rose looked up to find an enormous two-story house before her, its steep shingled roof reaching upward to kiss the overcast sky. She wiped the fatigue from her eyes, wondering if she was dreaming. When an elderly African woman opened the door and welcomed them inside, Rose knew it wasn't a dream.

The woman appeared glad to see Coleman, almost aching to hug him, but she kept the distance required of a servant. Coleman explained their situation and Rose heard her name mentioned. When the woman looked her way, her face erupted into a smile that lacked two front teeth.

Rose attempted a greeting, then thought a curtsy might be more appropriate, but her exhaustion held both her tongue and her actions.

"I must go up to Father," Coleman said to her.

"Of course," Rose agreed. "Do not worry about me."

"This is Cecilia," Coleman said, and the elderly woman bowed. This time, Rose found her manners

and returned the curtsey, which left the woman puzzled. Rose feared she had made an error in etiquette.

"Cecilia will get you something to eat, some clothes
to wear, and put you to bed," Coleman continued.
"I will join you shortly."

Despite his words to the contrary, Coleman
remained at her side, his arm wrapped protectively
around her waist. He had been like that since leaving
Opelousas, always worried about her welfare, never
leaving her side.

"I told you before I am not as fragile as I appear,"
Rose said, forcing a smile, even though she feared
she would faint on the spot.

Coleman reluctantly relinquished his hold, but his
eyes had difficulty leaving hers. "Go," Rose said,
touching his face.

As if to put him at ease, Cecilia pulled him away.
Rose imagined her long stream of lilting English was
to assure him she would take good care of his wife.
Coleman turned to the gallery staircase, then
bounded for the main floor, two stairs at a time.

Cecilia took one look at Rose and grabbed her
elbow seconds before Rose began to fall backward.
Then she placed a stabilizing hand at her back that
made Rose realize Cecilia was twice as strong as she
appeared.

"I guess both of our appearances are deceptive,"
Rose said. Surprisingly, Cecilia understood, answer-
ing with a toothless grin.

"Can't speak that language, but I understand it
some."

Her lack of French didn't stop the woman from

talking. She rattled on in English while leading Rose through the damp gallery up the stairs to the main floor.

The main house differed entirely from the dank bottom floor that met the street. Surrounded by paintings, elegant rugs, and fine furnishings, Rose felt as overwhelmed as the first day she had entered André's house. But Coleman's home had a more sophisticated air, as if an educated man lived here, one who did not spend his wealth to impress others. Still, she was impressed.

Cecilia led her through a library filled with leather-bound books, then to a room with a decidedly feminine feel—a "sitting room" she thought Cecilia said. In its center stood an enormous four-poster bed made up with crisp linens and topped by a mahogany canopy graced with a lovely carved pineapple. Rose had never seen anything so magnificent. What woman would want to "sit" on such an enticing bed?

A young African girl appeared, rubbing her eyes from fatigue. Cecilia shouted instructions to this "Poulette" and the young girl rushed out the door. It was clear who ran the household.

Rose felt faint again, so she reached behind her for the bed. Her fingers touched the soft cotton sheets, but the top of the bed hit her above the waist. How would she get into this enormous bed? she wondered. And how would she find the strength to remove her clothes? If only someone would place her head on those pillows, she would worry about disrobing later.

Again, Cecilia read her mind, hurriedly removing

Rose's clothes down to her chemise. The young girl entered with a cloth hung over her arm and a tray in her hands. Before Rose had time to object, Cecilia pulled her chemise over her head and replaced it with a silky clean undergarment that felt like heaven itself.

This is it, Rose thought, *sleep at last.* Cecilia helped her onto the high bed. Her feet dangled before her like a child. But when she tried to crawl beneath the sheets, Cecilia stopped her.

"Eat," the older woman demanded.

Rose hadn't the strength. "Please," she whispered in English. "Sleep."

Cecilia placed a maternal hand at her back and placed a small bowl at her lips. The lukewarm broth smelled delicious so Rose allowed herself a drink. Within seconds, the bowl was empty and Rose's belly was warm and satisfied.

"Now you sleep," she heard Cecilia say as she helped her into bed.

As soon as her head hit the pillow, Rose was fast asleep.

Coleman stared at the sleeping form of his father, a man who had aged a century since he had left Natchez. His hair had turned completely gray and brittle, and the lines surrounding his eyes and lips were more pronounced. He appeared a third his original size in the soft candlelight, his skin pulled taut over his emaciated body, his face sunken and dark.

Coleman placed a hand on Richard Thorpe's forehead to gauge a temperature, sighing with relief that his father's skin was cool. Falling into a nearby chair, Coleman watched the ragged breathing of the man he had vowed to despise until death. He remained angry, but now that his father's death was imminent, Coleman felt the battle lines fading.

"You look terrible."

Coleman glanced up to find his father studying him carefully. Despite his condition, the man's temperament hadn't changed a bit.

"Good to see you too, Father."

"Is this your new life?" Richard continued, pointing a feeble finger toward his clothes. "Is this the occupation that was to bring you prosperity and happiness?"

Coleman stood, ready to bolt. Even though he knew he could not stay away from his father's deathbed, for a moment he wondered why he had bothered to come. "I came as soon as I heard. Forgive me for not changing into formal attire. Is the King expected?"

Richard lifted his head and began to retort when a coughing fit overtook him. Coleman reached behind his father and helped him expel the irritant. To his horror, blood appeared on the handkerchief.

"What did the doctor say?"

Richard fell back against his pillows and sighed. "That I'm finished with this world."

Turning toward Coleman, his eyes glinted with awareness. "Is that why you've come? To pick up my pieces and obtain your inheritance? I told you I would leave you nothing, did you not believe me?"

Coleman shut his eyes to hold back his anger. It

took everything in his power not to walk out of that room and away from his family forever. But he owed it to his father, owed it to everyone in the household. "You forget, Father," he said firmly. "I'm not like you."

He had had enough for one meeting. If the fatigue of several days' journey had not exhausted his energy, this confrontation surely did. Coleman grabbed his hat and headed for the door, ready to signal the nurse to return to her duties.

"Coleman," his father whispered.

Pausing at the end of the bed, Coleman rubbed the bridge of his nose to ease a headache coming on. What was he doing? He knew there would be words between them, knew their anger would not be set aside simply because his father was ill. But he couldn't leave him. His father needed him, no matter how much he denied it. Coleman was the closest living relative for miles and his only offspring.

For days Rose had insisted he resolve the feelings between them. "Don't let your father pass without forgiving him," she had told him. "If you do, you will carry that pain with you for the rest of your life."

He wanted his precious Rose with him now; he ached for her comforting touch. She would know what to say, know how to handle such a demanding man, but he dreaded exposing his dear sweet wife to the verbal abuse Richard was sure to inflict. He even contemplated keeping the marriage secret.

"Come here," his father said, a note of urgency in his voice.

Coleman returned to his father's side, his hand

instinctively brushing the hair from the old man's ragged face.

"Are you well, my boy?" Richard asked softly.

"I'm fine, Pappy." Speaking his pet name for his father brought tears to his eyes. For an instant, he remembered the days of his youth, when his father was his best friend.

"You look good, despite those atrocious clothes."

Coleman offered a faint smile. "I'll change first thing tomorrow."

If he wasn't mistaken, his father's eyes had grown misty too. "Are you happy in this godforsaken Opelousas?"

Coleman thought of Rose and of the family who had welcomed him into their homes and hearts, despite his nationality. He remembered the disastrous hurricane and the months that followed when he had learned to farm. He recalled when he had found Rose at the stream and they had made love until dawn.

"I am, Pappy," Coleman answered. "I am married now."

Richard's eyes grew bright in the candlelight, and a ghost of a smile graced his lips. Then as if of their own accord, his eyelids slipped down and he fell into slumber. When Coleman pulled the sheet forward to cover his father's chest, he noticed tears at the corners of his eyes.

Even more surprising were the tears streaking Coleman's cheeks.

* * *

Almost an entire day passed before Rose awoke. Upon seeing Rose rise, Cecilia immediately brought forth a tray of food, which Rose wasted no time in consuming. A hot bath and freshly laundered clothes made Rose feel like a new woman.

Now that two days had passed and another morning was overtaking the city, Rose wondered where Coleman could be. Cecilia insisted he had visited her room while she slept, alternating between sitting with his father and checking on her. Rose worried he was not sleeping, worried he was carrying too much of the family's burden on his shoulders.

Or maybe it was something else.

Rose couldn't help thinking Coleman might be ashamed of introducing her to his father, might wish that his father pass without their meeting. She certainly understood his trepidation; Rose had been equally hesitant to mention to her mother that Coleman was their neighbor in Opelousas. But Rose was never ashamed of her love for him. And it hurt that he may feel otherwise toward her.

Rose sat on the settee in the library, staring at the rows and rows of books before her. Everything felt foreign, from the tapestries to the crystal chandelier. She felt as if she had entered a new world, one where she didn't belong. At any moment, she expected someone to enter the library and expel her from the room.

From across the hall Rose heard shouting, a man's voice berating a woman. The woman shouted back, a door opened, and a woman dressed as a nurse hurried through the library to the gallery stairs.

"He's impossible," she said to Rose in English before rushing down the stairs.

Rose stood and gazed out the library to the open door across the hall. Coleman's father lay dying in that room. With Coleman away on family business, the nurse gone, and Cecilia preparing breakfast in the kitchen across the courtyard, his father had been left alone.

"Is someone there?" the man asked in a husky voice that betrayed his fear.

Rose knew Coleman waited to properly introduce them, but this was an emergency. She took a deep breath and entered the room, ready to meet the man who might likely cast her to the streets.

Chapter Sixteen

Rose was astonished at Richard Thorpe's condition. Coleman had painted a picture of a robust commanding figure who took orders from no one, yet his father appeared as frail and weak as a child.

"Who are you?" he demanded.

Well, his voice still holds authority, Rose thought, noticing the man's attempt to appear stronger than he was.

"I'm Rose," she answered in English.

Richard tried to raise himself on his pillows to get a better look at her but failed. Rose quickly helped him sit up, placing an extra pillow at his back. "May I get you anything?" she asked, hoping her English words were correct and that he wouldn't comprehend who she was.

"You're French."

Nodding, Rose glanced around at the collection of medicine bottles and soiled handkerchiefs. "Would you like some tea?" Rose asked. "I make good a tea."

"I speak French," Richard answered in her native tongue. "There's no need to butcher my language."

Rose almost smiled at his brusque attempt at humor. For some reason she liked this man. *"Bon.* Then you will tell me what you need in a language I can understand."

Richard's eyes dimmed with an intense sadness and he looked away. "I need my life back," he said softly.

Feeling her heart sink, Rose gently pushed his shoulders back against the pillows to force him to relax. She placed the back of her hand at his forehead and found no temperature, then raised the sheet to cover a chest that rattled with each breath.

"Your son's here," she whispered. "At least you have a chance to resurrect your relationship."

"He hates me," Richard uttered.

"He doesn't hate you," Rose insisted. "He's angry. But every problem has a solution. Your differences can be resolved."

Richard looked at her as if finally realizing he was speaking to a live person. "Who are you?" he repeated.

She didn't know what to say. Now didn't seem the right time to introduce herself as his daughter-in-law. "My name is Rose," she answered. "I can make a tea that will help you breathe. Shall I brew one?"

Richard continued his intense scrutiny, but he nodded. For some reason, Rose imagined he liked her too.

After hunting down some peppermint and other herbs with Cecilia's help, Rose brewed a medicinal tea that spanned several generations of the Gallant family, no doubt learned from the Micmac Indians of her homeland. She brought the steaming liquid to Richard's bedside, but found him asleep. Very gently, she sat on the bed and placed a hand at his forehead.

"Why does everyone do that?" the old man bellowed. "I'm not dying of fever."

Again, his harsh tone did not scare Rose. She was usually startled by men of his temperament, but something in his soul reached out to her. She leaned over and poured a cup of tea, then slid a hand behind his neck and helped him sit up.

"I think it's because we're always worried about fevers and infections," she said, helping him sip the tea. "Or maybe it's because we know how comforting a hand feels on our forehead."

Richard sipped his tea obediently, but he frowned upon swallowing. "That's hideous."

"It is not," Rose countered. "I put honey in it to make it sweet."

Richard grunted but took another swallow. After several more sips, it was clear he was breathing easier. "Who are you? I could never be so fortunate as to have a nurse who's both smart and agreeable."

"I thank you, monsieur," Rose said, placing the empty cup on the tray. "I have a feeling compliments do not often pass those lips."

"I am not the horrible man my son says I am."

"Your son never spoke ill of you, monsieur," Rose said. "He has hardly spoken of you at all, which proves he doesn't hate you."

Richard rose on one hand, pulling himself up on his pillows. "Now how you do figure that one?"

"It's easy to speak of someone you dislike," she explained. "But difficult to speak of something that pains you. And if something pains you, it's only because you care."

His eyes shifted as he contemplated her words. Rose knew he wasn't convinced, but a light of hope glinted in his eyes.

"I have betrayed him," he said gravely. "I have caused him more pain than you know. He will never forgive me."

Without forethought, Rose took his hand. "I believe he won't forgive himself. And you are the only person who can help him erase that pain."

Richard stubbornly shook his head. "He won't listen to me," he said angrily. "He does everything I tell him not to. This Opelousas escapade at least has a chance of being prosperous, but to spend his mother's inheritance on a girl he would never see again!"

Rose dropped his hand as her heart sank. "What do you mean?"

"He met some French girl at the Spanish fort in Natchez," Richard explained. "She and her family wanted to go to St. Gabriel against the wishes of the Spanish government. So my son, in his infinite wisdom, pays for their passage with his slaves and money." He glanced at her briefly and smirked. "All this for a girl he could never communicate with, much less see again.''

As his words slowly sank in, Rose felt her world close in around her. She had always wondered why the Spanish had allowed them to join the other Acadians at St. Gabriel, why after weeks of protestations her family was given free reign in Louisiana and a boat at their disposal, while the other Acadians had to remain at Natchez.

It was Coleman who had made it all possible. That was why he disappeared immediately after they were told they could leave. He had paid for their passage, against his father's wishes, then left for Opelousas without hope of ever seeing her again. And was disinherited in the process.

As a tear made its way down her cheek, Rose thought of their long summer while Coleman waited patiently for Marianne to change her mind. At any time he could have told her he was the reason for their safe passage to St. Gabriel, but he never did. He chose to let Marianne judge him on his character and not on the power of his money. But he had gambled his happiness in the process.

Rose remembered her doubts of Coleman's sincerity regarding his family and felt ashamed. Besides her father, Coleman was the finest, most honorable man she knew.

She felt Richard's hand on hers. "What have I done?" he asked.

With her free hand, Rose wiped away the tears. "You have created a great man," she answered. "You should be proud."

"At this moment, I am not very proud of myself." He squeezed her hand so she would look at him. "You are that girl, are you not?"

Rose nodded. "We came to Louisiana in search of my father," she explained. "We heard he was at St. Gabriel, but we were forced to Natchez by order of the Spanish. After we were allowed"—Rose swallowed her emotions—"After Coleman made it possible for us to go to St. Gabriel, we learned our father had left the territory looking for us. So we traveled to Opelousas in search of his land grant, to wait for his return. Fate placed us as neighbors to your son."

"Your Acadian family allowed this courtship?" he asked incredulously.

Rose thought back on the many objections her family had raised. "It's been a long summer, monsieur. But yes, they finally agreed."

"Richard," he answered. "If I am your father now, you must call me Richard."

Father. How long had it been since she called a man by that name? Tears welled again in her eyes, then poured down her cheeks. "Why do you have to die?" she said, not thinking of what she was saying. "I have only begun to know you and I have so longed for a father."

Richard reached up and tucked a strand of hair behind her ear. His hands lingered as he gently stroked her hair. When their eyes met, Rose recognized the gentleness inherent to the Thorpe men. There was very little difference between the two men, after all.

"I'm afraid there is no hope for me," he whispered.

"But I will die peacefully knowing my son is happy in marriage."

Rose felt the tears returning, but she had to fight them this time. He had to realize what resolution meant to Coleman.

"Make peace with your son," she pleaded. "Please don't let him shoulder this grief alone."

Richard's eyelids grew heavy from a mixture of fatigue and sadness. His hands dropped to his side and he nodded before his eyes closed. When Rose left his bedside to return the tray to the kitchen, she heard a soft whisper.

"Don't leave me," Richard said, his hand reaching for hers.

Taking his hand once more, Rose leaned and kissed her father-in-law's forehead. "I will be right here."

In the course of two hours Coleman had met with the minister, hired a carriage and undertaker, and settled the family's account with the cemetery. Every minute had felt like a year. Now he was about to cross his father's threshold once again and relive memories best forgotten.

Coleman approached the bed, watching his father's labored breathing. He appeared to sleep more restfully, but he hadn't eaten in days. There wasn't much time. The doctor was surprised he had lived this long, more than likely waiting for Coleman's return.

Fatigue overwhelmed him and Coleman gripped the bed's frame for support. He wasn't ready to let his father go. So much conflict remained between them.

A soft hand snaked its way around his waist while a head of delicate brown tresses leaned against his shoulder. Coleman instantly pulled Rose into his arms and held her tight, breathing in her scent like a swimmer gasping for air.

"What are you doing in here?" he asked.

"Your nurse quit," she whispered.

Rose sensed something different between them and pulled back to examine him. Dressed in his finest clothes, including an imported silk coat that matched the embroidered waistcoat, Coleman knew he looked as foreign to her as he felt. The neck of his shirt was done up with a layered cravat at his neck that itched insufferably, and the three layers of clothes were soaked with perspiration. As much as he longed to rid himself of the suffocating garments, he had an image to uphold.

"He dresses up nicely, doesn't he?" his father asked her in French.

Rose seemed neither surprised at his father's comment—obviously they had already met—nor deterred from her original assessment of him in all his finery. He remembered Marianne's fears at the *bal de maison* that Rose wouldn't fit in with his family and friends. Was Rose thinking the same thing?

"He is a different man, *oui*," Rose answered softly.

Coleman began to refute that claim, but his father interrupted. "I don't know what you saw in him, filthy rags and all."

Coming to life, Rose strolled toward the head of

the bed and smiled as she placed a loving hand on his shoulder. "I saw the dear faces of your grandchildren."

Tears brimmed in his father's eyes as Coleman watched in amazement. So little was spoken, yet so much passed between the two of them. Coleman shouldn't have been surprised. Rose did that to people.

"How long were you going to wait to introduce us?" Richard asked him.

"To be honest, I didn't know how you'd react, and the doctor said not to upset you."

Richard grunted. "All that doctor cares about is his bill." Glancing up at Rose with awe, he added, "His medicines pale compared to that tea of yours."

"Shall I get you some more?" Rose asked.

The light shining in his father's eyes when he looked at Rose began to dim, and Coleman felt a shiver. Rose must have felt it too, for her back straightened and she bit her lower lip, the way she always did when faced with problems.

"I want you to do something for me, but not the tea," Richard said, his voice barely a whisper.

Rose leaned in close. "Anything."

"I want you to have Philip bring you by carriage to my tailor on St. Anne Street," Richard continued. "He will fit you with a proper mourning outfit and any other clothes you desire. Tell him you are my daughter. Tell him to charge my account."

Again, Rose's back straightened, but this time because of pride. "Are you ashamed of my clothes?"

Richard took her hands in his. "No, my dear, you

have mistaken me. There will be rich people attending my funeral. I don't want you to feel uncomfortable. I want my daughter to hold her head high with the rest of New Orleans society."

Now Coleman was hearing things; he was sure of it.

"Make sure this happens," Richard said to his son, making Coleman realize it wasn't a dream. "Write up a missive. Spare no expense."

Still half in shock, Coleman nodded.

"One more thing," Richard said hoarsely.

Rose leaned down so that her ear was next to his lips. "Grandchildren. Give me lots of grandchildren."

When Rose sat up, tears streamed from her eyes. "We shall name our firstborn son after you."

Richard fell back against his pillows, closing his eyes. Coleman placed his hands at the top of Rose's arms and lifted her from the bed. She turned and cried softly into his chest.

They left Richard's bedside, calling Cecilia to watch over him. When they reached the library, Coleman drew up a missive explaining his father's instructions, then led Rose down to the bottom floor and a waiting carriage.

"Give this to the tailor and he'll know what to do," Coleman told her. "He's a good man and he speaks French."

"But you'll need me," she protested.

Placing her safely on the seat, he kissed her hands, then closed the carriage door. "My father's right. People in society can be very cruel. He learned that from my mother's family. Go and choose anything you like. I must speak with my father now."

Through the open window Rose took his hand, her round eyes filled with sadness and love. "Any father who could raise a man as wonderful as you can't be all wrong," she said just before the carriage bolted into the street.

Coleman watched his wife disappear around the corner, as a knot of trepidation formed in his belly and began to grow. He quickly returned to his father's side, where Cecilia was lighting a candle and wiping tears from her face with the corner of her apron.

"He's not coughing no more, Mr. Coleman," Cecilia said between sobs. "That's not good. Mama always said the end was near when . . ."

"Thank you, Cecilia," Coleman said, trying to will away the image. "I'll sit with him now."

Coleman sat on the bed the way Rose had done, examining his father's face for signs of improvement. He knew there was no hope, but Coleman couldn't help watching for it anyway.

"Son," his father whispered. "We have to talk."

Talk was the last thing Coleman wanted to do. It was too final. "Why don't you try eating something?" he suggested. "I'll have Cecilia fetch some broth."

"There's no time, Coleman," Richard said. "There is something I have to tell you. It's about your mother."

Coleman rose and strode to the window, stretching out his arms on the windowsill and staring at the busy streets of New Orleans where people laughed, oblivious to the approaching death of one of its residents. He wanted to shut out the entire scene, forget the image of his emaciated father, go back to their quarrels because at least then the man had strength enough to be angry.

"I don't wish to speak of Mother," Coleman said, although he knew they must.

"I never wanted you to know this," his father continued. "I would rather have left the world with you being angry with me, but Rose said something that has haunted me, so I think you should know for your own sake."

Coleman fingered the iron mustache hinges on the window shutters. What could Rose have said that concerned his mother?

"She didn't love me," Richard began. "She had an unfortunate encounter with a married man in England and her family arranged our marriage to save her from scandal. Although I fell in love with her the moment I saw her at the Virginia docks, she never cared for me and always thought me beneath her. We had a nice life, though. You were born. Our plantation in Georgia was prosperous. I couldn't have asked for anything more."

Two women in evening gowns passed beneath their window. In the distance Coleman heard music playing. But all he could see were the happier days of his youth when his father taught him to play the violin and took him hunting. They had been inseparable, chasing the countryside for wild turkeys and deer.

While his mother had been indifferent.

Coleman shut his eyes. He didn't want to remember his mother's cold detached manner. There had been some happy times between the three of them, times when they played music together or read the classics. But she was never content with a farmer's life, always visiting the wealthy neighbors for tea and parties, while Coleman and his father remained at home.

Which made her death hurt that much more. He felt guilty enough for her passing. Remembering her in such a light raked him with more guilt.

"I really don't wish to speak of Mother," Coleman said bitterly.

"She had an affair."

His father's words hung in the humid air like death itself. And they struck at Coleman's heart.

"What did you say?" he asked, turning to look upon his father's face.

"That's why I took the job in Louisiana," Richard continued. "Even though she had visited my bedroom after years of not being intimate, I suspected another man. She denied it and I wanted to believe her, but I thought the safest thing to do was to remove her from the temptation."

Coleman felt his skin burn. His mother had despised the frontier worse than Georgia. "So you brought her to Natchez? To the frontier where a woman of her station would be miserable?"

Richard winced with pain and Coleman immediately regretted his outburst. The doctor had warned him not to get his father agitated. Coleman poured Richard a glass of water, sat at the edge of the bed and placed the glass at his lips. But his father pushed it away.

"It's too late," he said angrily. "You must understand."

"I understand," Coleman said, but he doubted his words. Why did he need to know of his mother's infidelity? What difference did it make now?

"You *don't* understand," Richard insisted. "I never would have left her that night had I known the truth."

The knot tightened in his belly. He hated asking, but he had to know. "What truth?" Coleman asked.

"I didn't know it was your mother's time," Richard said, tears beginning at the corners of his eyes. "She said it would be at least another month. She was covering for him, you see. She wanted me to believe the child was mine."

Coleman shut his eyes, trying not to remember that night when his hands were stained with his brother's blood. The blood of a child born at full-term.

"You know I'm right," his father whispered, his breath more labored with each word.

Coleman nodded, pain gripping his heart.

"I never meant for this to happen," his father said, his voice breaking. "I never would have left that night. I adored her, despite what she did."

Silence followed and Coleman swore he could hear the beating of his heart. Then his father uttered the words that were his undoing. "I never meant for you to shoulder this alone."

Wincing from his own pain, Coleman fought back the tears. "I couldn't save them," he said, reliving the torment of watching his mother and brother die. "I tried, but I couldn't save them."

Richard placed a feeble hand on his and Coleman

let his head fall against his father's chest. His father attempted to soothe him by placing a hand on his head, but his strength was failing. "You did your best."

"But I have wronged you," Coleman continued. "I have been a failure to you."

Richard's gasped with each breath, making it difficult to speak. "I'm proud of you, boy," he said softly, then his hand dropped to his side.

Before his chest fell for the last time, Richard offered one last sentence. "Take care of Rose. Be happy."

Chapter Seventeen

Philip opened the carriage door wide and held out his hand. Rose studied the carriage steps leading to the ground and wondered how she would balance herself while raising her long skirts high enough to avoid tripping.

"Take my hand," Philip whispered. "Raise your skirt with your other hand, putting that foot first."

Rose did as she was instructed and found herself safely on the courtyard's bricks. Feeling triumphant, she looked up to find the gallery stairs looming before her.

"Life is so much simpler with short skirts," she said to Philip, who waited for her to pass.

"Yes, madame," he answered.

As she climbed the steps, heedful of the black silk

gracing her ankles, Rose remembered the tailor's exclamations at her homespun skirt that fell at her lower calf. *Proper women don't show their ankles,* he had said. *Bosoms can be revealed, but never the lower leg.*

"Such nonsense," Rose muttered as she gingerly climbed to the main floor. "A woman could die of cold or fall on her head."

When she reached the top floor, Coleman stood at the other end of the gallery, bloodshot eyes staring off into the distance. He must have noticed the carriage's arrival, Rose thought. Why had he not come down to her? Why did he not acknowledge her presence now? For an instant Rose feared she looked as ridiculous in the massive yards of fabric as she felt. And Coleman was afraid to tell her so.

"Coleman?" she called out.

From the side of the staircase, in an enclosed part of the gallery where Cecilia lived, she heard muffled crying. Suddenly, Rose understood. She quickly closed the distance between them, lifting herself on her toes and throwing her arms around her husband's shoulders.

"Oh, Coleman."

Coleman came to life, hugging her so tight she could scarcely breathe.

"I am so glad you're here," he whispered.

Holding the sleeves of his coat, Rose pulled back to examine him. Dark circles stained his face beneath eyes that held no brightness. Gone were the sparkling blue eyes that glistened with affection every time they were together. Gone was the hopeful countenance that had carried him through a disappointing summer.

Rose ran her fingers through his blond curls, and Coleman dropped his head against her forehead while his body sagged with fatigue.

"You must get to bed," she told him. "I will see to it now."

Coleman straightened and shook his head. "I have to choose his suit, have to tell the minister. I must get Philip to contact the undertaker."

He was much heavier than she and a few inches taller, but Rose was determined. She tugged on his coat, pulling him toward her bedroom.

"I will take care of all that," she said. "You are going to bed."

Coleman moved a few steps, then halted. "But I must . . ."

"You forget, my dear," Rose reminded him, pulling him forward once again, "New Orleans is a French city. Who better to deal with these things than a French woman?"

Days of refusing sleep coupled with the pain of his father's death left Coleman dazed, so he followed her blindly. Rose led him to her bed, then removed his clothes and tucked him beneath her beloved cotton sheets. Even with his head against a pillow, he still could not welcome sleep. He stared at the canopy above him, his eyes hollow with shock.

Rose climbed onto the bed and placed his head on her half-exposed bosom. She kissed his forehead, caressed his hair, then gently pushed his eyelids shut with the tips of her fingers. She kissed his closed eyelids and sang "A La Claire Fontaine," his favorite Acadian ballad.

Many minutes passed before Rose felt the rhythmic cadence of his breathing. When she was certain he was fast asleep, she kissed him once more, left his bedside, and returned to the gallery where Cecilia waited, expecting orders from the mistress of the house.

Still feeling like an impostor and aching from the news that her new father and friend had passed away, Rose gathered up her courage. She remembered Richard's words about his daughter holding her head high among New Orleans society. She could do this. She *would* do this.

"Tell Philip to fetch the undertaker," Rose instructed. "After he has brought the man to the house, tell him to relay word to the minister that Monsieur Thorpe has left this world."

With her last words, Cecilia burst into tears. It was everything Rose could do not to join her. But she had work to do.

"Go," she told Cecilia, knowing that if they both kept busy they would survive the night. "Tell the kitchen staff to prepare for the funeral. We will have lots of people here tomorrow. We must be ready to feed them. I will put the house in order."

Cecilia curtsied, then descended the stairs still clutching her apron to her eyes.

As Rose watched the city settle into twilight from the back gallery, she felt a presence surround her, as if comforting arms circled her shoulders. She should have felt grief and sadness at his passing, but for some unexplainable reason her soul felt strengthened and confident.

Life continued despite death. She knew that now. Generations spanned the years, despite the tragedies.

Richard Thorpe was still alive in many ways, Rose thought, as she placed a loving hand on her belly. Her growing child was evidence of that fact.

By nightfall of the next day, Richard Thorpe was laid to rest and the house was filled with well-wishers and grieving friends. Rose knew Coleman took comfort in the number of mourners, both English and French, who came to pay their respects. Perhaps he had realized that his father was not the aggressive, career-minded soldier he had imagined him to be. Or maybe in those last hours, father and son had finally made peace.

Coleman refused to speak of his father; he barely spoke at all. He never strayed from Rose's side, wrapping a protective arm about her waist when speaking to his English friends, proudly introducing her to everyone.

Richard had been right, though. There were many raised eyebrows from the society ladies of New Orleans. Rose and Coleman had bridged a nationality chasm, and a social one as well. She didn't mind the innuendoes and patronizing glances. She held her head high, the way her father-in-law had instructed her.

By the end of the evening, Coleman's fatigue was evident. Rose was equally tired of the constant stress of organizing such a massive household and of the effort needed to translate the English words in her mind. When Coleman was called away by the family solicitor, Rose took the opportunity to steal into the courtyard and find a quiet spot to rest.

Her stays, two stiff pieces of fabric sewn over whalebone and wrapped around her middle, provided a nice smooth shape to the gown, but the tightness hurt her tender breasts. What she wouldn't give to rid herself of the entire gown with its endless cascades of material and crawl into that heavenly bed.

"Caught you."

Rose looked up to find Jean dressed in an elegant black coat and waistcoat, his hat in his hands. The sight of someone familiar, someone connected to family brought tears to her eyes. She jumped up and hugged the man who was twice her size.

"Oh, Jean," she said. "You are a sight to behold."

Jean held her close, patting her back the way Lorenz always did. For a moment, she feared the sobs collecting in her chest would erupt and unravel her.

"Are you holding up well, *'ti monde?*" Jean asked, raising her chin to get a better look at her.

Rose could only answer with a nod. Sensing her precarious emotional state, Jean led her back to her bench, joining her with his long legs stretched before him.

"Has anyone caused you insult?" he asked, his voice becoming stern. "If there is a person present who has caused you harm, I promise I will . . ."

Rose shook her head. "It's not that."

"Then what is it, besides the usual heartache of death? I fear something else is troubling you."

Attempting a smile, Rose thought of all the things that had happened over the past two weeks: André and his accusations at the *bal de maison,* the tiring trip downriver, meeting her father-in-law only to lose him the same day. But nothing compared to what the solicitor had informed Coleman that morning.

"Monsieur Thorpe," Rose said, then swallowed, "has left Coleman everything."

Jean brightened as she knew he would. "That's good news. Are you not pleased?"

Rose stood and paced the small area surrounding the garden bench. "His estate is this house, the plantation in Natchez."

Placing an elbow over the back of the bench, Jean seemed to understand her meaning. "You're worried Coleman will want to live in Natchez or New Orleans."

Rose stopped pacing and met his eyes. "Won't he?"

"I can't answer for him, Rose. He did say he never wanted to see Natchez again."

Rose sat down next to him and grabbed his sleeve. "But that was because of his anger toward his father. Certainly, he won't want to pass up a plantation as prosperous as this one."

Jean's eyebrows tightened. "Do *you* wish to live in Natchez?"

The anxiety that had threatened to consume her

all afternoon returned. How could she live without her family? Words refused to come and she could only shake her head.

Footsteps sounded on the slate tiles; the large stones had been used as ballast in the ships arriving from Europe. Coleman appeared, as glad to see Jean as Rose was. The two men shook hands, Jean covering their joined hands with another.

"It is good to see you, my friend," Coleman said.

"And you. My condolences."

Coleman nodded his head, then reached a hand toward Rose. She took it and he pulled her to his side, wrapping an arm about her shoulder. He hadn't lingered at her side all day simply to ease her discomfort, she realized. He needed her as much as she needed him.

"I can't stay," Jean said. "Forgive me, but I have some urgent business to tend to."

"You will be returning to the West, will you not?" Coleman inquired.

Jean gazed down at his hat. "No. I am close to retrieving my ship. If I am able to win her back from the Spanish, I must go to the Caribbean."

When Jean looked up, Rose knew a conflict raged within him. "I have left something in the foyer," he added. "Will you see to it that Gabrielle gets it?"

"Of course," Coleman said, holding out his hand once more.

As Jean took it, a mischievous glint appeared in his eyes. "If you need passage back to Opelousas, I can arrange it."

Rose held her breath, wondering how Coleman would respond. "Thank you" was all he said.

The couple saw Jean to the door, relieved to find the visitors gone. They walked up the gallery stairs to the library, enjoying a glass of port and the fresh cheese that Cecilia had left for them. Coleman approached the bookcases and ran his fingers appreciatively over several titles. Rose's heart constricted.

"Do you miss your books?" she asked.

"Yes, I do," Coleman replied.

When he turned and found her hands bunching the material of her skirt, his cerulean eyes grew large with worry. "What is it, my love? Are you worried I will miss my books?"

Rose swallowed, wondering how she would ask him. If he wished to stay, she wouldn't dream of separating him from the things he desired. But her spirit fell at the thought of it.

Coleman removed her hands from the knots in her dress and pulled her to his chest. There was so much material between them. Rose longed for the simpler days when they could watch the sun set from the back gallery of his farm, bare feet dangling off the side. Or make passionate love next to a slow-moving stream.

"I was planning on bringing them home with us," Coleman said, kissing the line of her cheekbone.

"Home?" Rose said, her voice shaking. "Which home?"

Coleman sighed and rested her head against his chest. "I know your worries," he said softly. "We have spent the entire summer wondering if we would marry and never thought about where we would live."

In all her contemplations of their future, she never once imagined they would live in English Natchez or the congested streets of New Orleans.

"I have spoken to my solicitor," Coleman continued. "I believe we can acquire a nice land grant in Attakapas. It may not be next to your father's, but it will be close enough."

Rose pulled back abruptly. "In Attakapas?"

Sliding a hand through the hair above her ear and caressing her cheek, Coleman leaned forward for a kiss. It seemed ages since they had shared affection, and his lips, so hot and longing, were evident of that celibacy. Rose wanted to lose herself in that kiss, but there were so many questions.

"But what about—"

"Opelousas?" Coleman managed a slight smile. "I must say I'm rather attached to that pitiful little farm, perhaps because I own such wonderful memories there. I would hate selling it, although I'm not sure what we will do with it."

Rose shook her head. "I meant your father's plantation in Natchez."

"My uncle wants it and he's more than welcome to it." His eyes studied her and he frowned. "Do *you* wish to live there?"

Rose almost laughed with relief. "No," she said grinning. "I thought you did."

Pulling her back into his embrace, Coleman sighed. "You're my family now, Rose. I want nothing more than to be with you and make you happy."

Rose closed her eyes and relished the feel of her husband's silky broad shoulder against her cheek.

They had yet to be married by a priest, yet to be given a proper ceremony. And by the time spring arrived, their family would increase by one. Life held such wonderful possibilities.

"I have given my solicitor free use of this house in exchange for his services," Coleman said, still holding her close. "It will be here for us should we need it. He has been instructed to regularly check the arriving ships, the hospitals, and government officials for signs of your father. I want to know the minute he crosses into the Louisiana Territory."

A tear slipped from her eyes, caused by shame for doubting her husband mixed with gratitude for having met such a remarkable man.

"I love you so much," she whispered.

His hand caressed her cheek once more and Rose sensed his sadness returning.

"You're my family now," he repeated.

Rose thought of the young life they had created with their communion by the stream. When they returned to Opelousas, she would tell him the news. To reveal her state now would only make him worry, and Coleman had had enough emotional hardships inflicted on him for one week.

"We are a family, my love," she said. "In more ways than one."

Thunder pealed and lightning lit up the sky as the rain fell in torrents upon them. The sheets of rain were so thick they couldn't make out the road. Rose pulled her bonnet down to shield herself from the harsh rain and leaned into Coleman's shoulder.

For the second time violent weather welcomed them to Opelousas. And they were so close. André's house had just come into view as the sky released its fury.

Coleman halted the horses. They had begun to rear at the noise. There was nothing to do but wait.

A figure appeared at their wagon, a large man in an oversized hat. He threw Coleman a blanket, then headed for the horses.

"Get to the house," he shouted. "I'll see to the horses."

Coleman covered Rose with the blanket and they ran toward André's house. When they reached the front gallery, they were too far from the road to make out the stranger in the rain.

"Who do you think that was?" Rose asked.

The door opened and Esther appeared. "Madame Rose, Monsieur Coleman," she exclaimed, happy to see them. "Come in out of that rain."

They followed Esther into the foyer, the same hall-way Rose had entered on her first day at the Opelousas Poste. The house had been stripped of its contents with only a few pieces of furniture scattered about.

"What has happened here?" Rose asked.

Esther shook her head solemnly. "Monsieur André is not doing so good. He shipped his things to Pointe Coupée, where his mother and sister are staying with relatives. Rumor has it he is to sell most of every-thing."

Even though she had plenty of reasons for despising André, Rose couldn't help but feel sorry for the man. She didn't wish misfortune on anyone.

"What about the plantation?" Coleman inquired.

"We still here," Esther said. "Monsieur André said he would take care of us, no matter what."

The front door flew open and André walked in, his bold figure soaked from his felt hat to his leather shoes. "The horses are in my barn," he told Coleman. "May I get you a brandy?"

Rose and Coleman exchanged glances, shocked at his congeniality.

"Please," André said, as if he sensed their discomfort. "Join me in the parlor."

They followed him into the room that had once housed magnificent furnishings, but now only contained two chairs and a few niceties. Rose recalled how her family had stared at such finery when they first visited his grand house.

André poured them each a glass of brandy, but his eyes regarded Rose. "The rain won't last long, but if you wish to change into dry clothes, I can try to find something of my sister's."

"I'd like that," Rose said, feeling a sudden chill. *"Merci."*

"Esther," André called out and the woman instantly appeared. "Show Rose to Darcie's quarters and give her anything she needs."

Esther bowed and led Rose from the room. Before she turned the corner, she glanced back at Coleman who looked as confused as she.

"More?" André asked, holding up the brandy bottle.

Watching his nemesis offering him brandy sent Coleman's defenses into action. Was there an ulterior motive behind André's sudden politeness? When Coleman studied the man's eyes, he noticed a sadness that went beyond financial ruin. He wondered if his change of heart might be the result of something else, something personal.

"Your family is at my overseer's house," André explained. "I believe Emilie and Lorenz have been living at your place, working your farm."

"Thank you for that," Coleman answered.

André shrugged and placed a foot on the ironwork of the fireplace. "I owed it to them," he said. "Believe it or not, I do stand by my word, even if I have nothing to pay them."

Feeling more at ease, Coleman leaned back in his chair. "It's not necessary. I have come into money."

André frowned, as if remembering something important. "I'm sorry to hear about your father. I lost my father a few years ago. It leaves an enormous hole."

The pain of the funeral returned and Coleman found it ironically comforting to have André share his anguish. They were definitely not made of the same cloth, but perhaps their differences weren't that vast.

"What about you?" Coleman asked. "What are your plans?"

André poured another drink, reminding Coleman of the days when all had seemed lost and he had regularly drowned himself on bottles of rum. "I suppose I must endure Pointe Coupée society and find a wife."

"It's not as bad as it seems," Coleman said with a grin.

"Well, not all of us are as fortunate as you."

Ever since André had welcomed them into his home, Coleman had the distinct feeling it was Rose who had caused such a transformation. Now Coleman knew it to be true. He shouldn't have been surprised; Rose could melt the heart of the most savage beast. But it still amazed him that André DeClouet had fallen in love with his wife.

"Is there anything I can do?" Coleman asked him. "May I lend you enough money to make it through the harvest?"

André studied him hard as if he had grown donkey ears. "After all I have done to you?" he asked. "I tried to ruin you, remember?"

Coleman kicked back the brandy and let the strong liquid warm his insides. "You said nothing that wasn't true," Coleman said. "Besides, I think I know why you did it."

The two men stared at each other, André hesitant to admit his feelings. Coleman decided to change the subject, for both their sakes.

"André, if I were French, you would accept, would you not?"

A smirk formed at the corner of his lips. "But you're not French, *L'Anglais.*"

Coleman laughed and poured himself another brandy. "I am now," he said. "In a few years I will be more Gallant than Thorpe."

Relaxing and enjoying the companionship, André smiled and slapped Coleman on the back. "I never would have believed it two months ago. You couldn't speak a word."

"Love will do that to you," Coleman said. "Love will make you do things you never thought you'd do."

André's smile disappeared and he stared into his brandy. For the first time in his life, Coleman felt pity for the man. Hadn't he stood in those very shoes weeks before? Only Coleman had the good fortune of having Rose's love in return.

"Take my offer," Coleman said.

Still, André hesitated.

"We're both gentlemen of means trying to survive the frontier. This will be a business arrangement between neighbors."

"What will you gain from this?" André asked, making Coleman realize the man was still the same arrogant businessman underneath.

"You will lend me your home for a day so that Rose and I can be properly married. If we travel on to Attakapas, you will look after my place for me. When you get back on your feet, pay me back."

"*If* you travel to Attakapas?"

Now it was Coleman's turn to frown. "I'm worried about Rose," he said softly. "She hasn't been herself lately. She's always wanting to sleep, and she eats very little. She's been sick several days on the trip here. She can't seem to keep her breakfast down.''

André leaned his head back and laughed. "You English are such idiots." He placed a friendly hand on Coleman's shoulder and leaned in close. "You're going to be a father," he whispered.

Chapter Eighteen

Coleman felt the blood leave his face at the same minute Rose arrived in the parlor, dressed in a light blue gown. She looked stunning, her wet hair set free about her shoulders, but the paleness that had plagued her usually rosy cheeks remained. Oh God, Coleman thought with horror, why hadn't he seen this? He should have forbidden her to travel.

"Esther," André called out. "Get Rose some biscuits or toast. And some milk. See if we have fresh milk handy."

Esther bowed and turned to leave.

"Wait," André called out, heading for the parlor doors. "I will get it myself." When he turned back toward the couple, he was smiling broadly. "I think you both should sit down. You are both on the verge of fainting.''

With those words, André was gone, closing the doors behind him. Rose sat on the chair opposite Coleman. ''What did he mean by that?''

In an instant, Coleman knelt at her side, staring into her eyes for confirmation. Rose answered with a questioning frown. When she bit her lower lip nervously, Coleman knew the truth.

''Why didn't you tell me about the child?'' he asked her.

Rose's eyes doubled in size. ''How did André know?''

''I mentioned your symptoms. Rose, why didn't you tell me? We never would have left New Orleans.''

Petite fingers grazed his cheeks lovingly. ''That's precisely why I didn't tell you.''

An intense fear threatened to cut off his air. Rose must have sensed it, for she cupped his face in her hands and kissed him.

''Don't worry, my love,'' she said. ''I told you before I am not as fragile as I seem.''

As hard as he tried, he couldn't dispel the dread gripping his chest. He couldn't forget the image of his mother's long journey through labor, then death.

''You are happy about this, are you not?'' Rose's sweet face exhibited almost as much trepidation as his, only of a different nature. Naturally, she only cared about the child.

''Of course I am,'' Coleman managed. ''I'm just concerned . . . ''

Rose silenced his lips once more. "I'll be fine," she said. "You must stop worrying about me so."

Coleman stood and paced the room. "That's impossible."

"We will be close to Maman," Rose offered. "Between the two of you, no harm could possibly come to me."

Pausing at the mantel, Coleman realized they had one more trip to take. He knew Rose would not approve of his next decision, but it wasn't an issue he would negotiate.

"We're staying here," Coleman said. "I'll see that your family is safely to the Attakapas Poste, but we will remain here."

However weak she might have felt that afternoon, Rose felt a sudden rush of blood to her cheeks. "Why?" she demanded. "If I made the trip upriver from New Orleans, I can surely survive a journey over land and bayou."

Coleman stubbornly shook his head. "I won't allow it. You are not to leave this place until you are feeling better."

This was absurd. Women survived childhood every day. Had Rose relinquished one overprotective family for another? She started to object further, when the parlor doors opened and André brought in a tray of toast and milk.

"There's someone here to see you," André said, then discreetly left the room.

Rose heard the familiar footsteps in the hall and knew immediately her mother was near. When Marianne entered the parlor, Rose threw herself into her mother's eager arms.

"Oh, Maman," Rose said, savoring the feel of her mother's embrace. "I have missed you so much."

Marianne drew back and studied Rose, her eyes brimming with tears of happiness. She hugged Rose once more, then held out her arms to Coleman.

"I am so sorry for your loss," Marianne said. "You may have lost a father, but you have gained a family. Always take comfort in that."

Coleman nodded, a pained expression still haunting his face as he glanced at Rose over her mother's shoulder.

Marianne stepped back and examined them both, still holding each of their hands. "What is wrong?" she asked, confirming Rose's suspicions that mothers knew everything. "Something is wrong between you. What is it?"

"Coleman wants us to remain at Opelousas," Rose began. "He wants the rest of the family to go on to Attakapas."

"She's not well," Coleman stated. "She's not up to traveling."

"I am fine," Rose insisted.

"It's too risky," Coleman countered. "I won't allow it."

While their bantering continued, Rose found Marianne's eyes boring into her. Rose knew she had to explain her predicament, but dreaded having her mother fuss over her as well. The brandy she consumed earlier burned in her nervous belly, and she felt her lunch threaten to rise. Rose grabbed the milk and gulped down a swallow.

"You're staying here," Marianne said flatly.

Before Rose could recover and object, Marianne held up a hand.

"Remember the day I gave you permission to marry? I said you must marry immediately, but I didn't say why?"

Rose briefly recalled such a comment, but what had it to do with their current situation?

"I had a vision," her mother continued. "I saw your father arriving in Louisiana. You were both there and married." Marianne's eyes grew misty and she took her daughter's hand. "I wanted you to be married quickly because I saw you big with child."

Relieved that her condition was out in the open, Rose sighed. "Then tell Coleman that babies are born every day and that I will be fine to travel."

Instead, Marianne shook her head. "You are staying here. Lorenz can bring Gabrielle and me south where we will wait on your father's land grant. Then Lorenz will return and the four of you will help bring in Coleman's harvest. That way Emilie will be here if you need a woman's touch. When you are well, you can travel again."

"But I *am* well," Rose insisted.

"You have been ill for days," Coleman interjected. "Most women are ill in the first few months."

A headache began at her temple and for a moment Rose wished to relent. She certainly wasn't up for another bumpy wagon ride or rolling voyage in a pirogue. If truth be told, she would be happiest sleeping most of the day on a soft, steady bed. But like so many times in her past, her family was deciding her fate.

"Darling," her mother said. "We love you and only want the best for you."

"But I'm not capable of knowing what's best, is that it?"

This time, Coleman took her hand. "No, my love. That is not it. You are so worried about the welfare of others that you cannot see your own needs. We are not trying to run your life. We are trying to save you from your own kindness."

The look Marianne sent Coleman was all the convincing Rose needed. Her mother placed a hand over her mouth while tears poured down her face. She had married the man her mother had always wished for, which proved she was capable of making some right decisions.

Or perhaps they were right, Rose thought as fatigue overtook her senses and the milk caused a bad taste in her mouth. Perhaps it was best to stay put for a while.

"I give up," Rose said. "But we will join you by Christmas."

"If you're up to it," both her mother and Coleman said.

Rose laughed, realizing that it was fruitless to escape the protective nature of the ones who loved her.

Marianne wiped the tears away and straightened. "Now let us speak of your wedding."

* * *

The ceremony was everything Rose had dreamed of and more. She wore a silk gown purchased in New Orleans, graced by an elegant kerchief around the neckline, and Coleman wore his finest waistcoat and coat. The entire poste turned out, including Commandant Courtableau, bringing food and presents while André offered up his finest wine and brandy. Henri and his portly wife arrived with a bottle of rum, pleased to see Coleman finally married, and Sostan and his family brought a cake shaped like a violin.

Even though he was the subject of the festivities, Coleman couldn't help himself. He performed several tunes on the violin for his guests, who all gratefully took turns around the parlor floor. By nightfall, Marianne slipped his violin from his fingers and ushered him toward the dance floor and his waiting bride. As Coleman took Rose into his arms, Marianne began a soft love song.

Staring into the blue eyes that had captured her heart months ago in a rustic Spanish fort on the Mississippi River, Rose couldn't believe how much had happened since then. Or how lucky she was. Coleman had helped her family get to St. Gabriel, had seen that her father was safely through Georgia. Now, his solicitor would find Joseph and send him home to the waiting arms of his family in Attakapas.

Coleman was the finest of men. And now he was her husband.

"What are you thinking?" Coleman asked her as they turned around the floor.

"That there is too much material between us again," she lied. "How will we ever rid ourselves of all these clothes?"

Sky blue eyes sparkled and he smiled coyly, sending delicious shivers through her. "My love, nothing will come between us tonight."

He pulled her close, allowing her to rest her cheek against the blond curls at his nape while Marianne sang of love everlasting. Rose thought of her father and how she wished he could witness her happiness. She closed her eyes and sent him a prayer.

"He's with us now," Coleman whispered, reading her mind. "They both are."

The song ended and the crowd cheered for the bride and groom. As a sense of bliss overtook Rose, Coleman reached down and met her lips, carrying them both to heaven.

Chapter Nineteen

The streets of New Orleans blurred from the fever, but Joseph knew he had finally arrived in the Louisiana Territory. His fever, contracted in Georgia, had returned full force, but he continued on, forcing one foot in front of the other as he made his way down Chartres Street.

He paused at the gate of the Ursuline Convent, an imposing structure fronted by a courtyard.

"May I help you?" a nun asked.

Through the haze Joseph recognized the dress of the Ursuline Order, but the face was indistinguishable, her voice echoing through his mind. He feared he would collapse on the spot.

"Help me," he managed.

The nun called out and two men approached, placing Joseph's arms about their shoulders. His feet gave way, and the men dragged Joseph into the building, then down a hall to a room full of people. He felt a bed beneath his back, but images flitted in and out of his mind like nighthawks chasing mosquitoes at twilight.

Where was he? He tried to remember. He recalled the English burning his village, the ships sailing into Minas Basin to cart them away. But he wasn't in Nova Scotia.

He remembered a land grant in a land of prairies, a giant river, and alligators the size of men. He remembered arriving in Maryland and beginning a long arduous journey that had spanned several colonies.

He slipped a tongue on his parched lips. Someone was placing a damp rag there to quench his thirst. If only they could quench his longing to be reunited with his family.

"Help me," he repeated.

A soft hand touched his forehead and he remembered his wife. She sat next to the bed, smiling, welcoming him home from a day in the orchards. Then she began to sing.

"Marianne?" he whispered, trying to sit up.

A strong hand pushed him back against the pillow. A masculine voice asked him his name. But all he comprehended was the lilting voice of his wife.

"There's not much hope," Joseph heard someone say. "He's not going to make it."

Thirteen years. It had been thirteen years since he held his true love in his arms, since his daughters had kissed him good night. After thirteen excruciating years, was it all coming to this?

Before darkness overtook him, Joseph managed to speak one final thought. "Oh yes, I will," he said, before all turned to black.

ABOUT THE AUTHOR

Cherie Claire never had problems dreaming up great characters for her Louisiana historical romances. A native of South Louisiana, she was saturated in the colorful culture and traditions of the Bayou State. A Web site journalist, Cherie makes her home in California with her husband and her two sons.

Cherie loves to hear from readers. Visit her Web site at www.geocities.com/BourbonStreet/Bayou/4745

Book Three
The Acadians: Gabrielle

Years have passed since the Gallant family was separated from their patriarch during the Acadian exile from Nova Scotia, but Gabrielle and her mother refuse to give up. They travel to the sleepy shores of Bayou Teche to wait for Joseph Gallant's return. Gabrielle also waits for a visit from Captain Jean Bouclaire, a Louisiana pirate who has stolen her heart.

Captain Jean Bouclaire has finally decided to settle down and he knows the right woman to ask. On his way to join Gabrielle, he is challenged to a duel that results in his exile from the Louisiana Territory. Now a fugitive, he must decide whether to flee the colony or risk his life for one last glimpse of his dark Acadian beauty.

Gabrielle will be available in April 2001.

COMING IN DECEMBER FROM
ZEBRA BALLAD ROMANCES

__A SISTER'S QUEST, Shadow of the Bastille #3
by Jo Ann Ferguson   0-8217-6788-7 $5.50US/$7.50CAN

When Michelle D'Orage agreed to be Count Alexei Vatutin's translator at the Congress of Vienna she was excited, but then she learned the handsome Russian's true reason for hiring her. Shaken and confused, she has little choice but to trust this mysterious stranger who holds the key to her past . . . and her dreams for the future.

__REILLY'S GOLD, Irish Blessing #2
by Elizabeth Keys   0-8217-6730-5 $5.50US/$7.50CAN

Young Irishman Devin Reilly had just arrived in America seeking riches to bolster the family business, but his fortune was about to change. After rescuing fiery Maggie Brownley he sees in her eyes that "Reilly's Blessing" will bind them together. Devin soon realizes that in Maggie's embrace he will find a love more precious than gold.

__THE FIRST TIME, The Mounties
by Kathryn Fox   0-8217-6731-3 $5.50US/$7.50CAN

Freshly graduated from medical school and eager to bury his sorrow over the tragedy in his past, Colin Fraser impulsively joins the Northwest Mounted Police. During a raid on a bootleg whiskey operation he finds Maggie, an ill bootlegger. Colin finds, while nursing the patient, the way to heal his own heart.

__HIS STOLEN BRIDE, Brothers in Arms #2
by Shelley Bradley   0-8217-6732-1 $5.50US/$7.50CAN

Wrongly accused of murdering his father, Drake Thornton MacDougall wants nothing more than to take revenge against his duplicitous half brother. So he strikes at the fiend the only way that he can . . . by abducting Averyl, his bride-to-be. In Averyl he finds the key to forgiving past wrongs and healing his tormented soul through pure love.

Call toll free **1-888-345-BOOK** to order by phone or use this coupon to order by mail. ALL BOOKS AVAILABLE DECEMBER 1, 2000.

Name _____

Address _____

City _____ State _____ Zip _____

Please send me the books I have checked above.

I am enclosing $ _____
Plus postage and handling* $ _____
Sales tax (in NY and TN) $ _____
Total amount enclosed $ _____

*Add $2.50 for the first book and $.50 for each additional book.

Send check or money order (no cash or CODS) to:

Kensington Publishing Corp., Dept. C.O., 850 Third Avenue, New York, NY 10022

Prices and numbers subject to change without notice. Valid only in the U.S.

All orders subject to availabilty. **NO ADVANCE ORDERS.**

Visit our Web site at **www.kensingtonbooks.com.**

Thrilling Romance from
Meryl Sawyer

__**Half Moon Bay**   **$6.50US/$8.00CAN**
   0-8217-6144-7

__**The Hideaway**   **$5.99US/$7.50CAN**
   0-8217-5780-6

__**Tempting Fate**   **$6.50US/$8.00CAN**
   0-8217-5858-6

__**Unforgettable**   **$6.50US/$8.00CAN**
   0-8217-5564-1

Call toll free **1-888-345-BOOK** to order by phone or use this coupon to order by mail.

Name _____

Address _____

City _____ State _____ Zip _____

Please send me the books I have checked above.

I am enclosing $_____

Plus postage and handling* $_____

Sales tax (in New York and Tennessee) $_____

Total amount enclosed $_____

*Add $2.50 for the first book and $.50 for each additional book.

Send check or money order (no cash or CODs) to:

Kensington Publishing Corp., 850 Third Avenue, New York, NY 10022

Prices and Numbers subject to change without notice.

All orders subject to availability.

Check out our website at **www.kensingtonbooks.com**

Put a Little Romance in Your Life With
Rosanne Bittner